UNDER CURRENT

Derek

UNDER CURRENT

SIMON LAWDER

MERCER books

MERCER books

First published in 2016 by Mercer Books
www.mercerbooks.co.uk

ISBN 978-0-9935733-0-9

A CIP catalogue record for this book is available from The British Library

Design by Reuben Wakeman
Printed in the UK by Acanthus Press

To Catriona for her motivation,
my writers' group for their wizardry,
and the creative spirit for my inspiration.

CONTENTS

CHAPTER 1

Deauville, Normandy, France

Suddenly almost everyone was on their feet; parents anxiously gathering their things together and ushering their offspring away, others preferring to stay and watch from a distance. A small crowd was already gathering at the water's edge as the inflatable rescue craft edged into the shallows, crew members jumped into the water, grabbed the side ropes and ran it aground.

Only one person had noticed the man, in the private area cordoned off for the Casino's clients, sit up and lift himself off his sun-bed. She had watched closely as he leaned down to say a few words to his wife, patted his two little girls on the head and walked the forty metres or so down the sand, his eyes fixed on some far distant point as he brushed past baking bodies, towels and parasols, to the water's edge.

The woman fiddled with something in her hand and smiled as the man strode purposefully into the water.

If anyone else had been watching him, they might have found it odd that, once the water was up to his waist, he didn't do the usual thing and dive in or start to swim: he just carried on walking, allowing the warm water to rise up to his shoulders, then to his neck, walking onwards, onwards until his face started to disappear, his expressionless eyes staring straight forward at the hazy horizon.

By now, his route had taken him some distance away from the other bathers, most of whom were engaged in noisy ball games or just floating on their back enjoying the hot sun on their skin.

When he disappeared quietly beneath the water, there was hardly a ripple.

It must have been at least ten minutes before a young man, a strong swimmer showing off just how good he was, came upon the body floating face down and shouted frantically for help.

It took four lifeguards to lift the stretcher from the life raft and carry it out of the shallows and up the beach. He was clearly a big man, well over six feet. The watching woman knew more than that: he was in his mid-forties, British and had kept himself in good condition.

She knew him as a charming man with an exceptional intellect, one of life's winners: a high-flyer in his student days at Cambridge, snapped up by one of the more fashionable Chambers at Lincoln's Inn, now he was a QC in the top fee bracket with a good, solid marriage; a man who, so the whispers went, had been identified by the powers-that-be for greater things.

And that, of course, was why he had to go.

As the stretcher-bearers reached a clear patch of sand and laid him down, the crowd, now three-deep in places, tried to edge forward to get a better look until two of the lifeguards barked at them to stay clear and give them space to work. Their colleagues had already started the life-saving routine, one pressing firmly on the man's chest while the other pumped oxygen into his mouth.

The shriek took everyone by surprise.

'Please, let me through. Please. Get out of…my…way, you idiots!' A woman was shouting in English, fighting to clear a path through the onlookers.

As she reached the front, she stopped, her hand on her mouth, her eyes wide.

'Oh my God, oh my God.' Instinctively, her elbow connected with the restraining lifeguard's solar plexus. The next second, she was on her knees beside the stretcher.

'Robert,' she sobbed. 'Robert, darling, what have you done?'

The watcher turned away. It was time to go. A busy few days lay in front of her.

For now, it was a case of 'job done'.

As she walked towards a quiet side street behind the promenade, nobody gave her a passing glance. She didn't mind; she had taken a lot of trouble disguising her distinctive mane of black hair and her perfectly-proportioned figure that morning. The cheap sunglasses did an effective job of hiding the look in her eyes – professional, determined, quietly satisfied. Sensual.

Sensual? Every time a job went according to plan, the thrill came in many forms.

No one could possibly have guessed that she had just earned herself a quarter of a million dollars by disposing of the next chairman of the UK's Independent Press Standards Organisation, the media watchdog that, over recent years, had acquired enough teeth to put the fear of God into journalists and newspaper owners.

London Euston station

He was early enough to catch the 4.15 train, and it was on time, for a change. That would get him to Stratford-on-Avon just after 5. Even allowing for the Friday evening traffic, he should arrive at his Warwickshire village home well before 6, with time for a refreshing shower before his wife appeared at the bedroom door and thrust an apron and the potato peeler into his hands.

It had been a pig of a week. Yet again, the economic forecasters – a bunch of complete wankers in his personal opinion - had got it wrong and it had been he, yet again, who was forced in as anonymous spokesman, facing hordes of cynical journalists and explaining, in the most optimistic terms, of course, why they had cocked up the numbers for the third quarter running.

Having to do all this in London had not helped. For one thing, it was uncomfortably hot and humid; and for another, any Brit whose salary came in Euros from the tottering European Union's coffers had to expect to be a target for the media's scorn. Although tomorrow's financial press would not mention him by name, all the financial analysts would know it was him. He would be the one they would blame in the wine bars of London, Frankfurt and Paris.

After phoning his wife to confirm his expected arrival time, the man found his seat in the air-conditioned first-class carriage. He stood aside to allow a tall, conservatively dressed woman to pass. She smiled, thanked him and settled into a seat three rows further back. Something about her made him turn as she took a small phone-like gadget from her pocket. He thought he heard a tiny beep.

The man removed his jacket, sat down and opened the Evening Standard.

Extraordinary eyes, he thought, then turned his attention to the business news.

Euro-prats get it wrong again, he read. He smiled. Sometimes a cliché really did fit the bill . . . the bill . . . the bill . . .

Four hours later, a passenger approached the train manager as they pulled out of Oxenholme station, in the picturesque Lake District, on their way to Edinburgh. After checking the restaurant car and toilets, the train manager phoned ahead to Carlisle to report some unidentified, possibly abandoned luggage.

The train had been too busy for her to notice other passengers, she'd told the train manager. And no, she couldn't recall much about any of them. She was tired and had dozed most of the way.

Someone was calling the man's mobile phone but she had already silenced the ring tone. She reached across and checked the screen – his wife again. Turning it off, she stood and walked through to the space between her carriage and the next. Opening the window he'd used earlier, she threw it down a steep embankment.

When she got back to her seat, the catering trolley had arrived. She bought herself another large vodka with ice, smiled her job done smile and settled down with her iPad to write her report.

Her employers should be pleased at the week's progress.

The man regarded by many as the dark horse to become the next head of the Basel Committee on Banking Supervision, the world's most powerful financial regulator, would never be seen again.

West Norwood, South London

Property in this street had been in high demand in the early 2000's as young couples and speculators, fuelled by easy cheap mortgages, decided this was to be the next boom suburb of commuter London. The houses had as much character as buyers could expect in a metropolis of ten million people: reasonable gardens, mature trees lining the pavements, and it was usually possible to park a car within a hundred metres of your own house.

A few residents had come unstuck when the banks crashed but not the owners of the house where the police car was pulling up outside.

Inside, a mother was doing her best to negotiate a deal with her twelve year-old, who was perfectly sure he could finish his homework, meet his mates for an impromptu game of cricket in the park, eat supper and practise on his trumpet before 8 p.m. At the moment when the bell rang, she felt she was getting the upper hand.

'Mrs Daniel?' enquired the uniformed officer, showing her his ID card.

'Yes,' she replied, wiping her hands on her apron.

'Sorry to disturb you, Madam. Do you think we could come in for a moment?'

A rash of burglaries in neighbouring streets had triggered a big effort by the police to get local residents to tighten up on their security. House to house enquiries were not uncommon these last few weeks.

'Of course.' She smiled. 'Come in, please.'

It was then that she noticed a female officer standing behind the man. Something about the woman's expression triggered a flicker of worry.

As the police car drove away, the mother was still sitting on the edge of the sofa, her head in her hands, in an advanced state of shock. The policewoman had done her best to console her but she had rejected her help and asked them to leave.

The sitting room door opened a fraction and a very frightened twelve year-old face peeped into the room. She looked up, her brain a mass of confused thoughts and emotions, her face showing every symptom of a secure, intelligent woman whose world had just imploded.

How could she tell him? He's only twelve, for God's sake. It just wasn't *fair*.

The silver Mercedes two-seater burst into life and pulled out as soon as the police car rounded the next turn. It was a beautiful evening. Jenna Dobrosova felt the need to celebrate: she pressed the button and lowered the sunroof, letting the warm breeze pour the perfume of a hundred gardens into the car's cockpit.

Three out of three.

Tonight she would enjoy herself. Oh, yes.

It would be several hours before the world learned that Jamie Daniel, the man some called a saint, others a genius, the mastermind behind the most powerful and well-informed corruption-busting website in Europe, had been caught red-handed soliciting young boys for sex in a copse in South London.

CHAPTER 2

Twenty years earlier
Beijing, China

Hong Jintao had been waiting more than an hour beyond the appointed time, which was not unexpected. A few magazines and some tea-making facilities would have made the wait more bearable but, on his arrival at the old imperial palace that housed the private offices of the most powerful men in China, he had been escorted to a huge barely furnished room and told to sit on one specific upright chair, even though he was the only person there.

In an attempt to overcome his nerves, he had already counted the dragons on the ornate murals four times. 173 or 174? He decided not to check them again; it would only make him worry more.

Hong had only a vague idea of why he had been summoned. At university, his speciality had been the history and culture of Great Britain and he currently held the relatively minor post of Cultural Adviser at the UK desk of the National Intelligence Agency. Recently, there had been the occasional rumour that the Politburo Standing Committee of the Communist Party of China was becoming rather irritated with Britain. But it was almost unheard of for someone of his lowly rank to receive a summons to this heavily guarded building.

At least, he reassured himself, *they're not going to fire me; they'd have kept that within the Department.*

Finally, a door on the far side of the room opened and a solemn faced, well-groomed young man waved silently, inviting Hong to follow him down a long corridor. He knocked on an unmarked door and ushered Hong into a surprisingly small office. A short, elderly man stood looking out onto the courtyard.

The man turned to welcome him and Hong had to suppress a gasp.

The 'invitation' had come from a middle-ranking functionary but here, walking round the desk to shake his hand, was one of China's most recognisable faces: the man widely credited with the success of the People's Republic's policy of investment in the developing world - Africa, Latin America, South Asia and the Middle East.

Country by country, year after year, China had bought new friends; as well as securing the supply chains for the vast natural resources they required, these countries' local politicians, both those in power and the local opposition, were now turning first to China for support, in preference to America or Russia.

'Good morning, Hong Jintao,' said Guo Dalong, shaking the young man's hand. 'Please, take a seat.'

'Thank you, sir,' muttered Hong, struggling to maintain at least some degree of calm in front of this great man.

Tea had quietly arrived and Guo served them both.

'I have heard much about your work,' said Guo, after sipping his tea. 'You are highly regarded at the National Intelligence Agency. Which is why I need your advice.'

Guo Dalong needs my advice? One of the six most powerful men in China needs my advice? Hong dug his nails into the palm of his hands to check that he hadn't died in the night and passed over into Paradise.

'I know you are a busy man,' Guo continued. 'So I'll explain quickly what I need from you. You are an expert on the United Kingdom of Great Britain, correct?'

'And Northern Ireland,' Hong intervened and immediately wished he had not bothered.

But the old man laughed out loud. 'Thank you for correcting my mistake.'

Now he was feeling more at ease in front of this evidently likeable man, Hong listened intently as Guo Dalong began to spell out why he was here.

'Hong, I have a problem with the United Kingdom,' he began. Hong could hear himself breathing.

'As I'm sure you are aware, it has been our long-term policy to develop cordial, and mutually beneficial, relationships with many countries in the Third World. Not for ideological reasons – we gave up on converting the world to Communism long ago and frankly, between you and me, while it works for us, it would be a disaster for most of these countries.

'No, our original motives were far more pragmatic. We needed land, food, minerals: it's the only way we can balance the books in this impossibly vast and diverse country we call China.'

Hong sat quietly, waiting for Guo to get to the point. He still had no idea why he was sitting in this office.

'We knew this would all take a very long time, but as you know, patience is a central character trait of the Chinese. So far,' the old man continued, 'it's been going pretty well. Clearly I can't share details with a man of your status but let's just say that we now control more than twenty global commodity markets as well as the political strategy of more than half the nations of Africa, large parts of South Asia, a dozen countries in South America, and several of the Gulf States.

'However, and here I come to the point of our conversation, we are still having a little difficulty with your British friends.'

Hong wanted to say something – although he had come to like them in many ways, the British were not his friends; he merely studied them - but this was not the time. Guo was in full flow.

'Let's be frank: the British are yesterday's imperial power, a tiny country that has already sold off its entire manufacturing base to foreign owners, riddled with social unrest, America's puppy dog. And yet, years after the demise of its mighty empire, it still clings to its front row seat in the global theatre, on the basis of nothing more than what they arrogantly regard as past glories. While we in China, despite quietly bankrolling the debt-ridden economies of the US and most of Europe with our investment funds and tourism cash, have apparently still not earned our invitation to join the really important world leadership forums.

'But . . . what about the United Nations?' Hong intervened.

'The UN? The Americans have an excellent phrase: all piss and wind, my boy. An expensive, long-running televised saga with next to no real influence over anyone. High-sounding resolutions that half the world chooses to veto or ignore and no power to intervene when someone steps out of line. No, the real debates, where the real leaders, the men who truly run world affairs meet, they take place elsewhere, behind closed doors, doors to which the British still have a key but we do not.'

Guo Dalong paused and watched the young man's face. Hong

Jintao was confused. *Why am I, a lowly apparatchik, receiving a detailed briefing on the behind-the-scenes world of global politics? When is he going to get to the point?*

'Now, Hong Jintao, I would like you to tell me how you think this frustrating state of affairs with Great Britain may be hampering our programme of Third World, shall we say, management?'

Now the pressure was on the young man: so this was the test he had been summoned here to undergo. This was the kind of opportunity that would never come again.

He looked the aging politician in the eyes, searching for clues as to the answer he was expected to give. Guo was smiling again, returning his stare, his eyes revealing nothing as he waited for Hong to respond.

Then an extraordinary thing happened. His mind cleared. Hong could see exactly what he should say. It was almost as if the older man was, in some strange way, transmitting his own thoughts to Hong's mind. But at the same time, he felt sure these were his own ideas; that somehow his thinking had moved onto a higher level. The answers seemed so obvious now, so evident.

He cleared his throat.

'Sir,' he began. 'It has to relate to the British Commonwealth. More than fifty countries, almost one-third of the world's population and a quarter of its land area.

'Even though almost every Commonwealth country has now gained its independence, they have each chosen, or perhaps been persuaded, to retain their membership. Why? Because they all still depend on Britain for trade and for aid funding. And, under Britain's wing, they can feel part of that voice at the top table too, something they could never dream of alone.'

Now he could see the logic of the argument stretching out before him, like a brightly lit flight path.

'As long as Britain retains its hold over the Asian and African Commonwealth countries, many of whom are rich in minerals and other resources, China will be never be able to bring them, or their leaders, into line.'

Guo sat back in his chair, spread his hands and smiled broadly. 'Well done, Hong Jintao. Your superiors were correct in their assessment of your talents. Have some more tea.'

Once he had refilled the exquisite bone china cups, Guo took up the story once more.

'So,' he continued calmly, 'the Politburo has formulated a long-term strategy, designed to resolve this little difficulty. It will take some time for us to see the benefits, but we are patient people. And, with your help . . .'

His voice was now barely a whisper.

'Your task, over the coming years, Hong Jintao, will be to unlock these doors for us, to break the chains that are holding us back from our ultimate goal – which is . . .' He paused, clearly for effect, his eyebrows raised.

When he spoke again, his tone was deadly serious. 'Our ultimate goal, my young friend, can be expressed in just a few words: control of the entire global economy.'

He paused again to allow this to sink in. Now Hong's head was a mass of tangled emotions – excitement, incredulity, mild panic, fascination – and he knew it showed.

Guo pressed on. 'The twenty-year plan we have formulated is, in our view, the only way to remove the British from our path.'

'Twenty years?' Hong couldn't help himself interrupting.

'Yes. As I said earlier, patience – the Chinese way. Death by a thousand cuts – they will hardly realise it's happening to them so they will not fight back.

'Guo Dalong, I am very honoured that you should be asking me to assume this great responsibility. May I ask you . . .?'

'Ah, such youthful enthusiasm. I have told you what our goals are. And now you are eager to know *how*. I will tell you. I would like to give you a short lesson in what is known as *realpolitik*.'

'*Realpolitik*?' the young man asked.

'A German word. It means politics based on power and the practicalities of life, rather than ideology. The reality of power, Hong Jintao. The practical application of influence; where the real power lies. Great Britain is like most Western countries, indeed like almost every country that employs the democratic system. The people go out to vote every few years, blithely believing that they are free to elect a government who will run their country for them. Poor souls, they are so deluded.

'In Britain, just as in the United States and in most of Europe, the people who really run the country, who control the law, business, the economy, the markets, the Commonwealth, and the elected government, they operate behind the scenes, well away from the public eye. They are sometimes referred to as the Establishment, sometimes as the ruling classes. In earlier times, it was the land-owning aristocracy, the power-brokers, and the academic elite. Now they have been joined by the bankers, the heads of the giant corporations and the media. Plus, of course, the heads of the nation's oldest families. In Britain, believe me, these are the people who choose, and remove, the party leaders and, once they are in government, their chosen leaders, naturally, do their bidding.'

'You talked earlier about the top table nations, sir,' said Hong. 'The really important world forums.'

'Yes, I did. These elite groups meet regularly, in private, with their opposite numbers from the other top table member countries. The elected heads of government are invited to attend a few selected sessions but only as guests. These meetings, Hong Jintao, are where the decisions that affect the lives of billions of people, and the movement of trillions of dollars, are made. And little Great Britain – their Establishment, not their government – still appears to win far too many of the arguments. Why? Some think it's to do with their immensely wealthy banking families, the power of the City; for me, it's also about the strange power the European royal families still hold over international affairs, even after all this time.'

Once again, Hong Jintao was puzzled. His studies had shown clearly that the royal families of Britain and Europe, most of whom were inter-related, were little more than symbolic, ceremonial figures these days, wealthy landowners of course, but with no real power in the late twentieth century. Now Guo was painting an entirely different picture.

Guo continued: 'Which brings us to the British Commonwealth. These power brokers still exercise considerable influence over what happens in their former colonies. They effectively control their cash-flow. Control the flow of cash and you've got them by the balls. And, as Theodore Roosevelt famously said: "If you've got them by the balls, their hearts and minds will follow."

Hong laughed. Guo did not.

'This, young man, is the true power base of the British and so, in our judgement, there lies the key to the arena where China must be present.'

He paused, not entirely for effect, stood up and leaned forward, his hands on the desk.

In the last few minutes, his eyes had completely lost the kindly twinkle.

'Hong Jintao, we have decided to infiltrate and then destroy the power of the British Establishment. And you have been chosen to lead the entire operation.'

Guo had stopped speaking and was now sitting back in his chair, catching his breath. He looked old, very tired.

Looking back in the days and years to come, Hong Jintao would never quite understand why he felt so calm. This was the moment that would change his entire destiny and yet already, the massive responsibility Guo was placing upon his shoulders felt both comfortable and exhilarating. He knew he was up to the challenge.

'Where do you suggest I start, Guo Dalong?' asked Hong after a minute or so.

The old man opened a drawer in his desk and extracted a plain covered file. He laid it on the desk in front of him.

'In here you will find details of three young British men. They have been selected after considerable research. Your mission is to recruit them, train them, with and without their knowledge, to become our instruments as they rise to positions of great power in their country.'

Hong reached across and took the file without opening it.

'Our instruments?' he asked.

'Yes, our spies. During the Second World War, the Soviet Union successfully penetrated British security and drained them of information for many years afterwards; others have done the same since, you can be sure, but, when the spies were caught, the British have managed to avoid any publicity. The men in this file are young now but, in twenty years' time, under your guidance, they will be our own Burgess, Philby and McLean.'

Hong had read about the unmasking of the so-called 'Cambridge group' of spies in the early 1950s but not until they had betrayed huge quantities of government secrets to their Russian masters.

'*Great* Britain,' Guo laughed at the word 'great', 'will be fatally damaged and consigned to history.'

Paris, France
A few months later

Dropping his heavy suitcase beside the elegant restored oak wardrobe, Gregory Bellingham fell backwards onto the bed and grinned. The hotel the department had selected was a classic example of Parisian *ancien régime*: a nondescript street door, tall and wide enough to allow a carriage to pass, opening onto a cobbled courtyard surrounded by three storeys of tall windows, a mass of colour cascading from the window boxes.

He entered a marble tiled reception area, hung with vast ornate drapes, scattered with aging furniture and an even older head porter, the smell of fresh bread and flowers almost masking the mothballs.

'Bonjour, Monsieur,' the old man croaked.

'Hello, my dear chap,' replied Gregory, waving his passport.

In common with almost every hotel porter and restaurant waiter in Paris, the porter, who almost certainly had a fair command of English, ignored him and, muttering something about '*petit déjeuner à huit heures*', handed Gregory his key and pointed to the lift.

Just large enough to accommodate one man and a case, it had taken almost a minute to reach the next floor. His brass bed, complete with a couple of loose knobs, felt wonderfully comfortable but creaked loudly as he sat up to remove his shoes.

On the face of it, almost a year away from the daily grind, here in Paris, studying for an MBA at HEC, Europe's top international business school, all at the Government's expense, with the 'cast-iron guarantee of a two-grade salary hike when you get back', sounded like a pretty damned good offer.

But Gregory Bellingham's brief career in Whitehall, after graduating with flying colours from Cambridge, had taught him to take very great care whenever anyone dropped phrases like 'cast-iron guarantee' into the conversation.

'You do realise, Bellingham, that an MBA from HEC is like winning the pools in these parts,' the Director of People Enhancement had said. 'People have been known to sacrifice their grandmother to get on that list. Fantastic opportunity. Wish I'd had the chance myself. Can't think why they chose you, though. Loads of brighter sparks around, in my humble view.'

The newly-crowned DoPE, who appeared to possess only one rather shabby tweed jacket, had discreetly unscrewed his new title from his office door within days of its triumphant announcement by the latest Minister for Loose Ends, as their department was unaffectionately known.

'New roles, new culture, new start,' had been the theme of the minister's address to the staff on his first day.

The suffix 'Same devious, demotivating, self-serving senior management' was offered by one wag on behalf of the signally unimpressed room, only just loud enough for the minister to hear.

'At least *People Enhancement* makes a change from the dreaded *Human Resources*,' commented Gregory's pal David Marksworth, over lunch the next day. 'Don't you think that said everything you needed to know about employers' attitudes to their staff in the 90's?'

He switched to his Whitehall grandee voice. '"Hello. Is that the warehouse? We need a couple more truckloads of human resources. Tomorrow, if not earlier. Medium grade, in brown or black, doesn't matter, as long as they're still on special offer." Yuck!'

Marksworth, whom Bellingham had known since Cambridge, had also been selected to go to Paris and Gregory was looking forward to renewing their old partnership. David had an unerring knack of attracting the company of well-heeled, attractive ladies, from a variety of age groups. Nothing to do with good looks; David's nose was a strange shape and his ears didn't match. It was the mischievous twinkle in his one good eye that was apparently irresistible.

This course was going to be hard work but it had every prospect of being a lot of fun too.

Lying on the pristine white linen, he allowed himself a brief smile before his mind switched back to the real reason why he reckoned that he and his friend David had been sent to Paris.

By common consent, HEC provided just about the best management education the world can offer. Every September, thirty of the world's brightest young executives were sent by their employers - multinational corporations, billionaires and governments - to complete their education. Thirty men and women, from twelve different countries, who had been singled out, some for their extraordinary potential, others for their impeccable breeding. These were thirty of the people, Gregory reflected, who, barring accidents, would one day be running the world.

Including me.

He decided to see whether David had checked in. When he arrived downstairs, there was no sign of the geriatric porter, so he wandered over to the desk and swivelled the guest registration file. The front page was headed *HEC MBA*. Around twenty names were listed, all male as far as he could tell. The women students had clearly been billeted elsewhere.

Each guest's room number and nationality was typed along-side his name. Germany, Russia, Ghana, Brazil, Saudi Arabia, India, China . . .

Running his finger down the list, and realising his friend had not yet arrived, he decided to explore the local *faubourg*.

He was only a stone's throw to the north of the Arc de Triomphe but, in that curiously Parisian way, the streets exuded a kind of genteel residential peace, the city's traffic noise but a distant hum. Elderly aristocratic ladies in elegant hats and gloves, each trailing an expensive small dog, seemed to be the dominant socio-economic grouping. The entire retail scene consisted of one florist, one shop selling nothing but a multi-coloured mountain of small macaroons and a historic clock specialist who wasn't sure when he'd return.

A slim figure emerged from the shadow of the hotel's staircase, crossed the foyer and took a quick look at the list on the porter's desk before slipping out of the door.

Reaching the street, the man spotted Gregory Bellingham taking a left in the direction of the Avenue des Champs-Elysées and set off along the same route. Bellingham glanced round instinctively but saw nothing.

CHAPTER 3

Sometime in the reasonably near future
Oxford, England

Patrick Cameron hadn't slept well but the usual cycling three miles to work would help to clear his head. He needed to be on time and in good form: Government inspectors had a habit of asking trick questions when they carried out a snap check.

He wasn't supposed to have prior warning of their arrival at the medical research lab he'd been running in Oxford for the last three years. Quite how Rowena, his PA, had discovered news of the impending 'enemy invasion' was not for him to know. When she waved her hands in the air, rolled her eyes and muttered something about receiving 'a message from my angels', he had thought it best not to enquire further.

He swallowed the last of his coffee, checked the kettle was boiling and poured water into the teapot. Half a dozen squat-thrusts later, the tea was ready and the last of the muzziness in his head had gone. Approaching forty, he needed to loosen up more these days before climbing onto his bike. But at least he still had all his hair and his waist measurement meant he could still get into his favourite trousers, at a squeeze.

Placing the hot mug beside the bed, Patrick leaned forward to kiss Angela on the forehead. He knew she'd been awake a lot too in the small hours of the night but she would need to get up in the next few minutes if she was to be on duty at school on time, pregnant or not.

Only weeks to go. This was not just his wife; this was the woman who had shown such incredible courage when he had asked her to help him infiltrate and bust open a plot by religious extremists to start a holy war – the most recent, and hopefully the final occasion the Security Service would ask him to go undercover and risk his life.

Now all that mattered was the baby, their first, a small person whose arrival, Patrick was sure, would lead them into a wonderful new phase of their life together.

By now, she had managed to manoeuvre herself into a sitting position, cup in one hand, the other pushing her naturally wavy fair hair back from her face.

'Let me take a look at you before you go. Those socks you wore with your green trousers yesterday looked awful. Couldn't you see?' She laughed.

'You know me, love. Grab the first ones I find from the drawer. Anyway, fifty percent of men are supposed to be colour blind.'

She gave her husband the once-over. 'You're a good-looking devil. Sexy without flaunting it. The mauve sweater would be better but you'll do. Such a shame about those socks. Nag, nag, I know what you're thinking. Off you go.'

'Bye, love. Have a good day. Give the bastards hell,' she mumbled as he left the room.

'You too,' he said, laughing.

Oxford was still coming to life as he pedalled past the historic colleges, cradles where countless brilliant men and women had nurtured their talents before moving on to change the world, each in their own different way.

The sun was already drying the overnight showers, the street cleaners had done their job, and he could smell the coffee and croissants from a hundred café doors. He stopped to pick up a morning paper from a street vendor and stuffed it into his saddle-bag.

Swinging round the corner into the lab's parking area, he was happy to see no strange cars: he had beaten the bogey men by arriving early.

A couple of his staff were already at their work, dressed in white coats, poring over the results of the tests they had run overnight.

'Hi, guys', he called as they looked up and smiled. 'Anything new?'

'Oh, hi Patrick', said Julian. Patrick had had one hell of a fight to stop this man being poached by the Security Service nine months earlier. 'When you've got a moment, you might want to take a look at this.'

Julian was his star man. A tousle-haired lad who always looked as though he had just climbed out of bed, not often his own. A strong contender for an award of scruffiest man in Oxford, Julian's unconscious ability to send attractive women, of all ages, into squirming paroxysms of lust for his body was the stuff of legend.

On a more professional level, his uncanny knack of spotting inconsistencies in a mountain of seemingly normal data had been the trigger that led to a breakthrough in the early diagnosis of breast cancer the previous year. But his real speciality was the brain.

In recent months, his work had focussed on trying to identify imbalances in younger brains that could later develop into the onset of dementia.

Patrick dumped his things in his office and strolled over to Julian's lab desk. 'What have you got, mate?' he asked.

'You remember I was analysing the brain scans of a sample of people with dementia? Well, just out of interest, I thought I'd run a comparison check against the scans of a few characters who everyone thought were quite "normal" . . .' he waggled his fingers. ' . . . but who suddenly, out of the blue, did something totally out of character. Like murder their kids or go on the rampage.'

'I'm with you so far,' said Patrick. 'Go on.'

'Well, the best way to explain what I'm rambling on about is to show you a few pictures.'

He clicked his mouse on a couple of icons and the screen started to scroll through a series of brain scans, side by side. On each scan, an area had been highlighted in red and a blow-up of the highlighted area superimposed in a box in the corner.

'The dementia sufferers are on the left, the others on the right. Watch carefully. Notice anything?'

'Run them through again, please, Julian. A bit more slowly.'

As the shot sequence ran once more, Patrick suddenly grabbed the young man's arm and said, 'Stop it there.'

'You've won this morning's star prize.' Julian smiled.

'Unless I'm missing something here,' said Patrick, 'the dementia victims fall into a number of distinct categories. But we already knew that. Now, when I look at the people with sudden behaviour change, I can see where your research is heading, except for this one.' He pointed to the scan on the right-hand side of the screen and asked,

'Who's that?'

'That, my friend, is today's odd man out. His name was Alistair Thomas.'

'*The* Alistair Thomas?' Patrick said, shock in his voice.

'The same. All set to be elected leader of his party, the man tipped to be our greatest statesman of the last fifty years, the "new British Kennedy". And what happens?

'At ten in the evening, he announces to his family he has to attend an urgent meeting, gets into his car and, stone cold sober, drives the wrong way up the motorway and dies under the wheels of a sixty ton truck.

'Thank God his brain survived the crash. Now, tell me: am I wrong or is his scan showing exactly the same pattern as the dementia patient on the left?'

He leaned closer to the screen.

'Yes,' said Julian. 'But why do none of the other "sudden change" examples show anything remotely similar?'

'Your sample size is pretty small, Julian. You'll need to run the same test with at least thirty of each. But, I agree with you, it does seem weird.'

While they had been talking, the lab had filled up with staff arriving for work.

Rowena, a woman never noted for subtlety, was looking down at the car park from a window. Today she had chosen to wear thigh length white leather boots beneath an astonishingly short skirt and a tee-shirt emblazoned with the words:

I LOVE giving my boss a hand.

Patrick wasn't sure but he suspected that her multi-coloured hair had acquired yet another streak.

'Achtung!' she exclaimed and started to goose-step around the room. The inspectors had arrived.

Patrick finished showing the 'men from the Ministry' (motto: We're here to help you) round the building and had seen them safely installed in a side office, surrounded by voluminous files and a plate piled high with cream buns.

Returning to his own office, he checked his emails, answered the urgent stuff and relaxed. He noticed the morning newspaper lying untidily where he had dropped it.

Picking it up, he scanned the front page. A by-line caught his eye: *Top whistle-blower in court. Alleged sex with minors. See page 6.*

Something made him turn to the full article. What he saw hit him like a rock.

He couldn't believe what he was seeing. There was Jamie Daniel, one of his great old university friends, a man with whom he had spent any number of raunchy evenings, possibly the most heterosexual guy he had ever met, being led from a police van to answer charges of importuning young boys! It didn't make any sense.

How come he had missed the news of his arrest a month earlier? He checked the date. Then he remembered: he and Angela had been on a long weekend break in Barcelona.

He hadn't been in touch with Jamie Daniel for years. But there had to be a mistake here. Either that or his old pal, who had the guts to launch his now notorious corruption-busting website while he was still a student, had been set up.

'Julian!' he called out. To nobody's surprise, one of the inspectors, a woman in her forties, married with considerable assets, was at that moment perched on Julian's desk conducting an in-depth interview.

'I'd like you to do something for me,' Patrick said when the mass of hair finally peeked round the door.

Assistant Commissioner Andy Fields of the Security Service had the same newspaper spread across his desk. But his was accompanied by a file of cuttings of other articles, each one announcing the death, disappearance or disgrace of someone in public life.

Taking each example at face value, there was probably a perfectly good explanation. Human failings were a fact of life; most people had at least one guilty secret, their dark side. And, since time began, fear of exposure or plain and simple pressure of work, had always tipped a few people over the edge,

What had caught Fields' eye in these cases, however, was in the detail. He had started to list the common factors:

In (almost) every case:

- *The individual concerned was about to be promoted*
- *The individual was expected, once appointed, to make radical changes, to clean the place up and/or to clear out dead wood*
- *The men or women who took their place were all on our MoleWatch list (low category level)*

The Exceptions:

- *All involved in campaigning – civil liberties, anti-corruption, etc.*
- *Question: had they over-stepped the mark?*

So far:

They all had, or were expected to, upset the status quo
Which means they all had, or were expected to, spoil somebody's plans
Plans for what?
To achieve power? Or to hold on to power?
For themselves? Or on behalf of someone else?

Fields sat back and pondered, steepling his fingers and tapping his chin. There was not much to go on, but . . .

He pulled a slim phone from an inside pocket and dialled a number; a number that changed every month.

The man who picked up the call had just come in from working on his vegetable patch. His back was hurting; he would need to ask his wife to rub something into his lower spine again. *Bugger this old age!*

He had not yet had time to wash his hands but the distinctive ring-tone told him he had to answer this call.

'Hello.' He listened for all of two minutes.

'I'll call the others,' he said. 'We'll let you know, when and where.'

He put the phone down and picked up the kettle.

Tea - that was the answer. He would have loved a cigarette too but his wife would cut him off at the balls.

No respect for senior rank these days. I was a bloody Air Vice-Marshal once, for crying out loud.

Oh, bugger old age!

CHAPTER 4

Paris, October 1996

Gregory Bellingham was already falling in love with Paris. He still had vague memories of the last time he was there, on holiday en famille. Being made to trail round musty old buildings with his irritating younger sister while their parents drooled over some hideous oil painting had taken the gloss off Paris in the spring.

Today, every intersection of narrow streets yielded new delights. Central London had long ago lost so many of its friendly family grocers, shops piled high with dozens of freshly baked loaves or cakes, butchers you could bank on for flavour and tenderness; but here they were everywhere, true craftsmen and women, knowledgeable, proud of their work, with all the time in the world to chat amiably to every client.

He checked his watch. Perhaps he had time for a quick 'snifter' before heading back to the hotel. Spotting a pleasant looking café, he took a seat at a pavement table.

A white-aproned waiter appeared.

'Une beer, s'il vous plaît,' said Bellingham, showing no embarrassment at his awful accent.

The waiter grinned, said, 'Sure buddy', and walked back inside.

'Do you mind if I join you?' A tall, slim man with Oriental looks was standing by his table, smiling.

Gregory looked up, surprised. 'Of course. Please take a seat.'

'My name's Hong,' the man said as he settled in. 'I think we may be attending the same course here. I noticed you in the hotel. I'm from China, by the way.' The man's English accent was perfect.

'The MBA at HEC? Well, well. I'm Gregory Bellingham. I'm from London. How do you do?' They shook hands and Hong ordered a beer for himself.

Within minutes, they were both laughing. They'd discovered

they both worked as low-grade civil servants for their own national government. By the time the second beers arrived, they were like old friends, sharing hilarious stories of irrational bosses, incompetent departments and silly regulations.

Hong said, 'May I call you Gregory?'

'My close friends call me Greg.'

'And mine call me Jin. It's short for Jintao but easier for Westerners to remember.'

They shook hands again. This time the Chinese man clasped Bellingham's arm firmly with his other hand.

'I think we're going to have fun together here,' he said, looking closely at Greg's reaction.

Greg wasn't at all sure what they had done for the rest of that afternoon. When he woke in his bed early the next morning, he could just recall watching himself, lying naked on a table in a darkened room, staring into a very bright light, while a voice, a woman's voice, the most beautiful voice he had ever heard, spoke close to his ear.

He couldn't remember what she had been saying; in truth, it didn't matter. He only knew that he felt entranced, utterly calm, but intensely aroused. Then, just as the honeyed words brought him to an inevitable powerful release, the image faded.

For some reason, he had a strong feeling, but no more than a feeling, that both his new friend Jin and David Marksworth, his colleague from Whitehall, had been in the room with him, sharing in the joy.

Lying there, Greg had never felt happier in his life.

Once they had begun their studies, Greg, David and Jin became inseparable. At first, they never discussed it openly, but it was very obvious to them all that a bond had been formed.

While several of their classmates seemed far more interested in the hedonistic pleasures of Parisian student life, they all threw themselves wholeheartedly into the programme of lectures, case studies and research.

And yet David, who the other two appointed as their social secretary, made sure their life wasn't all work and no play. Under his guidance, they scheduled enough time off to get to know every side of Parisian life, often in the company of some of their more lively female classmates.

For Greg, the memory of that strange first day in Paris had begun to fade. All that mattered to him was the here and now. He felt renewed, confident: there was nothing he couldn't achieve, the intellectual and academic challenges of his studies held no fears with Jin and David at his side.

Almost imperceptibly, Jin was becoming their mentor, the leader of the pack. Greg had no qualms about their relationship: there was something so natural and welcoming about his manner, he found it more and more easy to set aside what Hong always referred to as 'our silly political differences'. When he spoke to David about this, he agreed, but not quite with Greg's level of enthusiasm.

In all other respects, David seemed his usual self, always good company, sharing ideas they could add to their essays, reminding Greg to keep in touch with his family and the people at the office from time to time.

In private, what surprised Greg about himself was the level of commitment he was showing to his MBA studies. Both at school and university, his lack of application had always irritated his teachers.

Bright but bone idle had been the most succinct of his academic assessments, until Paris.

Outwardly, he blamed the others for his unaccustomed display of motivation. But deep within, when he awoke in the small hours, he knew there was something else.

It was more than that. *He* was something else now. For the first time, he had a purpose in life, a mission. If anyone had asked him to explain that mission, he would refuse because, so far, he only had a vague idea.

All he knew for certain was that, starting here in Paris, he was now on a trail that, one day, would lead to something quite glorious. Change the world? Well, maybe.

He found himself remembering one rainy afternoon, many years earlier, sitting with his Dad, watching a rerun of the 1960 western *The Magnificent Seven*. The image of the seven gun-slinging cowboy heroes walking into battle, in a line side by side, had stayed in the back of his mind for years afterwards and here it was again, filling his vision as he dozed off back to sleep.

Except that this time it wasn't seven, but four: Greg himself, David Marksworth, Hong Jintao and another figure he couldn't quite make out, indistinct, anonymous, in shadow.

Four names that, for sure, would go down in history. It was just a matter of time.

London, August 2016

David Marksworth, Permanent Under-Secretary at the Ministry of Defence, didn't need an appointment. He was so frequent a visitor to the office of Gregory Bellingham, the Permanent Under-Secretary for Commonwealth Affairs, that the staff had even allocated him his own teacup and laid in a stock of his favourite Jaffa cakes.

Since Paris, the two men's careers had followed a remarkably similar pattern. For anyone to reach the rank of Permanent Under-Secretary at such a young age was almost unheard of, and their fast-track promotion had earned them more than a few mortal enemies among the older time servers in Her Majesty's Civil Service.

No-one doubted their ability; it was simply that there had always been an established procedure for rising through the complex hierarchy - a chap had to win his spurs and then wait in line for years and years. This broke all the rules.

Rumours of 'unusual relationships' and 'proclivities' had been overheard in Whitehall wine bars, although nobody was entirely sure what a proclivity actually was.

However, what none of the gossipmongers could deny was that the two old friends both enjoyed the absolute confidence of their respective Ministers, which only infuriated them even more.

It was no coincidence that, in each case, the Minister concerned had only recently been appointed to his post by the new Prime Minister. In a barely concealed response to the pressures that had forced her predecessor to retire hurt, one of her first 'new broom' actions was a mass clear-out of what the press had started to call the Old Boys Social Club – the PM's close-knit inner circle, all men with a similar educational background and a weekend rural retreat located within a few miles of each other.

'Morning, ladies,' barked David as he breezed through the ante-room. 'Any chance of a spot of tea? My goodness, Charlotte, you've changed your hair. Looks great – it brings out the wild woman in you.'

The gales of laughter that followed him as he entered Bellingham's office without knocking were blotted out as soon as he closed the door, together with his cheery grin.

Without so much as a glance at Bellingham, Marksworth walked across to the window and stood looking down at the Cenotaph war memorial in the middle of Whitehall. His face had hardened.

'OK to talk?' he said.

Greg was starting to get a little tired of his friend bursting in unannounced and had decided to have a word with him. Clearly, however, this was not the right time.

'Yes, the silencers are on,' he said. A squad of technicians, posing as fire alarm inspectors and funded by a faked government purchase order, had installed a sophisticated circuit in that one room that ensured that, once it was activated, the conversation could not be overheard by any monitoring system known to man.

'Hong's not happy with you,' said David. His tone was brusque and business-like. There was no doubt who was in charge here.

'But David . . . Three in the last month . . .'

'You will speak to me respectfully when we discuss these matters.'

'I am sorry, *shifu*.' He used the Cantonese word for 'master'.

'Jin expected more progress. Three is not good enough. We both know that.'

'*Shifu*, what exactly did he say to you?'

'He said I was to remind you of your commitments, to our oath of brotherhood . . . and . . .' He turned and faced the other man.

'Yes, I know. The penalties for failure.' Bellingham's face fell.

They both knew. There was only one penalty – death.

He remembered all too clearly the day, shortly before the business school's 1996 winter break, when Hong Jintao announced that they were now ready to swear the ultimate binding oath of loyalty to each other: the oath of brotherhood, he had called it.

The wording was based on the legendary Oath of the Peach Garden, described by the author Luo Guanzhong in his 14th century novel *Romance of the Three Kingdoms*: three friends, assembled in the Peach Garden, took an oath that would bind them together for life in their mission to protect the Han dynasty from the Yellow Turban rebels:

We have come together as brothers. From this day forward, we shall join forces for a common purpose: to save the troubled and to aid the endangered. We shall avenge the nation above, and pacify the citizenry below. We seek not to be born on the same day, in the same month and in the same year. We merely hope to die on the same day, in the same month and in the same year. May the Gods of Heaven and Earth attest to what is in our hearts. If we should ever do anything to betray our friendship, may heaven and the people of the earth both strike us dead.

In the weeks and months that followed the lost hours of that first day in Paris, he and David Markswortth had spent long periods with Hong, talking politics. Gradually, the conversations began to converge on one single topic: the iniquities of the British Empire.

Gregory's entire upbringing had depicted the Empire as a force for good, Britain's mighty contribution to the spread of civilisation. But, since meeting Hong Jintao, his mind seemed to find it perfectly logical to see matters from a quite different viewpoint.

Then one evening, Hong had finally revealed to them their 'sacred mission – to free the peoples of the Commonwealth countries from the tyrannical control of the Royal Family and their clique of high-born lackeys.'

'For hundreds of years, these countries and their peoples were misled by the British colonisers into believing their lives would improve as they became more "civilised"; whereas in truth, they have been exploited, robbed of their heritage, their culture, and their mineral wealth, forced to submit to an alien culture and to abandon their ancient gods.

'As Bishop Desmond Tutu said, "When the white missionaries came to Africa, they had the Bible and we had the land. They said 'Let us pray.' We closed our eyes. When we opened them we had the Bible and they had the land."

'Now, under the continued patronage of the British ruling classes, their leaders grow wealthy while the people starve, and the corner-stones of their culture have become violence, crime and corruption.

'This has to be stopped. And I am proud to say it is you, my friends,' Hong had proclaimed, 'you who will lead the battle to correct these appalling injustices and to punish its perpetrators.

Great glory will be yours.'

The oath of brotherhood had seemed such a natural confirmation of their relationship.

The new Gregory, as he had come to think of himself since that dramatic day, never had any problem accepting the legitimacy of their sacred mission. Hong's passion for the cause and the logic with which he presented his case affected him deeply. He was a believer and he had a duty to honour his oath.

Hong's instructions were clear – to dedicate themselves to their career, to earn the trust of their superiors, and to await further orders. David Marksworth's appointment to the rank of shifu had come as something of a surprise. He'd always recognised that Marksworth had the stronger personality: Greg would habitually share his anxieties, both professional and personal, with David but it was never reciprocated.

He realised that, although they had been close friends for almost twenty-five years, and David's commitment to the mission was as fervent as his own, Greg didn't really know him.

'The penalties for failure,' said David again, approaching Bellingham's desk. 'The words of our oath say that, if one of us fails, we all fail.'

Greg looked up. He knew what was coming next.

'And I will not allow that to happen,' said Marksworth.

CHAPTER 5

London, August 2015

Jeanne Devereaux was enjoying her day. She felt alive, refreshed, free at last to spend her time doing exactly what she liked, where she liked. And for Jeanne that meant a stroll through a sunlit Kensington Gardens; meeting a few useful friends for lunch on the roof garden terrace of a nearby hotel; then back to the apartment, change, a fast run to burn off some of the excesses of the week before setting the table, lighting candles, a quick shower and dressing appropriately for an evening of good wine, canapés, laughter and long, slow, tantric lovemaking with her partner.

This evening it would be her current male partner, the voracious grandson of one of Africa's London ambassadors. *He does have perfect manners, though.*

She'd checked her roots before leaving. The cosmetic surgeon had seen to the rest. She was a hundred percent Jeanne Devereaux. Well, to the outside world, anyway.

She'd earned her break. The last few weeks had been very rewarding financially, but exhausting, both mentally and physically. The schedule her employers had laid out meant she had to plan and set up three projects, in quite different locations, all quite different in style and execution, with delivery dates within days of each other.

Even for someone as experienced as Jeanne, that was what the British would call 'a bit of a tall order' – a bizarre expression, she thought.

She couldn't have managed it all without outside help and outside help always entailed risk. Fortunately she had run enough operations in England in recent years to know that winning the cooperation of the people who mattered was all about who you knew and applying pressure in the right places.

Her employers knew all the right people. She had recruited her own small team of pressurisers.

And today was a beautiful day. Five minutes and she'd be caressing her first glass of cold Chablis.

Just as she was approaching the park gates, she felt her phone buzz in her breast pocket.

Damn! My day off. She knew she'd switched off the handset before leaving home; only a tiny number of her contacts had the means to reactivate it remotely and then only in a strict emergency.

As soon as she checked the screen, she turned and walked back into the park's open spaces. The babble of birds and children would mask her voice.

She had no need to speak. The familiar voice started as soon as she answered the call.

'Embankment, usual place, one hour.'

Shit! 'Not a good time for me,' she said.

'Plus ten percent,' the voice responded quickly.

'No, I don't think so.' She looked at her watch.

'Twelve and a half.'

'Two hours.'

'Agreed.' The phone went dead.

Jeanne looked at the blank screen for several seconds and then disconnected. She would still be able to join her friends for lunch, she'd just negotiated a substantial rise in her fee and sex with Ade would go ahead undisturbed.

She shrugged, smiled, reached up and released her hair-band. After a less than auspicious start, Jenna Dobrosova was becoming rather fond of London.

At precisely the time that Jeanne Devereaux/Jenna Dobrosova, now replete with good cheer, *sole meunière* and Chablis, left the restaurant and hailed a cab to take her to the Thames Embankment, Patrick Cameron left his lab in Oxford, bound for a small village in Gloucestershire, young Julian slumped in the passenger seat.

Her Majesty's inspectors had protested but Patrick had muttered something about a medical emergency and informed them that Rowena was now in charge. That didn't go down too well, especially when she retrieved a riding crop from her desk and cracked it against a metal filing cabinet, shouting:

'Get on with your work. Any more slacking and you'll get a taste of this!'

It had only taken two calls to find the address where Jamie Daniel had relocated his operations centre away from public eyes. The media hadn't found him yet but the media didn't have Patrick's phone directory.

In less than an hour, they swung in through the electric gates of Kerswell Manor, built by a Bristol merchant seaman in the 1700s from the proceeds of his nefarious but lucrative trade with Africa and the Americas, and now the property of a second generation Bermuda-based investment banker. The owner only used the house for five or six weeks a year so that he could ride, entertain friends and see his daughters at the nearby boarding school for young ladies.

And he was a clandestine funder of Jamie's web campaign to root out corruption among "the Great and the Good".

As they drove slowly up the long drive, four of the owner's magnificent hunters pricked up their ears and trotted across to say hello. A middle-aged man in riding boots, Barbour jacket and cords emerged from an outbuilding and waved.

'Dr Cameron?' When Patrick nodded as he climbed out of the small car, the man smiled.

'I'm Jim, the estate manager. I guessed it might be you. The other gentleman sounded like he would drive something a lot better than that.'

Patrick looked round at the lab's runabout. It was starting to look its age.

'The other gentleman?' said Patrick.

The man ignored him. 'Follow me. Jamie's working round the back. Craig, the owner's, idea. Away from them prying binoculars, you know.'

As soon as Patrick saw his old friend, he slowed down. It had been three or four years since they had last met up, although they tried to stay in touch by phone from time to time. But even so, he was struck by the change in the man.

It had to be recent: only three months ago, Patrick had seen him interviewed on television after his website team had exposed widespread price-fixing collaboration in the fuel markets – oil, gas and coal – and he'd looked really fit and well.

Jamie Daniel looked up, smiled weakly and hauled himself out of his chair. He hadn't shaved for at least two days. He didn't look as though he'd slept much either.

The room was a converted farm workshop, warm and well-lit, now buzzing with banks of servers, laptops and printers.

Apart from Jamie, three young people were working away at their screens. Each one looked up and smiled a greeting at Patrick and Julian.

'Hi mate. Thanks for coming,' said Jamie. The two men hugged each other before Patrick introduced Julian.

Jamie said, 'Sorry I didn't have time to dress for the occasion.' The state of his shirt, carpet slippers and corduroy pants illustrated his point perfectly.

'Coffee?' he said pointing to the coffee machine, which appeared marginally more space-age than any of the IT gear in the room.

'You can have it in any one of twenty-seven different concoctions, but they all taste the same, so I'd recommend Numero Uno.'

'What's that?' asked Jamie.

'Strong, black, hot, in a mug, like the old days. Drop of rum?'

'No thanks, a bit early for me,' said Patrick pressing button number 1, more in hope than expectation. He watched his old friend pull a half-empty bottle from a drawer and plant it on his desk.

Jamie studied the bottle for ten seconds and, quite suddenly, sobbed.

'Shit, what a fucking mess, Pat.' He looked up as the tears began to flood down his cheeks. His three staff didn't flinch or look up.

Patrick took the mug from the machine's tray, sipped, pulled a face and passed it to Julian who was studying Jamie Daniel from a distance.

'Tell me the story, Jamie,' said Patrick. 'From extensive personal observation, you were a fairly indiscriminate shagger in the old days but I'd swear to God that you always drew the line – it was the only line you did draw – at under-age kids and, in particular the male of the species.'

'Well, well, well, you do turn up in the oddest of places, Cameron.'

The voice from the doorway made everyone look up. There, standing framed against the afternoon light, stood the immaculately dressed, shaved and well-combed figure of Assistant Commissioner

Andy Fields, operational head of the Security Service and, on three notable occasions, the man who had come perilously close to getting Patrick Cameron killed.

He continued: 'Which is a polite way of saying "Oh bollocks, not you again."'

By now Jamie Daniel was looking extremely flustered; his three assistants had decided it was time for a smoke or something and crept out of the room.

As his friend had clearly never come across Fields, Patrick made the introductions, in a manner that went some way towards calming Daniel's nerves.

Fields made himself a latte/cappuccino with 'double something Italian' and took a seat. Finally, Jamie was persuaded it was safe to tell his tale.

It was late one Thursday evening, sometime after the pubs had closed. Jamie Daniel had left the bar where he had just met with a very frightened woman, a whistle-blowing accountant with one of the country's largest construction firms, and was walking through one of the quieter parts of South Clapham, tossing up whether to hail a cab or take the Tube home to Fulham.

'Was the pub busy?' asked Julian, who hadn't uttered a word since they arrived.

Jamie turned, looked at Patrick, who nodded, then said, 'Yes, thankfully. Hell of a noise in there. It meant what this woman had to tell me wasn't overheard. Quite a story, I can tell you . . .'

'Go on, Jamie,' said Patrick quietly.

'Just a second,' Julian interrupted. 'How were you feeling as you left the pub?'

'Now you come to mention it, I felt a bit odd. I'd only had one pint so it wasn't the booze.'

'Odd?' said Julian. Patrick decided to allow him to continue.

'Yes,' he looked around and almost whispered, 'incredibly horny, actually.'

He grinned sheepishly.

'It wasn't about the woman I'd just met. She needed protecting not seducing. More . . . I don't know . . . Have you ever thought about having sex with a man, Patrick?'

Patrick let him continue.

'As I turned a corner, I heard the sound of a commotion coming from a small wooded area on the opposite side of the road. I realised I was close to the edge of the Common and it sounded like a dog yelping with pain.

'Crossing the road, I peered between the trees. I couldn't see much in the light from the street lamps, so I pulled out the pencil torch I always carry at night – I'm getting a bit short-sighted and it helps me find the lock on the front door.'

He laughed, then stopped.

'Seconds later, I found myself surrounded by boys – kids? teenagers? - each one dressed in some kind of flamboyant blouson, *very* tight designer jeans, hair and mascara freshly touched up. You know the type.

'"Hello, darling, it's your lucky day,"' said one of the youngsters.

'They grabbed me and pulled me deeper into this clump of trees. I remember stumbling over dead branches and rocks. Then they pinned me to a tree by both arms, and I felt my trousers being unbuttoned and pulled down to my ankles, my underwear too.

'There was nothing I could do. Someone had placed a gag over my mouth and they were too strong for me to fight back.

'Patrick, I'd never felt more terrified in my life. Or randy.

'What was this about? What did they want? Money? My watch? My phone? They could take the lot.'

Then, he described how, to his horror, he felt a hand slide onto his cock and start to rub backwards and forwards. An expert hand.

'That guy had done this before.'

Slowly but surely, he felt himself becoming aroused, as the hand began to move faster, more urgently.

He'd closed his eyes, trying to shut out the image of what they were doing to him, trying not to accept the pleasure. Just then the hand released him and was replaced by a soft pair of lips, then a warm mouth and throat.

All of a sudden, the whole scene was flooded with light. When Jamie opened his eyes, all but two of the painted boys had vanished, and in their place stood five uniformed policemen and a man in a suit. A photographer was snapping off shot after shot of Jamie's face and lower parts.

'Mr Daniel?' The man seemed to know his name. How?

Even though Jamie hadn't replied, he continued.

'I'm arresting you for a number of sexual offences, in particular in relation to having sex with under-age boys.'

'Under-age?' I said.

'Yes, sir. Both of these young men,' he indicated the two youngsters, who were now standing to one side, smirking, 'are under the age of consent. Fifteen, to be precise. One of the others is only twelve.'

'You could have fooled me,' said Jamie to Patrick and Andy Fields. 'More like twenty-five, I'd reckon, when I saw them in the bright light.'

'Members of the Metropolitan Police,' said Andy Fields and looked at them both.

'And the woman you interviewed in the pub?' asked Patrick.

'I've tried several times to contact her. Finally got her husband on the phone. She's in intensive care at Charing Cross. Apparently, she never made it home. Beaten up and robbed by a gang of kids. Lucky to be alive, he said.'

'Where?'

'Clapham Common. No more than two minutes away from where those bastards nailed me.'

Exasperation was written all over his face. 'Patrick, you're a medic. What in God's name's going on? I've never touched kids, never had any interest in gay sex before or since. What's the matter with me?'

Patrick put his hand on his friend's arm and looked at Andy Fields.

'Hate to say it, Andy but, if you're thinking what I'm thinking . . .'

Fields nodded. 'A quiet word outside, if you please, Doctor Cameron. Julian too, please.'

CHAPTER 6

The Thames Embankment, London

Bellingham was already waiting when Jenna arrived, to all the passing world just another boring, bored middle manager on a late takeaway sandwich break by the river.

He didn't look up as Jenna strolled towards the bench seat nor when she asked politely if the other place was taken; he simply moved his briefcase. She sat, crossing her legs. As usual, he sneaked a glance as she smoothed her skirt. They both knew he would never make a move on her but she clearly enjoyed playing the game. She smiled and fished her iPad out of her bag.

She knew she'd annoyed him. He'd expected an immediate response to his early morning message:

"Guillemot will depart by the end of the week. Nutkin."

The conversation between two keen birders with silly nicknames had proved an effective language for their communications. Every target had been allocated a sea-bird identity: each 'arrival' and 'departure' signalled that target's location and, in time, the results of Jenna's special attention.

In the last month alone, Storm Petrel, Puffin and Manx Shearwater had been 'spotted' and 'moved on'.

Guillemot, on the other hand, was rather special, even in this company. In almost every case so far, the victim had risen to great heights in their own field but remained a relative unknown to the wider public. But this one was different and neither Bellingham/Squirrel Nutkin nor Jenna/Miss Tiggy-Winkle had expected Guillemot to move to the front of the queue so soon.

This operation would present particular challenges, hence the need for this risky face-to-face meeting. He needed to make it quick – too many other Whitehall staffers knew his face.

Without turning towards her, he replaced his case on the seat between them. Jenna was engrossed in something she'd found on her tablet.

'By Friday. No excuses,' was all he said.

As he lifted his case and began to stand up, Jenna simultaneously laid her tablet on the same spot.

A minute later, he turned and looked back as she checked her watch, appeared to realise she was running late, gathered her tablet, slipped it into her bag, stood and strode swiftly away in the other direction.

Guillemot's detailed schedule for the next four days had been delivered.

Gloucestershire

Julian turned to Patrick as they watched Andy Fields' BMW disappear through the gates and turn onto the main road.

Julian sighed. 'How come every time I finally crack it with a woman my own age, that bugger pops up and tells me I've got to save the frigging nation ... *again*?'

Patrick laughed. His young colleague's love life was impossible to ignore. Their colleague Rowena had taken it upon herself to post a daily bulletin next to the lab's coffee machine. Julian never drank coffee.

'You're the neuro-scientist, Julian. You know the old saying, "Physician, heal thyself"?'

'He's right, though,' said Julian, nodding in the direction of Fields' departure. 'Somebody out there is playing games with people's minds . . . again.'

Patrick knew exactly what he meant. The last time Andy Fields had "invited" Patrick to take a break from research and go undercover, the villains were using such sophisticated technology to induce groups of innocent people to turn into killers that it was only Julian's gadgetry genius that had managed to save any further slaughter.

But, for some reason, this one felt different. On the previous occasion, groups of victims had been turned, temporarily, into aggressive, violent mobs until they were "switched off" and restored to normal. While, in every one of the cases outlined by Andy Fields, including Patrick's friend Jamie Daniel, an apparently well-balanced, successful individual, on the point of an exciting, fulfilled future, had devised a bizarre and unique way to either end his life, disappear or destroy his own reputation. Permanently.

'All men, every one different in style and execution, but . . .' said Julian, echoing his boss's thoughts.

Before he left, Andy Fields had put a proposal to them. It was very carefully worded. They both realised they had no option.

Patrick said, 'Well, my friend, it's down to you and me now.'

Julian grinned. Patrick could tell why: their motivations for accepting the assignment were quite different but it didn't matter. It was the scientific challenge that intrigued the young man while, deep down, Patrick was far more interested in outwitting – analysing, anticipating, deceiving, out-thinking - whoever the opposition turned out to be.

The fact that these people, whoever they were, were obviously prepared to kill to achieve their goals only served to sharpen his wits. This was active service.

And he would still be back in time to straighten everything up at the lab before he took paternity leave.

What am I thinking?

He grabbed Julian, who was still packing away the test results and samples he had taken from Jamie Daniel, and shoved him bodily towards the passenger door of the car.

'Oxford, my son. At speed. My marriage could depend on it.'

China

Hong Jintao had decided to leave his official limo in the garage for this trip. He told his driver not to wear official government uniform today. The anonymous black Mercedes sped the few miles from his residence, turning off down an unmarked road, through a high security barrier and on towards the centre of the forest.

The compound was the size of a small walled town; its original Ming dynasty gateway was the only indication that this place was anything special. In all other respects, the thirty-foot simple walls made it look more like a vast state retirement home – which in truth was exactly what it was.

The fact that it did not appear on any official maps was for one very good reason: this was the official residence, some called it the last resting place, of China's veteran leaders.

Hong Jintao, the People's Republic's Foreign Minister, was widely regarded as one of the country's most powerful men: his rise to power had gone almost unnoticed by foreign observers, so the announcement of his appointment as the new head of China's international negotiating team had occasioned much digging through the files.

Only those closest to the political inner circle knew the key fact: Hong Jintao was the personal protégé of Guo Dalong. And Guo Dalong was still, at the age of eighty-seven, China's chief power broker – the man without whose *imprimatur* few, if any, of the country's leaders over the last twenty-five years would have got their jobs.

In the time since Guo's first meeting with Hong, China's influence in the world, in particular in Africa and Asia, had steadily grown. More and more countries were accepting massive Chinese aid to improve their infrastructure, their raw material needs had created chaos in many markets as shortages bumped up the price, and Chinese manufacturing now accounted for the majority of the goods that Westerners found in their local stores.

But, as Guo had predicted, many British Commonwealth countries still turned to Britain for political influence in global affairs. The Americans had thrown in everything they could to try and wean these countries under their own economic umbrella, but with little success: only Australia, Canada and a few Caribbean islands had been unable to resist the American dollar.

This driver knew where to go. Passing through the gateway, he turned left and slowly followed the elegant road, lined with manicured lawns that would not have seemed out of place in a private Californian golf club.

As the Mercedes drew up in front of the gates, they swung open, allowing access to the wide gravel path that led to the front door. Hong had never failed to gasp at the beauty of the gardens but, on this occasion, he had other matters on his mind.

The summons had made it clear that this was not a social visit to his ageing mentor's home. Guo Dalong had concerns and he wanted answers.

Guo's long-term butler, in frock coat and striped trousers, was waiting on the steps. A man in his sixties, Harrison was English. He had been spirited away from his home country just in time, before he would have been arrested for spying on his former employer, the British ambassador to the United Nations. Hong suspected that Harrison was now rather more important than a butler to Guo.

After the briefest of greetings, Hong was led to the rear of the house and to the terrace where Guo liked to spend his mornings, meditating in his favourite armchair, a glass of fruit juice at his side.

The older he became, Guo had come to resemble more and more a Mandarin from an 18th century piece of porcelain-ware, even down to the way he wore his long hair and his fine embroidered jacket. His eyesight was poor, he needed a stick to walk and he wore aids in both ears, but his brain was as sharp as ever. Nobody tried to pull the wool over those failing eyes.

As he approached Guo's chair, the old man looked up, smiled courteously and waved him to a simple wooden garden chair. This was not a good sign, thought Hong: usually he was offered a much more comfortable seat.

'Good morning, my friend,' said Guo. 'I trust you are well and you are finding the time to enjoy this weather.'

'Thank you, Guo Dalong,' said Hong. 'I am well but, sadly, time is in short supply these days.'

Guo nodded and said nothing. His gaze returned to the garden.

Hong understood that it was up to him to begin the meeting.

'Thank you for the invitation, Guo Dalong. It is appropriate that we discuss the latest developments in the United Kingdom.'

Guo nodded again.

Hong began his report. 'To summarise, our agents have made some progress: after a couple of removal operations, we now have our own people in positions of control in both the British media and their banking community.'

The new heads of both the Independent Press Standards Organisation and the Basel Committee on Banking Supervision were both on China's payroll.

'This of course is in addition to our earlier, shall we say, "adjustment" at political level.'

'Yes, yes, we don't need to spend time on that,' said Guo.

Hong composed himself once more. 'I am confident that, within a short space of time, our men will have persuaded British public opinion, and therefore government policy, to question the relevance of aid and investment in those Commonwealth countries we have identified as prime targets.'

'Public opinion?'

'Yes. This should be relatively straightforward, sir. There is already a strong view among the British people that pretending that Great Britain is still a leading world power, that it still has a duty to pour money into all these badly-run little countries, to help them fight their little wars, just because their great-grandfathers used to run a thing called the British Empire, is a nonsense.

'Worse than that, with a health service struggling to survive, a crumbling road system and an ever-growing underclass – their country can no longer afford it. People are now adamant that foreign aid is a complete waste of their tax money. As the media campaign grows in strength and top bankers question its relevance, public unrest cannot be far away and those in power know it well.'

'Ah, the British people seem to be coming to their senses, at last,' said Guo Dalong. 'What else do you have for me?'

'We detected that the British owner of a privately-run website was close to obtaining evidence that could have exposed some of our more clandestine surveillance activities. Our men have put him out of action too.'

'Is that all?'

The three words Hong dreaded hearing. He could feel the sweat trickling down the back of his neck.

Guo turned at last to face him.

'I seem to remember, Hong Jintao, that my instructions specifically asked you to go rather deeper than what you have just described.'

Rarely a week passed without Hong waking in the early hours and hearing once again, as if the old man was there in the room beside his bed, those words from twenty years ago:

'Hong Jintao, we have decided to infiltrate and then destroy the power of the British Establishment. And you have been chosen to lead the entire operation.'

He took a deep breath and did his best to return the old man's piercing stare.

Guo spoke again. 'My young friend, surely you recognise that I do not simply want to gain control of the British Commonwealth; I want you to punish, to destroy the British Establishment!'

His voice was as strong as ever.

Hong swallowed; he knew deep down that Guo was right. But not for the first time, he wrestled with the question that had been nagging away at his brain for years:

Is Guo only interested in helping his nation or does he have a more personal score to settle?

He spoke quietly:

'I have today issued instructions for one more individual to be executed, by the end of this week.'

Sitting in the passenger seat as the car swept away from the compound, Hong Jintao could feel his pulse returning to normal.

He had said the right thing, made the right decision. Guo, for the moment, was placated.

Now he had to rely on the men he had so carefully recruited and trained – Marksworth and Bellingham.

Plus, in case he were needed, the one neither of them knew anything about. The man Hong liked to call the Locksmith.

CHAPTER 7

Oxford

After dropping Julian off at the lab, Patrick grabbed his bike and, fifteen minutes later, climbed the steps to the late Victorian cream-fronted terraced house which he and Angela had scraped together the deposit to buy eighteen months earlier.

He loved it: three-storeys, with tall windows, spacious first floor sitting room, open plan kitchen-dining area and long, high-walled garden. They still had much work to do before it would be exactly as they planned, but their own bedroom was finished and the room next to it was all ready to receive its tiny new occupant.

Less than four weeks to go, according to the calendar on the kitchen wall. After her first weeks of maternity leave from teaching at the junior school she loved so much, Angela seemed to be getting used to being alone during the day. She wasn't sleeping well but, with her regular daily routine of rest and a little exercise, she was feeling and looking good – that serene air that some, but by no means all, mothers take on as the Big Day approaches.

How serenely she would take Patrick's news was the question. He could feel his tension level rising as he put his key in the door and stepped into the hallway.

'Hi love,' she called from upstairs. 'You're early. Everything OK?'

She was in the sitting room, stretched out on the couch, a magazine on the table beside her and her tablet perched on her lap, switched off.

He leaned down and kissed the top of her head.

'How's your day, pet?'

Angela looked up and smiled. 'Just like the others – lady of leisure. Karen dropped in for a coffee. Lots of nappy talk and whinging about men.' She laughed. 'How was yours?'

'So so.' Patrick smiled, went through to the kitchen, switched on the kettle, and returned.

OK. Here goes.

He sat down on the edge of the couch. Angela shifted to make room for him. She looked apprehensive. She knew him too well.

'OK,' she said. 'Out with it. What's happened?'

Patrick knew he looked guilty but he couldn't help it.

'If it's that bugger Andy Fields again, I'll wring his neck,' she said, looking him straight in the eye.

Shit! Hole in one.

Patrick didn't need to say a thing but he did.

'You know what he's like, Angel. "National security; safety of the nation; you're the only man for the job . . ."'

'But we're about to have our first child, Patrick!' Barely controlled exasperation.

'I know, I know.'

'Tell him to take a hike, man. He'll just have to find somebody else and screw up their family's life instead.'

Patrick said nothing. The last two assignments that Fields had roped him in to handle had both worked out well. And he'd been very well paid. But not before he had come close, on both occasions, to losing important parts of his anatomy, possibly his life. Not to mention his wife.

He knew Angela had vivid memories of the last "adventure": she had been there alongside him, all the way. She'd been magnificent, the consummate actress, but it had taken her months to fully recover.

'They want Julian on this one too,' he said.

'Oh, so that makes everything alright, does it?' The temperature was now at seething level.

'Honey,' he put his hand on her arm. Bombshell time. He hadn't wanted to say this – he knew it could be seen as emotional blackmail:

'Two of these people's victims had pregnant wives too.'

His wife's face stopped and stared. It was fully twenty seconds before she spoke. Very quietly.

'You'd better tell me all about it, hadn't you?'

The Reform Club, London

'Good of you to come, Andrew. I've reserved a room. This way.'

The last person to call Assistant Commissioner Andy Fields 'Andrew' was his headmaster, shortly before the end of his final term at the appalling boys' boarding school his father had chosen for him, solely on the basis of its reputation for rugby coaching.

If he had looked a little closer, father would have discovered a somewhat strange crew of teaching staff, all bachelors, freezing dormitories, cold showers and a disciplinary system modelled on *Tom Brown's Schooldays*.

Andy followed the old man down the corridor and into an oak-panelled room. Four more white-haired men rose, smiling, to greet him, each immaculately dressed in a tweed suit, club tie and white shirt. Despite their age, they all bore that bright-eyed, smooth-skinned look that somehow lingers on with those who have spent many years at the heart of affairs of state. These were men who had always inspired respect, not through the grand title on their office door, but because those who followed them did so out of utter loyalty: they were proud to be part of their team.

These were what is truly meant by the term 'leaders'.

The group bore no official name but was known amongst themselves, and a highly select number of others, as 'The Last Resort Squad'.

Formed in the aftermath of the alleged 1968 plot to remove Prime Minister Harold Wilson, the group received no formal government recognition or funding, their membership was chosen by an anonymous 'committee of the great and the good', and their precise role had never been formally defined. They reported to no-one but plenty of people reported to them, whether they knew it or not. Their purpose was simple:

"To protect the nation from harm at the hands of its enemies from within, by monitoring the activity and behaviour of those in positions of power, by gathering evidence by whatever means deemed necessary, and by intercepting, at the earliest opportunity, any identified plan that could pose a threat to the free, democratic social fabric of the United Kingdom."

The definition of "enemies from within" had been left deliberately vague.

Everyone took their seat. Fresh coffee was served by a waiter who had mysteriously appeared, then left silently.

'Thank you for joining us, Andrew,' said the man who Fields knew as Sir Norman, a former Chief of the Armed Forces.

'We've done a little digging since you called me but perhaps it would be best if you brought us up to date with your thoughts.'

Andy took a sip of his coffee and began his debrief: the odd circumstances of the beach suicide and the disappearance from the train; the apparent coincidence that the men who took these men's place were both under low-level *MoleWatch* surveillance; and his conversation with Jamie Daniel.

The men around the table listened carefully, each jotting the occasional note on the pad in front of them.

When he had finished, Sir Norman thanked him and said, 'Now Jonty, could you tell us what you've managed to uncover?'

Jonathon "Jonty" Mackenzie, Lord Harptree, a former Principal Private Secretary to two Prime Ministers, was best known these days as chairman of the British Winegrowers Association; his vineyard in Somerset was producing some remarkably good Pinot Noir which he sold in moderate quantities, primarily to the more discerning, and well-informed, Whitehall civil servants. A jovial fellow, his bluff manner disguised a fine brain.

'Cost me a few quid in free bottles,' he grumbled, 'but I've unearthed some interesting guff on those two blighters who stepped in when our two chaps kicked the bucket.

'Firstly,' he referred to his notepad, 'let's take a look at the fellow who took up the reins at the Independent Press Standards Board after the first man drowned himself.'

He held up an official-looking photograph.

'Ex-journalist, Beijing correspondent for the BBC, marriage problems a few years back, fond of young skirt, I gather. Not too partial about where he dips his wick.'

The others listened intently. They were all clearly used to Jonty's style.

He continued. 'But I guess you know all that, Andy. What you may not know, however, is that he was also virtually bankrupt. Until three months ago, that is, when he suddenly came into a great deal of money. I pulled a few strings and discovered that the windfall came from the same account to which he's been doling out a rather large monthly standing order for the last four years – a so-called investment trust. All apparently Kosher. Except that, when you look a little more closely, this one's biggest funders, behind the scenes, are the Chinese security people in Copenhagen.'

'So what does that tell you, Jonty?' Sir Norman broke the silence.

'A case of blackmail your man first, until he'll do whatever you ask, then bail him out, I reckon.'

Notes were being scribbled.

'And the other man?'

'Yes, the replacement head of the banking supervision committee. Equally odd, I'm afraid. On the face of it, impeccable qualifications, quite as good as the fellow who vanished. Couldn't find a thing, then by luck,' he smiled, 'I was talking to a friend who happens to live in the next village to where this chap spends his weekends. That part of Wiltshire's a regular little hotbed of civil service mandarins, if you'll excuse the pun.' He giggled quietly at his own joke.

'Anyway,' he resumed, 'it appears our chum is not too fussy about who he invites as weekend guests. The local gossip last week was all about how the old boy who delivers the parish magazine knocked on the front door and was asked to leave, not too politely, by a large bearded gent he'd never seen before. Before the door was slammed in his face, he heard what he swears was the voice of someone in great pain, possibly begging for mercy, he couldn't be sure.'

'Are we sure about this, Jonty?' asked one of the other men. George was a career policeman like Andy, whose formidable reputation for rooting out corruption in judicial circles had earned him three assassination attempts and a discreet twenty-four hour escort. 'Couldn't this old codger have been imagining things?'

Jonty laughed. 'Look who's calling someone an old codger, George. But this one's reliable, I think. Before he retired and took up magazine delivery, he was senior professor of something unpronounceable at Jesus College, Cambridge.

'But there was one other thing I should have mentioned. Remember I mentioned the big bearded bugger?'

Nods all round.

'He looked Chinese.'

Everyone looked at everyone else.

Jonty checked his notes to see if he'd missed anything.

'Now, what else? Oh yes,' he piped up, stabbing the page with his finger. 'How could I forget that? I must be losing my faculties.' He laughed to himself as the others waited.

'Our professor-stroke-postman had the common sense to memorise the registration numbers of a few cars parked in the drive. Apparently, it's a game he plays to postpone the aging process. Anyway, two of them were rather interesting - one registered to the Chinese diplomatic team in London . . .'

'And the other, Jonty?' asked Gerald, the fourth Squad member, an enormously tall, lean man, one-time head of the country's leading international business school. They all knew Lord Jonty Harptree was enjoying himself, teasing them.

This was clearly Jonty's big moment and he squeezed every ounce of drama from his final line.

'The other one, Stuart, belongs to the Permanent Under-Secretary at the Ministry of Defence, a Mr David Marksworth.'

On his way back to his office, Andy made three calls. He already knew the broad plan – that had taken no more than twenty minutes for the combination of five fine minds to hatch. By the time he was sitting at his desk, wheels within wheels were already in motion, men and women had their new orders and information was starting to flow.

He checked the national news on his screen. The top item - confirmed rumours of yet another Commonwealth country riddled with corruption, British aid funds going missing.

He sat back and drummed his fingers on the desk.

'Call me, Patrick Cameron. Call me.'

CHAPTER 8

London

It had not taken long. A quiet word in the right ear, a couple of tickets to the West End opening night of a smash Broadway musical and Gregory Bellingham was on the plane. Well, not exactly on the plane but his place was confirmed in the official party which would accompany a royal prince and the Minister of State for Commonwealth Affairs to the inauguration ceremony of the new president of India.

Under normal circumstances, Bellingham, as Under-Secretary, would have been expected to stay behind and mind the shop but India was different. Its ever-growing position as one of the great global powerhouses, and its political influence over the other Commonwealth countries in Asia and Africa could quite justifiably explain his presence in this high-powered delegation. Nobody seemed to question the change of plan: all it required was some last-minute juggling of the seating and sleeping arrangements.

As he packed his case before setting off to catch a specially commandeered RAF flight, he anxiously checked his private phone every few minutes. Two messages would set his mind at rest. Two simple messages, that was all.

Then, just as his ministry driver was pulling away from the house, his phone buzzed, then buzzed again.

Guillemot primed, read the first message.

The other one made him smile:

Nesting place OK. Tiggy.

He had no idea who "Tiggy" really was. It didn't matter. Hour by hour, David Marksworth's detailed plan would now proceed. If he and "Tiggy" did their job, by the time Bellingham was back in his office, the political climate would have begun to change. Britain's relations with the Indian government, whose pen was poised over so many huge commercial contracts, would be shaken to the core.

Enough for India finally to turn away from their old Imperial masters? We'll see.

If they did so, India could also decide to persuade other Commonwealth countries to follow suit; these days, staying friends with India was far more important than any historic ties with the British throne.

Then the United Kingdom would be teetering on the edge of the slippery slope, its power base badly holed.

And that should keep Hong Jintao quiet for a while.

A few years earlier, Julian would have stood out like a sore thumb. Fortunately, under Andy Fields' leadership, the Security Service had come to recognise that dressing their agents like FBI G-men – blue suit, white button-down shirt, tie, shiny black shoes - was not the most effective way of helping them to blend in with the great unwashed British public. So now Julian's untameable haircut and "interesting" clothing combinations went unnoticed as he and Patrick accompanied the Defence Department's Permanent Under-Secretary to his daily succession of meetings in different government buildings.

Unnoticed, that is, by all except the more lively-minded female members of staff. As Julian breezed past, conversation ceased, unable to resist a sudden *en masse* libido surge. Patrick had long ago given up trying to explain this phenomenon in scientific terms; it just happened with Julian.

Patrick, on the other hand, had needed a little more attention. He couldn't risk being recognised if he bumped into anyone from his undercover past. The ID team at the Service's headquarters had not taken long to convert him into a shaven-headed, shades-wearing, gum-chewing, tattooed bodyguard – a popular image among men of a certain age doing their best to look cool.

When the ministry's head of security had suggested to Marksworth that, in view of recent intelligence about the activities of a known extremist cell, it would be a wise move to increase his bodyguard from one to three, he had agreed immediately. The note to Andy Fields reported that Marksworth actually appeared rather pleased by the news.

'I reckon it makes the pompous little shit feel even more important,' were the precise words used in the SMS message.

So, from now on, Patrick Cameron would be Johnny Monks while Julian, to Patrick's chagrin, would rejoice in the name of Sebastian Neal.

'Hey, I'm far more of a Sebastian than he is,' Cameron had complained, but to no avail.

The third member of the team was an ex-military policeman, Mike Challoner, a white-haired veteran MOD man, who knew everybody and who everybody liked, with the exception of those he called 'The Spotted Hanky Brigade', which included David Markswor th.

Challoner was one of Fields' most reliable men, trusted to keep his eyes open, his mouth shut and his photographic memory in gear at all times. Meeting Cameron, he clearly recognised a fellow pro and was happy to share his thoughts and ask his advice.

On the face of it, Julian was the kind of man he would have dismissed in seconds but, from the very first, the two of them got on famously. Julian was no natural comedian but he made Challoner laugh and that was enough for him.

Patrick had read the background check on David Marksworth three times.

'Good family, good school', whatever that meant. Fast-tracked through Civil Service training, including a spell studying in Paris; top grades in the passing out exams.

Then later, when others reached their 'promotion plateau' – the point at which the system decreed that they needed a 'period of stability' – Marksworth had continued to move in a Northerly direction within the MOD.

Quite why he had done so well was not clear in any detail from the file, except for a suggestion, here and there, that he had been spotted by men and women of influence at important stages of his career. Cameron made a note of their names in the margin.

Just in case.

Nonetheless, there was enough seemingly impartial evidence that this was a highly capable man who made things happen – rescuing an arms procurement budget that was running out of control; persuading colleagues in other ministries to hold back on non-urgent plans so that he could secure the funds for upgrading ground troops' vehicle body armour; brokering a deal with the French on shared landing facilities in the Magreb . . .

Patrick switched off his desk light and sat back, stretching his arms above his newly shaven head. To his right, Julian was quietly combing through a pile of dossiers he had decided were worth a look.

'Anything?' said Patrick.

'Mmm,' came the response, usually a sign that the young man was onto something.

'Could be nothing,' said Julian, looking up at Patrick and stabbing a page with his finger.

Cameron stood and moved to where he could look over Julian's shoulder.

'How's your French?' Julian looked up again and grinned.

New Delhi

If you know where to look, there is no shortage of high quality private entertainment in certain quarters of India's capital city.

For the time being, however, life's little pleasures would have to wait. Jenna Dobrosova needed to focus one hundred percent on the mission.

New Delhi was not entirely fresh territory and it was good to be back. Early in her career, on secondment from the Soviet army, she had attended a global symposium of neuroscientists in the same city.

Looking back, it was her experiences there that had unwittingly set her off down two of the paths that would come to dictate her life: a demonstration by an Austrian academic of his ground-breaking work on neurotechnology – the use of technology to affect how people think and behave; and her introduction, in the expert hands of a beautiful Indian scientist, to the extraordinary erotic power of Tantra.

She forced herself to turn her mind back to the job in hand. There were still thirty-six hours to go before the appointed moment but her obsession with detail dictated that everything had to be checked, rechecked and confirmed, especially in a country where the locals had a habit of changing their plans at the last minute.

She felt comfortable about the technology. For the fourth time in the last hour, here in her hotel room, she picked up the tiny console and, using nothing more than her eyes, keyed in the test code. Once again, the correct signal appeared on the screen. The final check would now have to await the target's arrival in New Delhi.

Gaining access to the man's brain in London could have been tricky but Greg Bellingham had managed to find out in advance where he was having his pre-flight haircut and, from then on, it was a simple matter of calling in at the salon to make a spurious enquiry. Then, while the receptionist was away checking her stock, a stroll past the Minister's chair and the job was done.

Time to relax. Time for a little fun. Jenna picked up her phone, scrolled through the address book, found the name, paused for a moment, trembled, made her decision and pressed "Call".

CHAPTER 9

New Delhi, the following day

Any half-competent recruitment consultant would have argued vehemently against the appointment of George Butterley Floyd, Marquis of Dulwich as Her Majesty's new Minister of State for Commonwealth Affairs. And many of them did just that. *George Utterly Flawed* ran the headline in the satirical magazine *Private Eye*.

To ask the otherwise unemployable second son of one of England's wealthiest families to maintain cordial relations with the heads of the same countries his forefathers had ruthlessly exploited for centuries could hardly be termed a wise political decision; but George's father, the Duke of Sedgemoor, was so far up the pecking order of the British Establishment that not even the Prime Minister – in fact especially the Prime Minister – would dream of questioning his nomination.

In truth, Lord Dulwich was a charming, apparently decent chap – balding, a touch overweight but a decent horseman and a fine shot. Provided that his staff, led by Permanent Under-Secretary Gregory Bellingham, scripted his every utterance, word for word, in advance, his arrogant racist upbringing rarely emerged in public.

Bellingham and his colleagues knew this was a risky strategy: it was only a matter of time before Lord Minister George departed from their careful script and put his foot in it in a big way. Their only hope of a reprieve was that the recipient of the unguarded comment was sharp enough to recognise the limitations of the Minister's intellect and to shrug the insult off without taking offence.

It was Gregory's turn to open proceedings at the early morning meeting in the British High Commission.

'Your duties today will not be too demanding, Minister. All the visiting presidents and royalty, including our own HRH, will gather in the stateroom at the Rashtrapati Bhavan . . .'

'The what?' the minister interrupted.

'The president's official residence, sir. Formerly known as the

Viceroy's House. Three hundred and forty rooms, set in a hundred and seventy acres. Designed by Lutyens as a fitting symbol of British imperial rule.'

'Ah, that sounds more like it,' the minister chuckled. 'Those were the days, what? Our glorious empire . . .'

He looked round the table expectantly but received only a few embarrassed grunts from the assembled officials. At least he hadn't mentioned the word fuzzy-wuzzies this time.

'Do carry on, Gregory,' the minister said.

Bellingham cleared his throat. 'As I was saying, Minister . . .'

'Do you think I could have some more tea?'

A junior officer stepped forward and refilled the minister's cup while the others shuffled their papers.

Bellingham tried again, his voice barely concealing his frustration. 'While the bigwigs are being presented, the Foreign Secretary, yourself and the senior ministers from other countries will be taking their seats in the grandstand behind the saluting platform in front of the building. I've arranged for you to be placed next to the foreign ministers of Nigeria and Singapore, sir.'

'Nigeria and Singapore, eh? Any suggested topics of conversation for me? Rigged elections, perhaps? The state of the noodle market?'

'I was rather hoping, sir, that you might put in a word for a couple of our companies who are pitching for large construction contracts in those two countries, actually. We've prepared some notes for you.'

He passed two sheets of paper to the minister who looked at them cursorily, stuffed them in his jacket pocket and grunted.

Bellingham continued. 'There'll be the usual religious ceremony and speeches, a march-past, and then you'll all repair to the banqueting hall for lunch. No alcohol, I'm afraid. This is India.'

'Oh bollocks,' muttered Lord Dulwich.

'That's about it. But, before we go, there is one important area we need to discuss, Minister,' said Bellingham. 'Rather sensitive.'

His Lordship was starting to look bored, checking his watch and adjusting his waistcoat.

Bellingham ploughed on. 'In fact, highly sensitive, sir. The fact is that anti-British sentiment is growing fast among certain sections of the Indian political class. The recent violence in the UK against immigrants, but particularly against Indians, has brought a deep feeling to the surface among the current generation of educated Indians that the time may have come for India to break away from their old Imperial masters.'

The minister had started to mutter. Bellingham ignored him.

'For these people, Britain is yesterday's power, tied hand and foot to an inexorably declining America, our empire consigned to history, much like ancient Rome and the Ottomans.'

The calls of protest around the room were silenced by a simple hand gesture.

'Yes, I know. It's outrageously unfair. We still lead the world in many fields.' He couldn't think of more than three offhand.

'The point is, sir, that's the way we are perceived by many influential Indians. Allow me to demonstrate.'

He picked a newspaper cutting from his file.

'"How can any country that is seen by the rest of the world to be in bed with Britain – a culturally racist society living on past glories - ever be taken seriously in the global theatre?"'

He looked round the table and saw he was touching on an uncomfortable truth for those present.

'Gentlemen, we should remind ourselves that the new president's grandfather met his death, in a very unpleasant manner, in a British jail.'

He closed his file and waited.

'What are you saying, Greg?' asked one of the officials.

Gregory shrugged and lowered his voice. 'All I am saying is that we live in interesting times. So it is essential – essential – that nothing happens today which could make matters worse.'

He looked left and right. For almost everyone round the table, it was clear that he had made his point. Almost everyone.

Lord Dulwich spoke, his face lightening up, rubbing his palms together. 'Well, that's all very interesting, Mr Bellingham, but life goes on. After all, we did give them our legal system and teach them cricket. They should be bloody grateful. We mustn't let all this spoil a good party, must we? Personally, I can't wait to get stuck into a decent chicken Tandoori.'

He stood and prepared to leave the room. Watching as the minister buttoned his jacket, Gregory checked the tiny console concealed in the case of his iPad.

Fine. The weapon was in place and primed. And, whatever happened that day, he'd managed to cover his own tracks. David Marksworth would be proud of him.

London, UK

Patrick Cameron had no need of the French-English dictionary that Julian had installed on his desktop. The MBA end of year project report he was reading was dated 1996. In line with protocol at HEC International Business School, so he had learned from the cover page, the opening abstract had to be presented in both French and English. Patrick presumed this was a token mark of respect to the French language, which was fighting a losing battle with English at that time to be recognised as the international language of business.

The report itself was written entirely in English, the subject matter of little interest to Patrick.

One of its authors was a David Marksworth, which was why Julian had pulled it from the archives. The second name, Gregory Bellingham, rang only a faint bell until he saw the scrap of paper Julian had just dropped on his desk – Bellingham was another Permanent Under-Secretary, this time at Commonwealth Affairs. It was the third author's name that had Patrick reaching for his phone.

'Andy, we've found something,' he said when the call was answered. 'David Marksworth was at business school with a certain Hong Jintao. Isn't that the name of the Chinese Foreign Minister?'

Silence, then, 'You're sure it's that Hong Jintao? There must be hundreds of Chinese with that name.'

'Good point. One hell of a coincidence, though, surely, don't you think?'

'I'll have it double-checked and come back to you. So Patrick, what's your man Marksworth been up to in the last few days? Anything interesting to report?'

'Nothing yet. Just one odd thing - he carries three phones around with him. One for official stuff, one for friends and family . . .'

'And the third?'

'Presumably that one's reserved for conversations he'd rather the others didn't hear.'

'Any chance you can borrow it and take a look?'

'We'll give it a try.'

'And how's Julian getting on with the samples he took from Jamie Daniel?'

'He's waiting for the analyst's report. Hopefully tonight or, at the latest, tomorrow.'

'OK. Over and out. Oh, by the way Patrick, out of interest, how did you discover Marksworth has three phones?'

'Ah, didn't I tell you? Young Julian, in addition to his other talents, is also a member of the Magic Circle – specialist subject, picking pockets.'

Ending the call, Cameron breathed out and sat back in his chair. He hadn't realised how tense he had become in the last few minutes.

Well, well, we meet again, Hong Jintao. Recognised in international circles as the mild-mannered but refreshingly progressive voice of Chinese diplomacy – "Not just a man you can do business with, a man you want to do business with", someone once said. The politicians love him.

But, behind the facade, in the private opinion of a select number of security professionals, he's a very different man with a very different agenda: ambitious, ruthless, clever, content to play the waiting game, no matter how long it lasts, to achieve his ultimate goal.

So, Mr Hong – what is your agenda? What is your ultimate goal?

'Julian,' he muttered. 'Where's Hong Jintao now? Find out, can you?'

New Delhi

Hong Jintao had just finished briefing his own people about the plans for the ceremony. He had decided not to mention that the Indian president had requested a private meeting with the President of the People's Republic over breakfast at which, he had let it be known, he was about to confirm that Chinese companies would be the preferred contractors for two new nuclear power stations, in return for substantial, but confidential, contributions to the Indian space weapons programme. Hong wanted to maximise the impact of this diplomatic coup in his own time and he could not risk a leak.

He also wanted to finish the meeting early. He had other matters to attend to.

He returned swiftly to his suite at the embassy. There he accessed the status reports from his network in Delhi. Everything appeared to be as it should.

It is going to be all a matter of timing.

Every detail had been meticulously rehearsed but, on the day, they knew they had to be prepared for the unexpected.

He shivered, although the room was very warm. No matter how hard he tried, he could not shrug off the feeling that his every move was being watched – by a very old man with long hair.

It was time to leave the hotel. Jenna Dobrosova checked herself one last time in the full length mirror. Towards the end of an adventurous evening together, her companion had helped her perfect her appearance for the following day. Many European wives living in India had taken to wearing traditional Indian clothing at ceremonial occasions: it was considered acceptable, even respectful, by the locals.

Jenna was surprised when she saw just how much the full-length sari, the judicious application of make-up to her eyes and forehead, and a brightly coloured silk scarf around her hair changed her appearance. When she adjusted her posture and lowered her eyes, the confident, athletic Russian was now the quiet, unassuming wife of a minor diplomat.

Arriving in the hotel foyer, she discreetly attached herself to a party of Indian and European dignitaries' wives. All attempts to strike up conversation with her were greeted with a smile and a few words in Russian.

When the cars dropped them in the grounds of the presidential residence, she smiled quietly to herself: her judgement had been that these women's husbands were of sufficiently important rank to be seated where they had a clear view of the platform. She was right.

She scanned the grandstand housing the visiting ministers of state, which rose up behind the platform and was filling rapidly. She soon located the row she was looking for and was relieved to find her target already installed in his expected seat. Thankfully, the traditional eccentricities of Indian administration had not relocated him elsewhere.

A loud fanfare sounded. Preceded by a gaggle of kings, princes and presidents, the new president of India was escorted onto the stage by a ceremonial guard of honour. He acknowledged the crowd's applause with a nervous smile and a bow, his hands folded demurely in front of his chest. Here was a man who commanded huge respect among his fellow countrymen for his wisdom and political nouse, but this was also an elderly, very private man who hated the trappings of office and who, according to rumour, liked to clean his own shoes and cook supper for his guests himself, using vegetables and spices he bought earlier from stalls in the local market.

The first to take the microphone was the Chairman of the Rajya Sabha, the Council of States, India's upper house of parliament.

High on the roof of the north wing of the presidential residence, Sergeant Kumar Shakli was in position. He had a clear line of sight to both of his targets. Except that this was not Sergeant Kumar Shakli. The real Shakli was dead, lying face down in a culvert on the edge of town, stripped of his identity. The man who had taken his place in the presidential protection squad was one of Asia's most highly paid assassins. By midnight, he would be having a late dinner with his family on the coast of Sri Lanka, hundreds of miles away.

Each member of the invited audience had the text of the ceremony printed in their programme. The first speaker was drawing to a close. This would be followed by the formal investiture, a speech of acceptance from the new president and a military display. Despite the efforts of dozens of large cooling fans, the temperature was climbing steadily.

George, Marquis of Dulwich, his suit jacket beginning to crumple in the heat, was staring straight ahead, apparently paying no attention to the proceedings on the platform.

His mind was a total blank. Primed and ready to receive orders.

CHAPTER 10

London

'Patrick,' said Julian, walking into the room. 'I don't know if you remember asking me to find out Hong Jintao's whereabouts.'

'Yes, Julian. Exactly three minutes ago, if I recall.'

'Sorry it's taken so long,' retorted Julian, continuing the joke.

'Well?'

'Well what? Oh yes, Hong Jintao. He's in India, New Delhi. Some kind of big ceremony.'

'Yes, there was something about it on this morning's news.' Patrick picked up the TV remote and switched it on, flicking through to the news channels. Within seconds, a live feed from the Indian presidential installation ceremony was filling the screen.

'Well, that's no surprise,' said Patrick as the camera left the speaker's dais and scanned the rows of royals and presidents in the stands. 'Looks like a three-line whip for the great and the good.'

'Speaking of whom,' said Julian casually. 'Our third man is there, too.'

'What do you mean, the third man?'

'Gregory Bellingham, remember? The other member of the HEC Paris student group. I managed to access his diary online.'

Julian's mastery of lateral thinking was the stuff of legend but, on this occasion, Patrick said simply, 'Thanks, Julian.' He watched the screen for a few more seconds, then muted the sound and turned away.

He shrugged. 'But that doesn't mean anything, does it? Bellingham works in Commonwealth Affairs, Hong is China's foreign minister, so they're both going to turn up at big gatherings in places like India. Part of the job; nothing sinister about that.

'Come on, let's do something else. We can take a look at Jamie Daniel's medical report. It arrived ten minutes ago. Over there.' He pointed to a large envelope lying on a side table.

Julian collected the envelope and began to slit it open as he walked slowly back towards Patrick's desk, his eyes still focused on the TV screen.

'Get a move on,' Patrick said.

Julian was ignoring him. Something he had seen was drawing him closer to the wall-mounted TV. Dropping the envelope on the desk as he passed, he placed himself directly in front of the live broadcast.

'Julian!' said Patrick.

The young man waved his hand behind him, giving Patrick a hybrid "Shut-up-and-come-here" signal.

'What is it?' asked Cameron, moving to stand beside him.

'I'm not sure. Just thought I saw something odd. There!'

He pointed as the camera panned along the grandstand housing most of the visiting diplomats. In an attempt to keep cool in the blistering heat, many of them were using their fans, others flapping their programme in front of their face. One or two had broken with protocol and undone their top button or removed their jacket.

Patrick was trying and failing to see what had struck his colleague as interesting. 'For the life of me, I can't . . .'

Julian grabbed the remote and switched the monitor to touch-screen. Selecting a menu command with his index finger, he scrolled back the images from the previous few minutes, then ran them forward more slowly until he found what he was seeking.

The camera had halted its earlier pan along the rows of diplomats and homed in on one man. Julian turned on the audio.

As the speaker on the platform had switched to the Hindi language, the TV commentator was taking the opportunity to fill in with some background information for the audience.

'And there is the British Secretary of State for Commonwealth Affairs, the affable Lord Dulwich. His forefathers made their fortune here in India in the late 19th century. In fact, Lord Dulwich's great-uncle was Lord Chief Justice of India between the wars. It's good to see that the current generation of the family are on such good terms with today's government . . .'

The TV director had then switched back to the camera covering the speech. Julian turned to Patrick.

'Did you see it?' he asked.

'See what?'

'That man, there, what was his name? Lord Dulwich. Everyone around him was trying to stay cool, except for him. Look.' He scrolled back a few seconds once more. The immaculately dressed diplomats surrounding Dulwich were all, without exception, flapping a fan or a programme by their face; some were mopping their brow. Lord Dulwich, on the other hand, despite giving every sign of suffering far more than any of his neighbours – his shirt and jacket were soaked, his face dripping with sweat – was sitting bolt upright, elbows on the arms of his chair, hands folded under his chin. His face looked utterly calm, his eyes staring straight ahead at some far-distant point.

'Well?' asked Julian.

'So perhaps he's just doing his stiff-upper-lip act,' said Cameron. 'Showing the others how the Brits can take the heat.'

Julian sighed. 'Sometimes I despair of you, Doctor Cameron. Look more closely. There.'

He touched a point on the screen beside the minister's head.

Patrick leaned forward. Julian's finger was now close to the side of the minister's neck.

'Right there,' he said again.

Because of the camera angle, it was hard to make it out but there, quite clearly, he could now see a circular mark peeking out above the man's shirt collar. No larger than a telephone key, it almost looked like the tip of a much larger blemish.

Julian touched the screen again and the sequence rolled forward a few seconds. Using just one finger, Lord Dulwich was involuntarily scratching under his collar. The collar had slipped half an inch down his neck. Now the blemish was fully revealed. It was more like a white inoculation bruise: a small, almost solid white circle standing out clearly against the man's lightly tanned skin.

'What's that mark, Julian?' Patrick asked.

Julian smiled and whooped, mimicking Rex Harrison's Professor Henry Higgins,

'By George, I think he's got it!'

He tapped the screen again and the image was enlarged. With the 4G ultra high definition, it was now just possible to discern that the white patch contained five tiny red pin-pricks, arranged at even intervals just inside its circumference.

'Now, why does that ring a bell with me?' said Patrick. 'I'm sure I've come across that somewhere in my dim and distant past.' His brow furrowed as he stared at the image.

'I know exactly where I saw it last, Patrick. Nothing dim and distant about it – last week, on Jamie Daniel's neck. Same white patch, same red dot pattern.'

Patrick looked at his young colleague as the implications of what he'd just heard began to whirl round his brain.

'Give me the phone!' he barked.

'Andy,' he said moments later. 'We have a connection.'

Andy Fields was back in the Reform Club, this time in the oak-panelled dining room, having lunch with Sir Norman Tudway. Designed three hundred years ago, nobody had since seen any reason to modernise the club's décor. And the roast beef was quite superb.

When Cameron's call came through, he excused himself and took it in the club's lobby area.

He listened as Patrick related what he and Julian had discovered.

'So what's the connection?' he asked when Patrick had finished.

'Jamie Daniel and Lord Dulwich have identical marks on their neck, *and*, guess who's there right now with Dulwich attending the same event in India - David Marksworth's old business school buddies, Gregory Bellingham and Hong Jintao.'

Fields digested this for a few moments. 'It's a bit tenuous, isn't it, Patrick?'

'I know. But we can't ignore it, surely,' Cameron protested.

'Right. Leave it with me. I'll call you back.' He rang off, walked swiftly back into the dining room and quietly summarised what he had learnt to Sir Norman.

'I think we'll skip dessert, don't you?' The elderly man was quite calm. 'Come with me.'

Within a minute, they were installed in a small private room, watching the direct TV broadcast feed from New Delhi, while Sir Norman made three short calls on Fields' mobile phone, jotting notes and numbers on a pad in front of him.

'Do you mind if I make a long distance call on this, Andy?' he asked.

Before Andy could respond, Sir Norman had turned away as he

waited for the connection.

'Hello, it's . . .' He muttered a codeword, so quickly that Patrick was unable to hear. 'Can you take a look at Lord Dulwich? He's sitting in the main grandstand, three rows back, lightweight suit, balding, next to the African man wearing traditional costume. Found him? Good. I want you to get him out of there. Now. I don't care how.'

He put down the phone and turned to Andy Fields.

'It may be too late but, as we've got one of our chaps on the spot, we can but try.'

Fields' SMS message to Patrick Cameron was on its way:

TV. Now. BBC News.

The first speaker had droned on rather longer than planned, according to Jenna Dobrosova's briefing notes. When he finally turned away from the microphone to polite applause, the new President was ushered to centre stage. A liveried official stepped forward bearing a beautifully embroidered cushion, on which lay an ornate chain of office.

The leader of the Upper House then intoned the words of the oath, repeated phrase by phrase by the President, who finally bowed his head to receive the Presidential chain, to rapturous cheers from every part of the arena. A band struck up a fanfare.

On the giant screen, Jenna could see the cameras switching quickly around different parts of the audience, all of whom were now on their feet applauding, their faces wreathed in smiles as they watched the ceremony unfold and the new President approaching the microphone.

She counted silently to ten, reached into her sari and located the console's buttons. She knew she had to remain cool at times like this, but the thrill of the moment, the enormity of what she was about to unleash, always got to her. She felt her hand tremble – the usual, almost erotic power surge through her body.

Up in the stand reserved for the most senior diplomats, Hong Jintao's eyes were switching from the President to Lord Dulwich to the roof and back again. His facial expression was calm but his brain was in overdrive. He could almost feel the controlling hand of Guo Dalong on his shoulder.

Don't let me down, Hong Jintao.

The President had unfolded his notes and was using his arms to invite the audience to resume their seats, smiling a beatific smile as he did so.

This was the moment.

Now! Now! Despite himself, beads of sweat were forming on Hong's brow.

Gregory Bellingham was feeling the heat, emotionally as well. He had been so careful to check and double-check every tiny detail of the plan. Yet still he offered up a short prayer to the gods of happenstance, the masters of the unexpected.

Please, stay out of my way a few moments longer. Only a few moments longer.

Jenna located Lord Dulwich in the stand once more. He had stood up with everyone else but, unlike them, was apparently paying no attention to what was happening on the platform, staring upwards to the sky, a puzzled look on his face.

She knew this was her moment. Slowly, she moved her finger onto the button, looked up one final time, and . . . froze.

Another man, smartly dressed, had appeared beside the minister. To her horror, the man grasped his Lordship's arm and whispered in his ear. As she watched, Lord Dulwich turned obediently and allowed himself to be directed along the row of seats towards the stairs.

Dulwich appeared totally bewildered, moving like a zombie. People near him were taking their seats, some now looking round, wondering what was happening, their attention distracted from the opening words of the new President's address.

The Nigerian foreign minister had to stand again to allow the two men to squeeze past his voluminous robes.

Jenna could not believe her eyes. This was not in the script. Her carefully constructed plan - 'a touch of genius' Marksworth had reluctantly admitted to her - was in danger of collapse. Quickly, she gathered her wits.

She had only two choices: take emergency action or abandon ship, now.

She looked down at the console, made her decision and pressed the button.

Instantaneously, Lord Dulwich stopped, then pushed his guide to one side. He reached inside his jacket and withdrew a thin, silver coloured cylinder. Holding it aloft, he raised his head and bellowed at the top of his voice:

'Rule Britannia! God save the Queen, Empress of India!'

At that very moment, a loud crack echoed around the arena. The Nigerian foreign minister clutched his shoulder and collapsed onto his seat.

The Indian President had stopped speaking. There was a moment of deathly silence. Then officials and guards rushed to his side and began to usher him off the platform.

Within seconds, all over the arena, people were on their feet, scrambling for cover, men and women shouting, some shrieking in fear. Officers were hurriedly moving their men into position, trying in vain to restore some form of order.

Jenna Dobrosova looked helplessly at the far grandstand. The mayhem there was at its worst. Several people were on their knees, surrounding the stricken African, while a medical team were fighting their way against the tide of people, as everyone else headed for the exits. Lord Dulwich and his silver cylinder, his sophisticated suicide bomb, were nowhere to be seen. There was nothing to be done.

She waited a minute or two, then turned, bowed her head and quietly joined the back of the crowd of distraught women queuing to leave, after carefully disengaging her console; the police at the gate were making everyone undergo a full body scan before being allowed through.

Gregory Bellingham was the only one left in his row of the grandstand; seated, head in hands, as his world fell apart.

Hong Jintao allowed himself to be escorted to safety by a member of the Presidential Guard. His place now was with his own President, he explained politely.

'Most unfortunate. Such a beautiful ceremony. I'm sure he will be a superb President,' he muttered to those closest to him. The hand of Guo Dalong on his shoulder had tightened.

Andy Fields and Sir Norman watched the chaos unfold in New Delhi. The television broadcast switched back to the London studio where a panel of hastily assembled commentators were trying to make sense of the events of the last few minutes.

'Phew, we cut that one rather fine,' Sir Norman muttered to himself. 'What do we make of all that, Andrew?'

Andy rubbed his eyes. 'I'm not sure. I know what I saw but I have no idea what would have happened if your man hadn't intervened. Have you? And did I really hear that man shout "Rule Britannia"? Where did he go?'

The television producer had reacted slowly to the rumpus in the grandstand as cameras swivelled around trying to locate its source, and the noise of the shot created even more confusion. By the time a cameramen latched onto the right area of the stand, the Nigerian was already lying wounded. Lord Dulwich and Sir Norman's man were disappearing from view.

'Rather eccentric, Lord Dulwich, always was. We'll have to wait until we hear a detailed report from our agent,' said Sir Norman, pointing to his phone.

'Who was he, by the way? Your agent, I mean.'

Sir Norman looked at him, smiled gently and said, 'If I told you that, I'd have to kill you, as the old saying goes. Let's just say that the Last Resort Squad likes to keep an eye on things. Just in case, you know.'

'But it was pure luck you had a man on the spot in Delhi.'

'No such thing as luck, old boy.' He smiled again as Fields opened his phone and called up Patrick Cameron.

CHAPTER 11

Whitehall

'I'm on my way, Minister.'

Buzz.

Seated at his London desk, David Marksworth's brain was so stunned by what he had just seen that, for a moment, he struggled to remember where he kept his other, off-the-record phone.

Without needing to look at the screen, he already knew who had sent the message.

Explain.

It only required that one word. Authority, fury, urgency, menace: that one word conveyed them all.

Marksworth shivered. Suddenly, the room felt cold. He closed the screen, located "Nutkin" in the contact list and typed. One word:

Explain.

There was a knock on his door.

Andy Fields was making it very clear. 'I want you to stay as close as you can to Marksworth, Patrick. Invent any excuse, use your ingenuity. Or, failing that, use Julian's; he seems to be on a roll right now.'

Standing in the lift with Julian, Cameron replied, 'Marksworth just called us in, Andy. Something about shit hitting fans. He's been summoned to Downing Street and he wants us to get him there without being intercepted by the media.'

'Yes, I'm not surprised. The Government will have gone into panic mode after what we've just seen on TV. If India decides to punish Britain for that fiasco, cancelling a few defence contracts would make a good start. And that's bang on Marksworth's job description.'

'We're on our way now,' said Patrick.

'Good luck. Did you manage to get a look at his third phone yet, by the way?'

'No, but it's top of our shopping list, I can assure you.'

Mike Challoner, the other bodyguard, was waiting for them outside Marksworth's door.

'He's ready to leave,' he said. 'Looking a bit frazzled. Must be a panic on. We'll need to use the rear entrance.'

At that moment, the door opened and David Marksworth emerged, storming straight past them without a word, his coat hanging off one shoulder.

Julian hung back a yard or two as they left the building, brushing aside the small group of reporters. He seemed so deep in thought that Patrick decided to leave him to it. He and Challoner took up station on Marksworth's offside and nearside as they weaved their way through and around government buildings on the three-minute walk to Number Ten.

'Just a minute, please.' Marksworth stopped suddenly, looked at his escorts and said, 'I need a few moments.'

'Sir,' said Challoner, 'you don't really have the time.'

'That's for me to judge!' he barked.

Marksworth moved a few yards away, removed a phone from his pocket and listened for fully forty seconds while the others waited. Patrick looked round at Julian, surprised to see he was also on the phone.

Without a word, David Marksworth ended the call, replaced the handset in his coat pocket and rejoined them, striding out ahead.

Patrick sidled up to Julian. 'What . . .?' he whispered.

'Just checking something,' the young man replied.

As they approached the side door to the Prime Minister's offices, it opened silently and Marksworth marched in. The three guards made their way round to what was always known as the Tradesmen's Entrance - a nondescript door reserved for junior staff, visitors' guards and drivers, behind which a dear lady named Lottie brewed one of the best cups of tea in London.

Patrick was one of the very few people Andy Fields trusted enough to know that Lottie was in truth a highly regarded undercover informant. Over the years, her sharp ears had overheard many snippets of information which had later proved very useful. She did keep the more scurrilous stuff to herself, however.

While Patrick and Mike sat chatting over their tea, Julian stood apart, leaning against a wall, his eyes fixed on his phone, his fingers working the screen at high speed. Patrick decided to ignore him; when Julian was ready, Julian would talk.

He certainly wasn't doing anything trivial, like tweeting his friends. Not with that phone: that phone was far too special to be wasted on idle chat.

David Markswortth took his seat at the conference table beside his boss, the Secretary of State for Defence. Senior representatives from the Trade ministry and the Foreign Service were already in their places, together with the Secret Intelligence Service, formerly known as MI6. Assistant Commissioner Andy Fields of the UK-focussed Security Service would not normally have been asked to attend a discussion about an international crisis but a brief word from Sir Norman in the appropriate ear had secured him a seat.

The door opened and everyone stood as the Prime Minister entered. A nasty head cold had forced her to send her deputy to New Delhi but now she looked clear-eyed and determined.

'Good morning, ladies and gentlemen.' She took her place and got straight down to business. This woman was no Maggie Thatcher – she liked to rule by consensus – but, when the situation called for it, she drove the carriage of state with a firm, steady hand.

'I have just been informed by our ambassador to India that the ceremony has been cancelled. The new President has convened an emergency cabinet meeting. Meanwhile four of our most senior diplomats and one of our Trade Ministers have been taken into custody, pending an inquiry into today's events.'

The outcry came from every side of the room. The Prime Minister raised her hand.

'I know, I know. Diplomatic immunity. I understand the Indian government are claiming that Lord Dulwich's extraordinary behaviour was an act of terrorism, which means they are entitled to suspend our people's immunity.

'I have issued instructions for His Royal Highness and all of our other senior people to be flown out of India without delay, leaving only our High Commissioner and his closest aides to secure their release.

'Now, before we talk about what happened and why, I would like each ministry to give me their assessment of the possible consequences of a major diplomatic row with India. Can we begin with trade, please?'

A senior civil servant spoke. 'Three billion pounds in large civil engineering contracts alone, Prime Minister. It's difficult to estimate potential losses in other fields but our exports to India are running at about five billion a year. However, it's the other side of the coin that should give us just as much cause for concern: Indian companies employ more people here in the UK than in the rest of Europe put together, and dozens of their larger companies are listed on the London Stock Exchange. All in all, we need them more than they need us.'

'Thank you. And I gather we had some bad news today about arms contracts, even before the tragic events happened.' She looked directly at Marksworth's minister.

'Err, yes, Prime Minister. I regret that, despite our best efforts, they have decided to do business with China.' He looked fixedly at the table. Everyone knew how much "financial leverage" had been offered to Indian government negotiators to secure the deals, but clearly to no avail.

'Any security risks, Mr Tamworth?' she asked the head of the SIS.

'Apart from acute embarrassment, Ma'm, none.'

Andy Fields was watching and listening intently, without appearing to pay particular attention to David Marksworth.

'Right,' said the PM, turning to her notes. 'The Foreign Secretary's advice is that I despatch a note expressing our sincere regrets, *not* apologies, for what happened today. Without, of course, indicating that we are to blame in any respect. Plus a small but well-publicised donation to their public health vaccination programme. We will, of course, be launching an inquiry into Lord Dulwich's behaviour which, with any luck, should keep the lid on things for a few months. He would like to use the time to smooth things over with our Indian friends. They are after all, he reminds us, loyal pillars of the Commonwealth.'

A general rumble of approval followed.

'If I may say so, Prime Minister . . .' David Marksworth spoke.

The PM looked up sharply. An audible collective sharp intake of breath filled the silence in the room. This was most irregular. Civil servants of Marksworth's rank were not expected to enter these discussions unless invited to do so.

'Excuse me; could you remind me who you are?' asked the PM.

'Marksworth, Permanent Under-Secretary at the Ministry of Defence, Prime Minister.'

'And . . .?'

'With great respect to everyone present, and in particular to the Foreign Secretary, I would suggest that his proposed strategy will only make matters worse.'

'And why is that, Mr Marksworth?' The Prime Minister sounded just a little tetchy.

'May I speak frankly, Prime Minister?'

'If you must.'

'From what I understand of the political climate in India these days, if you go ahead and do what has just been suggested, it will be seen as just another load of British imperialist patronising bullshit.'

Howls of protest were silenced by the Prime Minister's hand.

When she looked up, she was smiling quietly.

'Thank you, Mr Marksworth. I wonder whether you would be kind enough to contact my private secretary after this meeting.'

Ignoring the looks of surprise, she addressed the rest of the room. 'Now: Lord Dulwich. Do we have any information which might explain his behaviour?'

A senior Foreign Office official replied, 'Unfortunately, none of our people were looking in his direction at the time and the Indian TV cameras were slow to react. We're trying to talk to anyone who was seated near him and, hopefully, we'll have better pictures at some future date. All we can assume, Prime Minister, is that he had some kind of mental breakdown.' He shook his head, exasperated.

'Where is he now?'

'I understand he's being looked after in an appropriate manner. I'm assured he's in safe hands.'

Only Fields had been present when Sir Norman had spoken to a number of people on the phone. The Last Resort Squad had tidied matters up.

Fields looked across at Marksworth. He had the distinct impression that the man was looking rather pleased with himself.

'Right, that's it. Meeting closed.' The Prime Minister was gathering her papers.

'Err . . . Prime Minister.' The Foreign Office man was looking flustered now.

She stopped and turned round and addressed him. 'I want a new strategy on my desk, Mr Farnham, in thirty minutes. Bullshit-free this time.'

With that, she left, a faint smile on her lips.

As soon as the door had closed, huddles of officials gathered in all four corners of the room, each engaged in heated discussion.

Andy Fields was the only one to notice David Marksworth slip out through another door. He opened his phone and wrote a swift message to Patrick Cameron, before excusing himself and following through the same door.

Marksworth was standing no more than ten yards away, engrossed in reading his own phone. His face had turned very pale and his hand was shaking.

Fields continued past him and disappeared round the next corner.

Down in the Tradesmen's Entrance tea lounge, Patrick read Fields' message and showed it to Julian and Mike Challoner.

'Looks to me as though our man's making his mark with the PM.'

Julian held up his own phone for them both to see. 'Looks to me as though someone's making his mark with him.'

He slipped the phone to Patrick, out of sight under the table. A text message was showing on its screen:

"Explanation unacceptable, shifu. Failure cannot be tolerated."

'Who . . .?'

The young man gave a shy smile. 'I finally had the opportunity to locate Mr Marksworth's third phone on the way here, that's all. I've hacked it. No big deal.'

Patrick looked at Julian in astonishment. 'So that message is on Marksworth's phone? Let me see it again.' He reread the message. 'Any idea what *shifu* means?'

Mike Challoner piped up as he was taking a call. 'I worked in the Far East for a while. It's Chinese. Literally, it means master but it's sometimes used to mean a high rank, like captain, as well. Come on, guys, time to go. Our *shifu* is calling.'

The plane taking the Chinese delegation back to Beijing had just reached cruising height. The President had left in a smaller aircraft so, in deference to his seniority, Hong Jintao was alone in the forward cabin; which was fortunate, as it meant that the more junior staff were not able to witness their leader venting his anger, marching up and down, kicking seats and tables, hurling files.

The coup he had so carefully planned, the one that would surely satisfy Guo Dalong, had turned into a complete farce. The explanation he had received from David Marksworth had done nothing to improve his mood.

"Unforeseen events . . . most unfortunate . . . no apparent breach of our security . . ."

Hong suspected the clumsy hand of Gregory Bellingham. The man was weak, he'd always known that but, given a clear set of instructions, he had consistently delivered on time. Until now.

And yet . . . and yet. Perhaps there was a glimmer of hope in the darkness. That idiot Lord Whatever-his-name-was had made such a fool of himself before being apparently arrested that relations between India and the UK could well have been damaged after all, at least to some extent. Not as dramatically as if he had detonated the suicide bomb – the deaths and the perceived humiliation to India of such a catastrophic security failure in front of a distinguished international audience would have been intolerable. Britain would have been punished, in the severest manner possible. But perhaps . . . Hong shook himself back to reality.

But . . .that is not what I promised to Guo Dalong!

His phone buzzed. A message was coming through. Marksworth.

"Invited to private meeting with PM. An opportunity I shall not fail to exploit."

Hong Jintao stared at the message and felt his anger - fear? - start slowly to ebb away.

CHAPTER 12

George Butterley Floyd, Marquis of Dulwich looked round in bewilderment. He felt as though he had just awoken from a long night's sleep but he didn't recognise the brightly lit room. When he tried shaking his head, nothing happened; so he tried sitting up, and discovered that, for some reason, he couldn't move. His arms wouldn't work; they seemed to be pinned to his side. Kicking his feet – same problem.

I know. I'll close my eyes, then open them again. That usually works. There. No, it isn't a dream.

In the far corner of the white, featureless room, almost out of his range of vision, something was moving – a shapeless white figure with its back turned towards him, leaning to the left, then to the right and back again. From George's viewpoint, it looked more animal than human, blurred, almost furry. Cuddly?

I'd love a cuddle right now.

He started to tremble. The walls and ceiling were trembling too. He felt panic rise up from his gut to his throat. He opened his mouth but his throat was so dry, he only managed a dull croak.

He closed his eyes again. He decided to keep them shut: he felt safe now, safe in his own little world, away from all those horrid people who had told him to leave that big party because he'd been a very naughty boy.

Naughty? All I did was sing Rule Britannia.

It was one of his favourite songs - his best party piece at family gatherings. Mother said he had a beautiful voice. But this time nobody else had joined in and, *oh dear*, he was in trouble again.

To be fair, the nice man who had shown him the way out hadn't seemed at all angry. As soon as they reached the foot of the stairs, he had given George a nice fruity drink. After that, he couldn't remember very much. But he was safe now, with his eyes shut.

'Hello, George.' *Arrgh!* The white blob was standing beside him now, a monster looming over his face.

Oh no, it's removing its head!

He cringed down under the sheet.

'George. It's alright, you can come out now.' The voice sounded almost soothing.

He pulled the sheet down from one eye.

Phew, it wasn't its head; it was only a hat. What a nice, kind-looking, fuzzy lady. I wish Mummy was here, though. I wonder if this nice lady would like to give me a cuddle instead.

The "nice, kind-looking, fuzzy lady", Medical Officer Denise Pitts of the Royal Air Force Medical Services, reached forward and removed the dark glasses Lord Dulwich had worn since his arrest. Their dual functions of disguise and sight impairment were no longer necessary now they were airborne. He was her only patient on the long flight back to RAF Brize Norton airbase.

Actually, it was a rare pleasure to have a patient for once on a diplomatic mission. Every time a large delegation of British politicians or big-wigs went overseas, the RAF was ordered to position an Aero-medical Evacuation team nearby, just in case somebody important fell ill and needed to be flown home. Flying around the world empty had become the norm.

The call ordering Medical Officer Pitts and her colleagues to prepare to receive a patient had come from the RAF's strategic operational HQ in the UK. By the time the black Jaguar rolled up alongside the plane, the team had their fully equipped field treatment room ready. All they were told was that the patient had undergone a traumatic experience, was in a poor mental state and should be checked thoroughly for the presence of psychoactive substances.

The British security officer stepped out of the car into the hot sun and guided a very confused Lord Dulwich up the aircraft's steps. The man was clinging to the officer's arm, whimpering, a pathetic sight.

Within minutes, the patient was stripped, sedated and sound asleep, strapped onto a bunk, ready for take-off.

The officer's instructions were very clear. He didn't introduce himself.

'This man's name is George. He is under high security arrest. You will run this series of tests on him and give the only copy of the results to me.' He handed her a folded printout. 'Once I have the full report, you will delete the test data, permanently. I will be in the forward cabin when you've finished.'

Denise Pitts had plenty of practice treating traumatised servicemen in war zones. She knew that, in this case, the possibility of encountering psychoactive substances meant she had to take particular safety precautions.

The last occasion had been on her final tour of duty in Afghanistan. A worrying number of front line troops had started to behave very strangely on their return from the field and her team had been called in by their Army colleagues for a second opinion. Nothing definitive had been diagnosed, so the reports were inconclusive. But several colleagues privately suspected that someone – the Russians? Chinese? Islamists? - had developed a new form of narcotic drug. How it was transmitted, nobody had managed to work out, but the effects on different victims' behaviour were so diverse that she had even heard speculation that the victims were being controlled remotely.

Today, as the senior medic on duty, she decided to undertake the more dangerous tests on the patient alone, asking her team to wait and observe from the next room. After donning a head-to-toe protective suit, she removed samples of the man's blood and DNA and ran them through a series of sophisticated analyses.

No recognisable toxins showed up in the first run so she repeated the procedures. In cases such as this, a second, back-up set of tests was always recommended, for comparison purposes.

George, if that was his real name, remained quite docile throughout. None of the tests caused him any discomfort and Denise found that, if she stroked his forehead from time to time, he stayed relaxed, cooing like a baby and humming tunelessly.

When she compared the two sets of results, they were almost identical. Something told her to check her archives which she kept stored in a password-protected section of the personal data interface her employers had supplied to her a month ago to replace her aging tablet.

Two voice commands were all it took to locate the file she was looking for: a forensic study of six servicemen whose psychological reaction to war-zone action had been very similar, serious enough for them to be flown home. It was not unusual for trauma victims to exhibit persistent childlike behaviour for a while but very unusual for their brain to suddenly, instantaneously revert completely to normal. No explanation had ever been offered.

Scanning the results she had just obtained from George, she used a pattern analysis tool to check for any characteristics that were common to those found in the six soldiers. The initial search threw up far too many coincidences.

It was when she narrowed her search to look for any traces of chemical substances that things became more interesting. Again, there were a number of matches. She was able to discount the vast majority, as they were typical of a wide range of well-known medications. In the case of each of the soldiers, one specific molecular pattern had been checked and checked again. The trace was tiny and already fading. They had never seen it before or since, as far as Denise was aware. When it disappeared shortly afterwards, nobody had even bothered to give it a name and they concentrated their efforts on the overwhelming evidence pointing to post-traumatic stress.

And yet here it was again. The identical pattern.

She looked around. She'd become so engrossed in her work that she had completely shut herself off from her surroundings, in particular from George, who was now becoming increasingly agitated, struggling against the straps that bound him and muttering under his breath:

'I hate you . . . I wanna drink. I wanna play . . . I wanna go pee-pee . . .'

Denise put down her pen and walked over to the bed.

'It's alright, George. I'm here. I'll get you something to play with.'

She found an old computer tablet in a work bench drawer and located the inevitable games programmes. Handing it to George, she watched as the man purred with pleasure and, within a few seconds, he was shooting down alien spacecraft.

'Bang! Gotcha! Boom! Missed!'

Denise went to the door and asked someone to fetch the security agent. Five minutes later, her comparison analysis was on its way to London.

'Boss?'

'What is it now, Julian? I was just going to put my feet up for half an hour.'

The two men had not been happy when David Marksworth gave them the rest of the day off but there was nothing they could do. Back in the Battersea flat that Fields had put at their disposal, Julian was checking emails.

'Where did we put those Jamie Daniel results?' he asked.

'Shit! I forgot all about them,' said Patrick, jumping up from the settee and fishing out a large brown envelope from under a pile of papers.

He handed it to Julian who tore it open, pulled out the contents and sat down again at the screen.

'What is it?' asked Patrick.

'Something or nothing.' Julian pointed to the screen. All Patrick could see was a stream of algebraic formulae and symbols, until he looked more closely.

'DNA analyses?'

'Yep, and blood. We're looking at the nutter who shouted out at that Indian ceremony. Andy sent it over. Now, let's look at Jamie Daniel's profile.'

He ran his finger down the pages of results he had just opened, muttering to himself.

'Mmm . . . Right . . . Nothing there . . .'

He turned to the last page, looking back at the screen from time to time.

'Here we are. Boring . . . boring . . . nope. Aha!'

He turned to Patrick. 'I hate to say it but I think we may have struck a little gold, my friend.'

'I'm your boss, young man, not your friend.'

Julian pulled a face. 'Oh, pooh. You're no fun anymore, Dr Cameron. But seriously, what do you make of this?'

He pointed to a line of data on the screen with one hand and a line in the Daniel report with the other.

'Whatever it is, it looks like the same stuff in both cases. "Unidentified matter", it says here. Does it ring any bells with you?'

'Hold on,' said Cameron. He ran his finger along the line of numbers and symbols. 'I'll have to check to be sure. But if I were to take a guess, it's some kind of psychoactive drug.'

'And if both Jamie and the ghastly Lord Dulwich had the same drug in their veins, it's a fair bet it was put there by the same people.' He smiled.

'Well done, Julian, we'll make a scientist of you yet.'

Julian smiled his most charming smile. 'In the nicest possible way, boss, fuck off.'

'You're fired.'

'Oh no, not again.' He grinned.

'Right,' said Patrick. 'I'm going to call Andy Fields and you, you cheeky sod, are going to dig deep in the files to see if this nasty stuff has turned up anywhere else. OK?'

'Aye, aye, Captain. You make your call and I'll set the wheels in motion. Then, do you fancy a beer at the pub round the corner?'

'Julian, that blonde barmaid's married with three kids.'

'Ah, but they've all left home, and her husband's on a North Sea oil rig.'

New Delhi

The British High Commission was almost deserted. The place was a mess. Since the evacuation order had been given, the building had been placed under armed guard by the Indian authorities who had prevented the cleaners from entering. So the debris from the hasty departure was everywhere and it took James Goddard, the High Commissioner's Deputy, several seconds to locate the ringing telephone.

It was the New Delhi police.

'Mr Goddard, would you please send a car down to the central police station?'

'Why?' he asked.

'We have a British national in custody, sir. One of our patrols found him by the river asleep. He's been drinking, sir. Rather heavily.'

'It's not a Mr Bellingham, by any chance?' Goddard asked, trying to remain calm. Ever since the calamitous events at the President's palace, Under-Secretary Gregory Bellingham had been missing. The High Commission, not wishing to embarrass the British any further, had conducted their own search, but without success.

'Yes, sir, Mr Gregory Bellingham. We think he may have been trying to take his own life.'

CHAPTER 13

London

David Marksworth needed time to himself. Too much depended on how he handled the next few days. He had always known that he would face defining moments like these, when only his own speed and clarity of thought would determine the success of the mission. He had often wondered how he would feel when the time came. Now he knew.

Sitting at the desk in his private study, he closed his eyes and began to breathe deeply. Hong Jintao had instilled regular meditation into the brotherhood's daily routine; for David, it was the time when he could reflect on the historic, sacred duties that had been entrusted to him, on the admiration he had developed over the years for the wisdom of the Chinese ancients. Chinese spirituality was deeply engrained in his approach to life.

By contrast, he felt no hatred or even scorn for what his own nation had become, for the complete loss of spiritual integrity, or for the obsession with material wealth: there were far more Chinese multi-millionaires, after all.

No, theirs, the brotherhood's, was a far higher purpose: decades after losing its way in every field of human endeavour - cultural, commercial, military, artistic - Britain still presumed it had the right to tell everyone else how to run the world. Now he, David Marksworth, would begin their re-education, starting with the self-destruction of those who laughingly called themselves "leaders", the group who perpetuated the myth.

Yesterday, after the disaster in Delhi, doubts had begun to creep into his mind; now he realised how stupid that was. He should trust the fates: everything was ordained. Especially now that he would have the ear of the Prime Minister, no less. The road was clear. He could step forward with confidence.

He, in partnership with the most intelligent and spiritually pure culture the world had ever known, would proudly lead his fellow-countrymen towards a future founded on the acceptance that there was a better way, a more honest way for the country to regain its dignity. It would mean putting aside their arrogant imperial past and settling for the humble reality that Britain was just one more small nation, yesterday's imperialist. It was time to delegate to others, to the mighty economic and cultural powers of today, the management of world affairs.

As for Gregory Bellingham? For more than twenty years, the two men had shared everything, life, laughs, loves, dreams: almost like brothers. Their careers too had followed a remarkably similar pattern: both had risen through the ranks much faster than their contemporaries. Marksworth had often wondered whether somebody had been working behind the scenes on their behalf.

Even their private lives had run in parallel: each had married into a "good family", only to see their wife walk out, exasperated at sharing a home with a slightly distracted workaholic. Neither had any inkling that the man in their shared bed was also a spy.

But now his old friend had failed again - once too often. Surely the man could no longer be tolerated. Marksworth would await his orders. They would come soon enough. Whatever he was required to do, he would do it, swiftly and cleanly. He had never quite got used to the sight of blood.

New Delhi

Gregory Bellingham read the email again. In deference to his rank at the Department, the last few people in the High Commission had given him one of the best offices in the building, vacated earlier by the Trade Commissioner who was now on his way back to England. None of the staff had presumed to mention his drunken state or the report from the Indian police. A fresh set of clothes had been found and a selection of medications. His brain was working enough for him to maintain what he thought was a dignified silence, simply thanking them for their attention before retiring to the office for a snooze.

His head still hurt like hell as he downed yet another glass of water and poured himself some tea. He imagined someone had informed London that he'd turned up so, when he checked his Inbox, he wasn't surprised to see an encoded message from his Minister waiting for him. What did surprise him was the tone.

Dear Under-Secretary Bellingham,

You will remain in New Delhi and await the arrival of the small delegation we are sending to negotiate the release of our staff and smooth matters over with our Indian friends. Their ETA is 18:00 India time today.

He checked his watch. Another hour and a half. He read on:

Please be aware that you are suspended from all duties on full salary until further notice. You will make no contact whatever with the Indian Government nor interfere in any way with the work of our staff in New Delhi.

Suspended from duty? Why? He'd only gone for a walk and missed a plane, for God's sake. Hardly a capital offence.

Or . . . He shivered involuntarily.

Or do they suspect I had something to do with yesterday's cock-up?

Memories of Lord Dulwich's extraordinary behaviour came flooding back once more: it had all started so well, the drugging, the planting of the suicide bomb, the singing. Then he had been forced to watch, powerless to prevent the peer being led away, the shooting of the wrong man, as his carefully constructed plan fell apart.

His immediate reaction had been anger, confusion, then a sense of utter, overwhelming failure; although he had absolutely no idea what had gone wrong or why. All he knew was that, in Hong Jintao's eyes, under the terms of the oath they had all taken so many years ago in Paris, failure on this scale was completely unacceptable.

After he left the Presidential palace grounds, he'd found himself in an expatriates' bar filled with the typical garrulous whisky-chaser drinkers that populated every expatriates' bar all over the globe – men and women who had spent so long in the Tropics that they could never conceive of returning to live a normal life back in Europe; drinking away their days and nights in animated debate over the failings of their house steward, the England cricket team and "the youth of today".

They had all ignored him as he consumed double after double and his mood darkened. It wasn't his fault! But failure was failure. How could he face Hong Jintao and David Marksworth again and expect them to trust him to play any more responsible part in their plans?

He had few other friends, no wife, no family, no *life* beyond the Civil Service. What was the point of going back? What was the point of any damned thing anymore?

He could just recall leaving the bar and wandering down by the river, being accosted by beggars, his wallet stolen and not giving a damn.

He had never considered taking his own life before so he wasn't sure how to do it. The river looked so filthy, perhaps if he jumped from a bridge? Did he have the guts?

A knock on his door brought him back to the present. It opened and a man he vaguely recognised walked in. He couldn't place him although, for some reason, he felt he had known him for years. Well groomed, in his fifties, well-cut tropical suit, clean brown brogues, a neatly trimmed moustache. The sort of chap you'd bump into on most days in one of the better gentlemen's clubs in London.

'Come with me,' the man said without introducing himself.

'Who are you?' asked Bellingham without getting up.

'I'm the advance party,' was all he said. 'Now, I won't tell you again. Come with me.'

There was something about the man's manner. No, it was his eyes. That's what he remembered, the eyes. As though he was looking at you from a long, long distance away.

Bellingham stood, donned his jacket and walked towards the door.

Outside, the corridors were deserted. When they reached the front door, a solitary guard let them out without comment.

The heat was oppressive even though it was late in the day. Holding Bellingham's arm, the man guided him towards the gates where an Indian soldier allowed them to leave, again without a word.

Reaching the street, the man looked to the left and made a gesture with his hand. Bellingham looked in the same direction and saw an ancient American saloon, a 1970's Buick or something like that, he guessed. He used to play with a toy model like that when he was little.

The driver gunned its engine, set off from the side of the road, did a series of fast gear changes, the tyres squealed and Gregory felt encouraged to step into its path. Whether he was pushed or not didn't matter; he just knew that this was inevitable, the fates were doing their work.

No fear, just let it happen, Greg.

The car was doing upwards of forty miles per hour by the time it hit him, tossing him into the air, breaking his neck and carrying him along the street before his body crashed into the dust almost a hundred yards away, then driving off.

The man turned away as a small crowd converged on the inert Bellingham. He handed a small bundle of notes to the Indian officer in charge of guarding the High Commission, straightened his jacket and hailed a chauffeur-driven Jaguar parked across the street.

The Locksmith had proved exactly why he had been recruited by Hong Jintao all those years ago in Paris – to lie very low, then to intervene in exceptional circumstances. He would now return to his day job and await the next call, which could be years from now.

Checking his watch, he leaned forward and asked the driver to get him to the airport as quickly as he could. He wanted to be home in time to celebrate Mother's Day with his old Mum.

London

David Marksworth didn't know what to make of the evening news broadcasts. The morning papers had carried minor reports of the events in New Delhi - a corruption scandal involving a senior British government minister had taken precedence - but now the journalists had got their teeth into the wider implications of what had occurred and the Indian government's angry response.

News that India was overlooking British companies for big money contracts and the arrest of the diplomats and the minister had been greeted by some with furious outbursts condemning "ungrateful regimes, riddled with corruption, who learned everything they know about democracy from the British". There were even calls for retaliation from the more sensationalist commentators – one of the more eccentric even suggesting that his audience should all boycott Indian restaurants and take-aways.

The more thoughtful pieces, on the other hand, were speculating whether a breakdown in relations with the booming Indian economy would hit Britain's balance of trade and put people in Britain out of work.

He switched to another channel. The host had just opened a

studio debate on "whether the Commonwealth means anything these days and what value we gain from the millions of pounds we pour into aid programmes".

Marksworth smiled when he saw one of the invited guests – a charming, highly articulate writer, one of several people he was paying to influence public opinion.

As he watched the discussion develop, his mood changed. His man was doing his best to wipe the floor with the other guests by destroying their arguments brick by brick. And, in the process, delivering a damning verdict on the Establishment for "living in a bygone age, out of touch with world affairs, misreading the mood of the British people, wasting taxpayers' money . . ."

But the programme host, a highly respected, shrewd veteran, wasn't allowing Marksworth's man to hold the floor, countering his points with equally persuasive reminders of the need for strong international relations in a global economy. The studio audience was becoming increasingly animated, loud applause greeting each pronouncement.

Three-all, after extra time, he thought as the debate closed. *At least we've got people talking. If only . . . I need to talk to Greg. He was there.*

Then a news flash popped up on the TV screen:

Gregory Bellingham, Permanent Under-Secretary for Commonwealth Affairs, killed in a tragic road accident in New Delhi today.

He stared at the screen, stunned.

How the hell did that happen?

Wasn't Bellingham on the plane home with the others?

Why did he stay behind?

Then an awful thought started to dawn on him:

What if this wasn't an accident? What if it was . . . an execution? Only Hong could have ordered it. But who carried it out? I was Gregory's controller. That was my role. We are brotherhood. I am brotherhood. Aren't I?

He felt a creeping coldness infuse his skin, as if his life support system had just begun to fail.

Updates were coming in so thick and fast that Andy Fields was struggling to keep up. Julian matching the psychoactive drug in Jamie Daniel's and Lord Dulwich's blood had been followed by news of Bellingham's death. In suspicious circumstances?

Andy had immediately sent a seemingly routine message ordering a DNA blood sample to be taken from Bellingham before his body was flown home. The body was due in from New Delhi the following afternoon and one of his people would meet the plane and deliver the sample to Patrick and Julian's lab.

He accessed the limited-audience news feed that was collecting everything and anything relevant to what the Government was now calling, in private only, *The Indian Bummer* incident.

One new report quoted an Indian government source: the gunman who fired the shot that wounded the Nigerian Minister had admitted, "under questioning", that he had been paid by a "woman from England who said she was working for someone high up in Government". The man was insisting that the Nigerian was not his intended target but the report – that he was "only meant to frighten someone" – gave no clue as to who that someone was.

An Indian government spokesman was online: 'We are not sure that this was a deliberate attempt to humiliate India, to remind us that we are a second-class nation, because everyone knows that we are now one of the world's leading industrial nations,' he was saying. 'Our investigation will reveal the true culprits. In the meantime, I want to assure the world that we will stand firm, alongside our friends in what people in the West patronisingly refer to as the developing nations, against any kind of bullying. Those days are over. In our culture, when you humiliate a friend, that relationship is finished.'

Wow. Powerful stuff, thought Andy. *But at least they're trying to keep the temperature steady. For now.*

He dialled Patrick's private phone.

'Hi Andy, I was just about to call you.'

'Before you go on, Patrick, I want you to listen to me. We've got to nail David Marksworth once and for all, fast. Gregory Bellingham, his buddy from the days in Paris with Hong Jintao, has been killed in India today. I checked and he didn't make it back with the others on the plane, for some reason. We have to assume he was in on the Lord Dulwich plot and that they wiped him out before he was picked up and questioned. Too much of a coincidence. Heaven knows what they're planning next. But, if Marksworth starts bending the Prime Minister's ear and gets access to her level of information, well . . . I don't have to spell it out. Now, what have you got for me?'

'Phew. Another Kim Philby, eh? Message received and understood. Right, we've got a new DNA match and I want you to check out another name for me.'

'A new match? Who?'

'You remember Alistair Thomas?'

'Who doesn't? Tragic case – such a glittering career ahead of him. Didn't they call him the new British Kennedy?'

'That's the one. The outstanding man of his day. All set to be our best PM for fifty years then one day he gets in his car and causes a mega-smash driving the wrong way up the motorway. Julian examined several brain scans when we started on this case, including Thomas's. It didn't fit the pattern so we discarded it. Well, on a hunch, he just had a sample of Thomas's post-accident DNA analysed and, guess what – traces of a psychoactive drug.'

'Not the same one as Dulwich or Jamie Daniel?'

'No, but close enough. The same family, the same author's signature, if you like.'

Fields sat back, put the phone down on the desk and said nothing. This was a total bombshell. He needed a few seconds to think it through.

Finally, he picked up the receiver. 'OK Patrick. I'll get Thomas's case file sent over. Now, you said you wanted me to check out another name.'

'Yes. You remember the John McLean case?'

'Of course I do.' The previous year, an American extremist Christian billionaire had set up a complex conspiracy to persuade the West to start an all-out holy war. Fields' and Patrick's team had played a leading role in foiling the plot. In that case, the conspirators had used nanotechnology to alter temporarily their victims' behaviour and make them commit atrocities.

'We could be wrong but it's worth checking out. Julian and I detect the hand of a certain lady in this.'

'A lady? Ah, that bitch who bent the brains of those kids, turning them into temporary terrorists,' said Fields.

'Yep, that's the one. Jenna Dobrosova. Can you see if you can track down her movements over the last week or so?'

CHAPTER 14

Jenna Dobrosova was just waking from a comfortable sleep in the business class cabin of an Air India flight to San Francisco. On her way to New Delhi airport, she'd taken the snap decision to lie low for a couple of weeks and managed to switch her London-bound ticket. Everything she needed for the next phase, equipment, drugs and explosives, was safely tucked away in London so she was free to do a little networking, both social and business.

She had gone through passport control, using one of her seven passports, without incident. Everything she had used for the New Delhi operation had already been safely destroyed, so her luggage was clean. A week or so looking up old clients and a little naughtiness with friends in California would allow the dust to settle until she learned more.

How bad was the fallout from the botched bombing? How would her paymasters adjust the remainder of the plan?

Checking her personal data terminal, she was not surprised to see there had been no contact from London or Beijing. Hong, Marksworth and Bellingham would be frantically reassessing the whole project but she was confident that, whatever their final objectives were, she would be needed again.

She idly scrolled through the latest news headlines. The shooting in New Delhi was beginning to slip down the list already: the Indian government were talking tough but it was clear they didn't intend to impose any sanctions. While they had not yet released the British diplomats, the commentators expected them to be on their way home in a day or so. By then, a firm slap would have been delivered to Britain's wrist.

She ordered a Bloody Mary from the flight attendant and accessed the British diplomatic service's internal mail site: Marksworth had given her the password sequence in case she needed to check her targets' movements, although nothing Top Secret was available to her.

What she read almost made her knock the drink off the attendant's tray:

Under-Secretary Gregory Bellingham fatally injured in a traffic accident in New Delhi.

She scrolled down the rest of the item. Apparently Bellingham had been killed trying to cross the road outside the British High Commission. There was no suggestion as to why he had not left Delhi with the others or what he was doing at the High Commission.

Jenna worked through the mail server but found nothing that clarified the story. She sat back and took a long swig from her drink. This was the man who had passed on her final instructions in London. Despite his high rank, he was clearly working undercover for Hong Jintao in some capacity. He was a mole. But wait a minute . . .

Neither Bellingham nor David Markswortth knew how well I know Hong Jintao. As far as they've been concerned, I am just the sub-contractor designated by their masters to undertake a series of operations. If, and it's a big "if", Bellingham was killed as a punishment for the Delhi operation going wrong, who ordered it? Why wasn't I involved? And, where does that leave me?

She didn't like it when clients went behind her back. On more than one occasion, she had walked out on the contract, in her own way: the client in question would not have the opportunity to cheat her again, mainly because he was dead.

But this time it was different: Hong Jintao held too many strings, his commissions were largely responsible for her current lifestyle, and he knew too much about her little "foibles". She needed to think, to rethink. Risk assessment - that was her special skill: every time she planned an operation, she assessed the risks in the minutest detail and devised ways of minimising them.

This time, for the first time, I'm going to need to be my own client. I have to be one step ahead of them if they come for me.

She checked the graphics on the large wall screen. The plane would be landing at San Francisco International in ninety minutes.

'Could I have another Bloody Mary, please?'

London

Alistair Thomas' file arrived on Fields' desk an hour later, a large, fat bundle of papers. He could have read it online but he always liked to see and feel the handwritten notes and photographs for himself. He opened it.

The series of photographs showed a strikingly handsome young man with dark hair, a strong chin and intelligent, rather cheeky eyes. Alistair Thomas was the son of a Weston-super-Mare vicar. One of four children, he had been educated at Wells Cathedral School on a church scholarship. He was a lively lad, according to his end of term reports: he played the clarinet well, won the school debating prize, played rugby and cricket for the first team, and managed to win another scholarship, this time to St John's College, Oxford to read law.

According to his tutors there, he was not the most dedicated student, "far too easily distracted", which, in their view, led to the "disappointing" third class degree when a first had seemed quite achievable.

The distractions in question were only alluded to but appeared to include trying his hand at busking in some of Oxford's noisier pubs, the Oxford University Dramatic Society, and women. But not quite in that order. Politics had not seemingly entered his head at this stage.

Fields found himself liking this young man already.

On leaving Oxford, Alistair was offered a graduate traineeship in the legal department of one of London's merchant banks, only to leave within a year citing, in a later newspaper interview, his frustration that the bank's directors seemed to favour Old Etonians and "frankly, I was bored to tears".

Some of his drinking pals at the pub he frequented in South Kensington worked in advertising. In the same interview, he outlined his professional reasons for becoming interested in joining the ad world – "They were earning more money than me and having more fun."

Within weeks, he found himself in the offices of the J Walter Thompson agency in Berkeley Square, proudly sporting the title of Junior Assistant Account Executive, assigned to the team working on a famous brand of frozen foods. His big break came later when he quietly pointed out to his boss that their proposed name for a new frozen fish product could have unfortunate connotations. *Crispy Cod-Pieces* hit the shelves under a different name and Alistair Thomas' name became something of a legend in the industry.

One of the agency's directors was also a talent spotter for the Conservative party. He saw something special in Alistair Thomas. At that time, the party was becoming increasingly out of touch with the new generation of electors: Blair had swept to power, promising to create a fresh, vibrant, modern Britain, shattering the aging Tories' illusion of their God-given right to govern. A small group of forward thinkers recognised that it was time for a strategy and image makeover and had set about the task of identifying and grooming a group of photogenic, articulate, highly intelligent young men and women.

Alistair fitted the bill perfectly and, within a couple of years, he had been seconded to a senior Shadow Cabinet minister's office. From there, it was only a matter of time before he was found a safe Parliamentary seat and was installed as the party's candidate for the next election.

When the incumbent MP became too ill to continue, a by-election was called and Thomas became one of the youngest Members of Parliament in the House, elevated by the media to the status of minor celebrity, for a week at least.

That was when Andy Fields first saw him, at a Westminster reception organised by a couple of grandees who, he discovered much later, also had close links with The Last Resort Squad. He was impressed.

Over the following months and years, the party's PR machine found regular opportunities for men and women from the "fast-track" group to speak against the government on news channels, chat shows and the more serious late evening discussions. As time went by, their names and faces, with Alistair Thomas' well to the fore, became noticed and talked about.

When the PM of the day finally took the country to the polls, the Opposition crept back into government, promising to put the country back on its feet.

After failing to honour a clutch of pre-election promises, the media and the country turned against them. Senior party figures persuaded the new PM to stand aside, called a party conference and instituted a leadership election. Of the three candidates who made it to the final run-off, all the news channels agreed that young Alistair Thomas won the televised debates hands down.

Two days before the final vote, the man whose style, gentle humour, and vision of the future had captured the mood of the country, young and old, male and female, across a remarkably broad spectrum of voters, took his own life.

At the coroner's inquest, his wife testified that he had seemed tired and rather distant over dinner. When he left home to drive to Birmingham for one final meeting, he inexplicably drove his Audi onto the wrong side of the M1 motorway and hit an oncoming articulated truck at a combined speed of a hundred and twenty miles per hour.

Andy Fields could clearly remember the stunned reaction when people heard the news; even the newsreaders appeared genuinely upset. Why would a man within days of his moment of glory kill himself? All kinds of speculation flooded the media as to what might possibly have been going on in Alistair Thomas' life that he could not live with – sex, drugs, corrupt deals – but nothing concrete ever emerged.

Andy made discreet enquiries around the security community – nothing suspicious had cropped up, no dark secrets; the consensus view was that this was "a straightforward while-the-balance-of-the-mind-was-disturbed" affair.

He remembered thinking at the time -

How can anyone ever call a suicide straightforward? There's no such thing. Each one is different; each one is the culmination of a unique mix of highly personal tragedies.

Days later, Jane Beaumont, a relatively inexperienced forty-something MP, the current Minister for Women, was elected party leader and entered 10 Downing Street as Prime Minister. She had made a promising start, restored her party's popularity ratings. But now she too was facing critical questions from all sides of the political scene. One by one, many of the Cabinet ministers she inherited from her predecessor had committed blunders which were quite out of character and been forced to resign.

Their replacements were, to say the least, unexpected; dry, charisma-free technocrats from the traditional side of the party. As someone flippantly remarked one morning on breakfast TV:

'I don't know where she gets them from. Some remote Chinese robot factory, perhaps?'

Fields flipped through the rest of the file: glowing obituaries lamenting the loss of "Britain's new Kennedy", the autopsy report and the coroner's judgement. Again, nothing suspicious; no mention of anything odd in the brain scan.

He was about to close the file when something made him turn back to the police report of the motorway accident. Opening the database, he typed in the names of the traffic cops who attended the incident and the officer who had signed the report. All three had retired early within months, two of them on the grounds of ill health.

He made a note of their home addresses, sat back and stared out of the window, deep in thought. Then he made two calls, using his private mobile.

As he left the office, he told his PA he was going for some fresh air. He didn't say where.

Whitehall, London

The following morning, Marksworth decided to summon his security escort for the short walk back to Downing Street. Mike Challoner received the message that the Prime Minister's office had called: the PM had cleared a "window in her diary" and Marksworth was expected for coffee at 10.30am, sharp.

'Put the boys on standby please, Challoner,' said Marksworth. 'Top priority, no hiccoughs.' He seemed much more nervous than usual.

'No hiccoughs?' said Patrick when he heard the news. 'What did you have for breakfast, Julian?'

'Beans on toast.'

'Oh, no. Mike, I suggest Julian stays downwind of our lord and master today.'

They were all still sniggering like schoolboys when they arrived at Marksworth's office. Their man was wearing the suit he obviously kept for very special occasions, nervously adjusting his cuffs and fiddling with his silk tie. He smelled strongly of something so unsubtle it had to be conspicuously expensive. Julian sniffed and backed away a yard but Markswoth didn't notice.

'Right, gentlemen, off we go, into the lioness' den,' he said and everyone laughed dutifully. He adjusted his tie again and checked his hair in a mirror.

Patrick could see that the man's hands were shaking, a gleam of sweat on his forehead.

No one spoke on the short walk to Downing Street. Julian's downwind position allowed him to keep an eye on his intercept of Marksworth's phone.

A hundred yards from their destination, Marksworth suddenly halted, removed a phone from an inside pocket and tapped the screen. They all halted.

Within seconds, Marksworth switched the device off, returned it to his pocket and set off once more. Or rather, he took one step forward, stumbled, stopped, collected his wits and resumed walking normally. Patrick drew alongside him. The man was looking straight ahead but his face was deathly pale and he appeared to be shivering. He stumbled once more.

'Are you alright, sir?' asked Patrick.

'Absolutely perfect, thank you, Monks. Never better.' Marksworth had hardly ever addressed him by name so Patrick had almost forgotten his own alias.

'Yes, fine. Never better,' Marksworth repeated and turned towards the main door of Number Ten as it was opened to admit him.

Patrick turned to Julian. Mike Challoner joined them as they walked round the corner to the Tradesmen's Entrance.

'What was all that about, Julian?' asked Patrick.

Julian showed them his phone. They could both clearly read the short message:

LHR 17.30 Thursday CA937. Cancel all appointments.

'The boss-man is on his way,' all three said in unison.

CHAPTER 15

'Richard? Do you have a moment?'

'On my way, Prime Minister.'

The familiar figure of Richard Merriott slipped silently through the private office door. Tall, sandy greying hair, three piece dark suit, stiff collar and striped silk tie, immaculate as ever, her Special Tactical Adviser stood awaiting instructions.

'Sit down, please,' said Jane Beaumont. 'My apologies for bothering you so soon on your first day back in the office.'

This was the man she had come to rely on for those not infrequent moments when she needed to bypass the "system". The regular Downing Street staff were all extremely capable with many years of experience of how government worked but they always took so long: apparently, nothing could ever be accomplished without a written brief, a planning meeting and continual use of sentences that began with 'We always have to bear in mind, Prime Minister'.

Merriott's job description was deliberately open to interpretation and, what was more, she thoroughly enjoyed his company. She would never call him devious but she made extensive use of his talents.

'Please don't apologise, Prime Minister. I've already cleared the accumulated clutter. How can I help?'

She smiled. 'I would be most grateful for your advice on a meeting I'm about to have.

The Prime Minister was alone waiting to greet him as David Marksworth was shown into her office. She looked him directly in the eyes, smiled in welcome and showed him towards a comfortable chair near the fireplace.

'Good morning, Mr Marksworth.'

'Good morning, Prime Minister.'

'Would you prefer tea or coffee?'

An attendant, who had followed him in, took his order and disappeared.

Marksworth took his seat, perching on the front of the chair. The PM settled more comfortably into hers. Her jacket and matching skirt were both feminine and professional; less severe than Margaret Thatcher, her silk blouse was open at the neck and a simple square pendant on a fine silver chain reflected the room's discreet lighting. She looked utterly relaxed, in command, commenting on the weather and an article she had read in the morning paper speculating on the Queen's health.

If anyone would know if the Queen was ill, it would be the Prime Minister; she has an audience at Buckingham Palace every week, he thought. But she revealed nothing.

She waited until the coffee arrived, then opened the conversation, asking him about his work at the Defence Department, seeking his views on a range of topics, from equipping the armed forces to the deployment of British troops in the world's trouble spots. She was trying to put him at his ease while testing him out at the same time.

He was itching for an opportunity to check out where she stood on Britain's declining role in the world but he bided his time.

'I wanted to thank you,' she said, 'for bringing a healthy dose of fresh air into that meeting about India the other day. What was the phrase you used? Ah, yes, "British imperialist patronising bullshit".' She laughed out loud. 'That certainly set the Foreign Office's pants on fire. They had a brand new paper on my desk before you could say "pomposity".'

Marksworth smiled his self-effacing smile. Then they both laughed, Marksworth a little nervously.

She returned to business. 'Look, I wanted to ask you something – may I call you David, by the way?'

'Of course, Prime Minister.'

'Good. Tell me now, I know you have a certain reputation for plain speaking but I'd like to ask you to expand on your "patronising bullshit" remark. What precisely was behind that comment?'

Marksworth cleared his throat and sat forward, taking a sip from his coffee. It gave him time to think. The PM waited patiently.

He said: 'I think that sometimes we all need to remind ourselves that this is the twenty-first century and there comes a time when we have to stop expecting the rest of the world to be eternally grateful to Britain for our model of parliamentary democracy, our legal system, Shakespeare, Byron, and the Beatles.'

'I see,' she said thoughtfully. 'But what about Queen and Commonwealth? After all, India has become an immensely powerful nation and surely our longstanding links with them, and with all the other Commonwealth countries, are a huge mutual asset, particularly for them.'

'Prime Minister,' he said, warming to the debate, 'from what I understand, we were not universally popular when we ruled India and the current generation of educated young Indians regard that part of their history as, dare I say it, of dubious value. As for the Commonwealth countries - these days their market is the entire world. They really see no benefit in any trading or defence alliance based on tradition, culture or language. They'll go where they can negotiate the best deal. And they prefer to leave attending Commonwealth meetings to their grandfathers' generation – a nice chance for them to meet the Queen but, in their view, increasingly archaic and irrelevant.'

He felt a moment of panic, wondering whether he had gone too far. He knew he'd been exaggerating in what he said and he hadn't meant to speak so bluntly. It had just come out that way.

The PM, expressionless, had allowed him to finish and was waiting a few seconds before responding. 'Hmm. I wouldn't allow Her Majesty to hear you say that. But, I have to tell you that, at least in one respect, I agree with you: one of the great failings of we British is our obsession with hammering on about our past glories. To ask for universal respect because, for example, a Scot happened to invent the telephone nearly a hundred and fifty years ago – while he was working in America, actually - just makes us look stupid in the eyes of the rest of the world. You don't hear the Chinese continuously reminding us that they invented gunpowder.'

Marksworth's ears pricked up. *China? Why did she pick on China?*

He noticed that she was now watching him even more intently.

'Anyway, thank you for explaining that, David. The other subject I wanted to touch on this morning concerns you. Or, to be more precise, your loyalties.'

Marksworth knew full well a look of trepidation was crossing his face: there was nothing he could do about it. If she had spotted it, the PM gave no sign.

'I was studying your file. You've had a remarkable career since you returned from your MBA course in Paris.'

'Paris?' Trepidation rating up two more notches.

'Yes,' she continued. 'To reach the level of Ministerial Under-Secretary so quickly is very rare. I'd be most interested to hear your thoughts on why you were picked out for such rapid promotion.'

By this time, David was struggling to think straight.

'Err, umm, I really don't know, Prime Minister. Perhaps I was just in the right place at the right time.' He smiled weakly.

She smiled, too. 'I'm sure there's more to it than that. And wasn't it curious that your friend Mr Bellingham, who I see was also with you in Paris, climbed the ladder equally fast? Such a shame about his road accident, by the way. You must have been terribly upset.'

She was still looking him directly in the eyes, seemingly searching for clues.

'Err, yes, Prime Minister. Quite tragic. He was a good man and a dear friend.'

Where is this leading?

Her tone hadn't altered. 'I assume somebody identified something special in the two of you. Almost as if you were both selected for great things while you were still quite young, in Paris perhaps. Don't you think?'

Marksworth simply nodded. By now, he was incapable of rational thought and his throat had closed up.

The woman seems to be enjoying herself. Or am I imagining it?

'David, I have a suggestion for you.' She leaned forward a little; she seemed to be making sure she had his full attention. David gripped the chair's arms in an effort to control his shaking.

'I was wondering whether you would be willing to allow me to write to your Minister, and to your Permanent Secretary, asking them to agree to your being seconded to my private office here for a year or two.'

Bam! Am I dreaming? Where am I? Pull yourself together, man, for God's sake!

'Are you feeling alright, David? Would you like some water?'

'Forgive me, Prime Minister. This has come as rather a shock. I would, of course, be honoured. But, could I ask, what would be my duties?'

'I thought I would give you the title of Acting Secretary for Internal Communications, otherwise known as Government Bullshit Buster.' She laughed again, obviously delighted by her own wit.

David was doing his best – and failing miserably - to reflect on all the differing implications of this posting, particularly on his work for Hong Jintao.

Internal Communications: that could mean access to departmental files across the whole span of Government. Confidential? Secret? . . . His head was spinning.

The PM was speaking again, more slowly this time. 'Right, I'm glad we've sorted that out. And now I have one other assignment for you; but this would be strictly between the two of us. Do you understand?'

'Yes, Prime Minister. I understand.' Curiouser and curiouser.

'I am convinced that there is a group of traitors, undercover agents for the Chinese, working at a senior level in my Government.' She paused, her eyes now stern, boring into his skull.

'I have not discussed this with anyone, as there is a distinct possibility that they have also infiltrated our security services. My information comes from a very private source, the identity of which must remain with me.

'I have decided to ask you, David, using the broad access this new post will give you to the heads of every department, to find these people and bring their names to me, and only me. How does that sound?'

How David Marksworth managed to conclude the meeting, shake hands and thank the Prime Minister 'for the confidence you have placed in me', he would never know.

Outside, he slipped into the nearest restroom which, thankfully, was empty. Leaning with both hands against the hand basin, he stared at his reflection in the mirror and took several deep breaths, trying to force his pulse rate to settle down.

So many thoughts were racing through his mind:

She wants me where she can keep an eye on me.

She wants me to identify and expose the Chinese spy ring.

What kind of game is she playing?

What does she know, or at least suspect?

Who's she been talking to?

Or am I just getting paranoid?

He checked his watch, took out his private phone, and composed a message. The door opened just as he finished. A well-groomed man in his fifties brushed past him as he turned to leave.

'Good morning, David. Keeping well? How did it go with the PM? Is she in a good mood today? She was really snappy yesterday, I gather. Something bugging her, I suppose.'

'Oh, hello. Yes, fine. Sorry, can't stop; late for my next meeting. Talk soon, I hope. My regards to err . . .'

Back in the busy corridor, he called Mike Challoner and asked them to meet him in the street outside. As he walked down the stairs to leave, he had almost forgotten the conversation with the man in the loo. His only last thought was:

I don't remember him having a moustache.

'Where's what's-his-name, Challoner?'

'Oh, you mean Johnny Monks, sir?' Patrick was nowhere to be seen. 'He had to slip away for an hour or so. Doctor's appointment. Something to do with some blood tests.'

'Can't he do these things in his own time?' said Marksworth.

'Well, you know the Health Service these days. Snowed under with old folks and paper-pushing. You're lucky to get to see a quack in under a month. Did I ever tell you about my Dad? He'd almost snuffed it by the time a doctor got round to seeing him.'

'Yes, yes. Thank you, Challoner. I seem to have heard the story of your father a few times before.' He walked on ahead.

Julian watched the exchange with some amusement. Mike liked to pretend to Marksworth that he was, as he put it, 'dependable but a bit thick and boring'; Mike reckoned that, if he didn't think he was too bright, he might let something indiscreet slip out from time to time.

They both knew full well where Patrick had gone.

At exactly the appointed time, Cameron saw Andy Fields' cab pull up in front of the Reform Club in Pall Mall. He crossed the street and accompanied Andy up the steps.

'Thanks for coming so quickly, Patrick. There's someone I want you to meet.'

A uniformed steward showed them into the Library. Thousands of beautifully bound books lined the panelled walls. Stewards moved noiselessly between tables. The members present seemed far more interested in their morning paper than chatting. As they entered a tall, grey-haired man got up from one of the studded leather armchairs, folded his newspaper and turned to greet them. Despite his age, Patrick guessed he was in his late seventies, he knew instinctively that the man was ex-military.

Andy said, 'Hello, Sir Norman. May I introduce Dr Patrick Cameron?'

'Delighted to meet you, Dr Cameron,' the man said. 'Andrew speaks most highly of you.' He smiled. 'I've reserved a small room. Follow me, please.'

A pot of coffee was already warming on the sideboard when they arrived. Sir Norman did the honours before opening the discussion. 'Dr Cameron,' he said. 'I'm sure I don't have to confirm that this meeting must never be discussed outside this room.'

Patrick nodded.

'All you need to know is that I represent people who have the nation's welfare close to our hearts. Andrew here is a highly trusted associate. He recommended you to us. I gather you have performed well on certain other missions in which I and my friends also took a close interest.'

Patrick understood now: Sir Norman had told him, without telling him, that he was part of the highly secretive Last Resort Squad, Britain's ultimate guardians. Andy Fields had referred to them obliquely on more than one occasion in the past. He remembered him explaining how few people could be entirely trusted these days.

Sir Norman continued. 'I know you are aware that the mission in which you are currently engaged is highly sensitive. What I'm going to tell you now is why I invited you here today. It's important that you hear it directly from me.

'Dr Cameron, it would be no exaggeration to say that, in our view, the success or failure of this mission will have a direct bearing on the balance of power in the world.'

Patrick couldn't take his eyes off the old man. All he could think of was that, if what he was hearing were true, then he, Patrick Cameron, father-to-be in only a few weeks, was likely to be in grave danger. Angela's worried face flashed before his eyes.

Sir Norman continued: 'This is not simply a matter of Britain's standing in the world – that is changing, quite rightly in our view, every year. We see little point in clinging onto a prominent but increasingly unjustified place at all the world's top tables. What does concern us, however, is who controls those tables. It is critical that freedom and democracy survive, for the sake of humanity.

'In the last hundred years we have come perilously close to a world dominated, first by Fascism and later by Marxism. In both cases, thank God, they failed. What we are left with now is a messy compromise – democracy sounds wonderful in principle but elected politicians have their weaknesses, and there are still far too many rogue states – but on the whole it works.'

He smiled at Patrick. 'Do forgive this long lecture but you need to understand the context. In the last twenty years a new threat has emerged. Countries that formerly were content to trade peacefully with the rest of the world have adopted new priorities. Just as the larger international companies have used aggressive acquisition to create vast empires, "in order to compete on a global scale", as they describe it, so certain national leaders see the need to take control of large parts of the developing world, primarily in Africa and in Asia. They reason that, if they buy or bully their way into these countries, it will be only a matter of time before they achieve political control. That way, they'll effectively own all their natural resources, their workforce and their armies.'

He relaxed, sat back and took a big gulp from the glass of water at his side. He looked tired.

Patrick sensed it was time for him to react. 'We're talking about China here, aren't we, sir?'

'Of course. And the question you no doubt want to ask me is: so what's new? China has been investing vast amounts of cash in developing countries for years. You are right, they have; but our information tells us that they have now moved to a critical new stage. Tell me, do you recall the Cambridge Four?'

'I certainly do - they were a group of Russian spies, weren't they?'

'British spies working for the Soviets, to be accurate. Traitors. Guy

Burgess, Donald Maclean, Kim Philby and Anthony Blunt. Recruited by the Russians and converted to Communism while they were at Cambridge in the 1930s. For more than twenty years, they passed thousands of our secrets to the Russians until Burgess, Maclean and Philby escaped to Moscow before they were exposed. They all held important posts in government; Philby was so highly thought of he could well have become head of MI5.'

Patrick interrupted. 'Excuse me sir, but one thing's always bothered me about that story: it seems inconceivable that, since the Cambridge Four scandal, there have been hardly any other enemy spies working inside our government or security services. Why can I only recall hearing about a couple at the most?'

Sir Norman passed a satisfied look towards Andy Fields and nodded.

Fields took up the story. 'You're right, of course, Patrick. Just as we have always had people passing information about them to us, we know they have their own over here. To be honest, most spying these days involves people with access to economic and technological information making a few grand on the side. We've been pretty effective at picking them up and quietly putting them away without any public fuss. The more dangerous areas of spying – security, military secrets, sensitive diplomacy – on the other hand, are entirely another matter.

'You will understand that we can't discuss individual cases, but I can assure you that there have, as you say, been a number of highly-placed foreign agents in government circles over the years and those we have identified have been quietly removed from circulation. No fuss, no publicity. It would be foolish to say that we have caught them all. But I'd like to talk about the present day.

'We have suspected for some time that there are elements within the Chinese hierarchy who have one simple goal – to control the world's economy. But don't imagine that this is just about political power – for example, they are facing colossal energy shortages.

'We also believe that they have had a cell of agents, "deep sleepers" as we refer to them, implanted in government circles here for many years, waiting to be activated. They were recruited and converted to Communism as young men, following Russia's Philby-Burgess-Maclean model from the nineteen-fifties to the letter.

'We believe these sleepers were behind the series of recent unexplained deaths and disappearances you have been examining. Including that of Alistair Thomas some years ago. Now, it seems we can safely assume that your man Marksworth is one of them. We need to identify the others quickly. I can assure you that the recently notorious Lord Dulwich is not involved. Some of us have known him for years. Not the brightest of sparks. But Gregory Bellingham almost certainly was.'

'And Bellingham is dead,' said Patrick. 'Big question: if his death was not an accident, who killed him and why?'

'Now you understand why I can't pull Marksworth in for questioning,' said Andy Fields. 'There are certainly more of them out there and we would only scare the others off.'

'But, come on Andy, Marksworth is about to join the Prime Minister's staff!' Patrick exclaimed. 'He's bound to have access to the most confidential stuff.'

The other two men looked at each other and chuckled quietly.

'Actually, that's exactly where we want him,' said Andy. 'With you, Mike and Julian looking over his shoulder and another friend of ours close by . . .'

'Another friend? In Downing Street?' asked Patrick. 'Who?'

''Fraid I can't tell you the name. But you'll know who it is if and when the time comes. '

'Now gentlemen, I suggest we use the next hour to work on a few details,' said Sir Norman. 'Let's start with Alistair Thomas' death, the car crash: we need to talk to the three police officers.'

CHAPTER 16

As the China Airways jet flew across Western Europe, Hong Jintao was deep in thought. The Central Politburo Standing Committee of the Communist Party of China (the PSC) had summoned him to their weekly meeting two days earlier. In itself, that was not unusual: he was used to giving them regular updates in his role as Foreign Minister.

But as far as he was aware, only the President and his Premier were being kept informed about the plan to undermine the United Kingdom. So it had to be some other matter, extremely important and urgent, for him to be called in at such short notice.

He was ushered punctually into the room, where seven men were seated around a large circular table. Each had his own area of ministerial responsibility; their faces were familiar to everyone in the country and their joint decisions had the force of law.

Only one man stood, the President of the People's Republic.

'Welcome, honoured Foreign Minister.' Hong thought the President looked quite drawn on this occasion. For a man burdened with the massive responsibility of running the world's most populous, multi-cultural society, he had an extraordinary knack of making people he met feel that everything was under control. Not that day.

'We wish to take you into our confidence on a matter of the gravest importance, Hong Jintao,' he explained, once Hong had taken his seat. 'You are aware, of course, of our ten-year plan for China to become self-sufficient in energy.'

Hong acknowledged with a nod of his head.

'It has been brought to our attention that certain elements of that plan may not, after all, be workable. In simple terms, our so-called experts are now telling us that it will not be practical for us to achieve our medium-term industrial objectives, while maintaining the level of agricultural output we need to feed our people. A simple matter, one would have thought: it appears that we – they - have drastically miscalculated the country's requirements for water.'

'Water, Mr President? Or energy?' asked Hong.

'Water, Foreign Minister. The water needed to cool all of our new power stations is much greater than we – they - had calculated. So great that, if the situation were allowed to continue, we would not have enough to water the land. I do not have to explain to you the importance of maintaining our own food supplies.'

Hong listened quietly as his President outlined in more detail the mismatch between China's available water and its domestic, industrial and agricultural consumption. The picture he painted was so bad that only one conclusion could be drawn – if nothing was done, China would slowly but surely grind to a halt – it would quite literally run dry. And, if that happened, the social and economic consequences were too frightening to contemplate.

'We will deal with the incompetence of these experts as a separate issue,' the President continued. 'The more pressing need is for us to close down a number of our power stations, as soon as possible, and replace them with new secure sources of energy from elsewhere. At a price we can afford to pay, naturally.

'The strategy we have formulated to remedy this situation implies a radical rethinking of our foreign policy. We have considered a number of alternatives but, regrettably, none of them would deliver the resources we require within an acceptable timeframe at an acceptable cost.'

He paused to take his breath. Hong sensed that what the President was going to say next weighed heavily on his shoulders.

'We have decided to take political and economic control of a specified number of countries. We already have many of these countries in our pocket, although not wholly under our control, through our friendly investment programme over recent years. But we need more – more countries and more control. Now, the question is - where will we find these countries?' He looked directly at Hong, whose eyes had widened. The President smiled.

'Yes, Hong Jintao, you know the answer already – the Indian sub-Continent, South Asia, Africa . . .'

Hong watched a list of countries appear on the small screen in front of him, his thoughts travelling down several channels at once.

Almost every one is a member of the British Commonwealth of

Nations! They want to take control of – to destroy - the British Commonwealth? Exactly what Guo Dalong wants me to achieve, but for different reasons. But this time it's not about revenge, about destroying the British Establishment; it's to save the Chinese nation from catastrophe.

Or so it would appear. I wonder . . . do they know nothing of my work for Guo Dalong? Has he been operating alone? Who is really pulling the strings here?

His first thoughts were to doubt that what he was hearing was the whole truth. He decided to test his doubts with a question.

'Mr President, many of these countries are located at a great distance from China. Surely they're . . .?'

The President interrupted him with one hand.

'Too distant from China for us to use a pipeline like the one that now delivers gas from Russia? Or a cable? Of course, you are correct, Hong Jintao. But, by good fortune, we have discovered that the Americans have been secretly working on a new form of technology that will enable energy to be transmitted over great distances, wirelessly, in very large volumes. Thanks to a little cunning and ingenuity of our own, our people have succeeded in capturing and replicating their research.

'Naturally, as these countries have strong historical and political ties to the UK, we will only succeed if they are persuaded to turn away from history. I use the word "persuaded" in its complex form.'

For the first time, the other great men allowed themselves a quiet laugh.

'Hong Jintao,' the President's tone had now changed. 'We are looking to you to lay the groundwork for loosening the bonds that tie those Commonwealth countries to Britain. Use your agents in whatever way you deem necessary; you will have all the support you need from our intelligence agencies' network of students and academics in the United Kingdom.'

The flight attendant offered Hong another drink which he refused, turning back to his notes. The plan that had been forming in his mind was almost complete – a very different plan from the one he had in mind before the PSC meeting.

Strangely, he had heard nothing from Guo Dalong since his return from India. He had tried to contact him but without success.

Which placed him in a serious quandary: should he continue to comply with Guo Dalong's instructions or did the President's orders override Guo's?

It was the President's closing remark that changed everything - the words that had kept Hong Jintao awake all night:

'Be very clear, very clear indeed, that, while we would much prefer all this to pass off peacefully, if we deem it necessary, we are prepared to resolve the matter using military force.'

In other words, you are prepared to risk a major East-West confrontation – a war – to save your own country. Now where have I heard that before? was Hong's unspoken response.

As the plane started to slow, he buckled his seat belt and looked down on the usual blanket of rain clouds covering the South-East of England, one thought rattling back and forth, over and over, in his mind –

If I succeed, I will save my country and its people but hasten the downfall of a great civilisation. If I fail, hundreds of thousands, perhaps millions, will die.

San Francisco, USA

The temptation to ignore the message that had just flashed up on her phone was almost as great as the temptation of the delicious, naked creature currently spread-eagled across the bed in her hotel suite. But sadly, the distinctive ring-tone tipped the balance and, sighing, Jenna Dobrosova rose from her knees and walked across the room, elegant in her black leather basque and thigh-length high-heeled boots.

She read the message in silence, turned and looked back at the bed, at the feast that awaited her and decided she had to partake of at least the hors d'oeuvre – and maybe just a morsel or two of the main course - before showering, packing her cases and taking a taxi to the international airport for the next plane to London. After all, the psychoactive drugs she had used to create this scenario were not cheap. It would be a shame to waste them.

At least she had managed a few days of Californian fun, looking up a few old friends and making a new one.

Heathrow airport, London

Leaving the plane, Hong Jintao found David Marksworth waiting in the diplomatic lounge. His regular embassy driver was also at the terminal but he had been instructed to collect his bags and remain outside until the Foreign Minister was ready to leave.

'Good morning. I have reserved a small private room for us,' said Marksworth. Hong merely nodded and followed Marksworth, a shaven-headed, shades-wearing, gum-chewing, tattooed man a discreet distance behind.

'One of my personal bodyguards,' explained Marksworth, noticing the Chinese man's questioning look.

'My people swept the room for bugs before I arrived, Hong Jintao,' he said as soon as the door was closed.

'How have you explained to your department about your need to meet with me, David?'

Marksworth's chest swelled as he announced, 'I am now attached to the Prime Minister's private office, Foreign Minister. In effect, I can come and go as I please, with my own personal bodyguards.' He nodded in the direction of the door where Patrick Cameron's – or Johnny Monks' – back was visible through the glass.

'I see,' said Hong. 'Now I suggest we get right down to business. As you will learn, we have little time to waste.'

How the remarkable Julian had managed to secrete the tiny transmitter on David Marksworth's person without it being noticed by the Government's surveillance men was a mystery to Cameron. But his concealed earpiece was receiving a clear signal, the voices of Marksworth and Hong Jintao coming through loud and clear. Andy Fields and Sir Norman would be able to hear too and record the conversation.

'Firstly, *shifu,* I need to hear you reconfirm your absolute loyalty to the People's Republic of China and your willingness to dedicate and, if necessary, sacrifice yourself to the great mission with which you have been entrusted. Will you swear once again to our oath of brotherhood?' Hong Jintao, seemingly unaffected by the long flight, had fire in his eyes.

Marksworth nodded.

'Repeat after me . . .' Hong then pronounced, phrase by phrase, the oath they had both shared with Gregory Bellingham all those years earlier:

We have come together as brothers. From this day forward, we shall join forces for a common purpose: to save the troubled and to aid the endangered. We shall avenge the nation above, and pacify the citizenry below. We seek not to be born on the same day, in the same month and in the same year. We merely hope to die on the same day, in the same month and in the same year. May the Gods of Heaven and Earth attest to what is in our hearts. If we should ever do anything to betray our friendship, may heaven and the people of the earth both strike us dead.

Marksworth repeated every word.

'Thank you, David. *Shifu*.' He seemed satisfied. Marksworth, for his part, was feeling immeasurably moved by the sanctity of the occasion.

'We should now remember in our prayers the courage and loyalty of our brother Gregory Bellingham who has sadly left us,' said Hong.

'We remember him with gratitude,' said Marksworth, all the time thinking,

I still believe he was executed but I dare not ask. And Hong still hasn't convinced me that I'm in the clear.

The briefing then began in earnest. First Hong dealt with the approaching energy crisis in China. Rumours had been circulating in Whitehall but Marksworth had never heard the bald facts. Then he explained about the need for China to take ownership – 'ownership, not partnership' - of the energy resources in a number of countries many of which, for the moment at least, were members of the British Commonwealth.

'Here is a list of the Commonwealth countries we have identified as our targets.' He tapped the screen of his tablet and passed it to Marksworth, who scanned it and sat back, puzzled.

'Yes, I know,' said Hong, reading his thoughts. 'Some of these countries are large and powerful in their own right. But they are also rich in minerals and, in almost every case, their government is politically vulnerable. So it is realistic to include them.'

'But these places, the distances . . .' He pointed to a couple of names on the screen.

'Trust me,' said Hong dismissively. 'They are all legitimate targets. Now, to the plan. I have taken the liberty of listing the key points here.' He tapped the screen again. 'I want you to read it now and to commit it to memory. You may take no notes. If, for any reason, you are apprehended, there will be no record of this conversation.'

Marksworth, feeling slightly annoyed that Hong had refused to answer his last question, took Hong's tablet and read through three pages of short bullet points. It was brilliant, he could see that. As and when the entire plan was carried out, Britain would become the pariah of the world; no self-respecting government would want to be associated with the British. The road would be open for China to make its moves.

And yet, after reading it through several times, the same question kept recurring in his mind. This was going to require a great deal of planning, diversions synchronised and doors opened to which he currently had no keys.

'But who . . .?' he began.

'There's no need to concern yourself. The names of those in high places here who have already been recruited to our cause will be made known to you. You don't really believe that you and Bellingham were the only British who agreed to become our agents in the last twenty years, do you? All you need to understand at this stage is that, among their number, there are individuals who occupy positions of such extreme influence that we dare not risk exposing them, now or at any time in the future. That is why I am placing you in charge of the execution of this plan.'

Ah, I get it now. I am the one who is deemed expendable. What the Americans call the fall guy. Terrific! thought Marksworth with a shiver.

'May I ask you a question, Hong Jintao? What I have read tells me clearly what you want to happen but not how.'

'How is entirely your affair. For example, you are already familiar with the skills of our expert in psycho-active materials.'

'Yes, Jen . . .'

'She will be operating under a different identity when she arrives back in London tomorrow. The name Jeanne Devereaux has outlived its usefulness. You will be informed of her new name. You will also be given assistance with the recruitment of people with other skills. Now, I need to be absolutely sure you have correctly memorised everything you have read.' He took the tablet and opened another file.

'Here is your test paper,' he said, handing the tablet back to Marksworth. 'Please type the correct answer alongside each question.'

Ten minutes later, the two men left the room and headed off in different directions, David Marksworth followed obediently by the shaven-headed bodyguard Monks, who seemed a little preoccupied.

CHAPTER 17

Sir Norman removed the headphones, stood up and stretched. He walked to the window and looked out across the garden he and his wife had spent so much time, energy and passion recreating after they bought this house. That was when plain Captain Tudway, as he was then, was still a serving officer. Originally planned as their weekend bolthole, it became their home years later when he retired as Chief of the Armed Forces, although they still retained a small apartment in central London for those nights when they needed to be up in Town.

He had always loved the South Wiltshire countryside; he had grown up in a village near Salisbury, where his father was the local doctor, and met his wife-to-be Meg while he was stationed at a camp on Salisbury Plain as a young officer. So it had seemed quite natural, when the time came, for them to choose to retire there, only an hour from London by train. Village life suited them both well: he was churchwarden of the local church and chaired the village residents' forum, while Meg served as a parish councillor as well as helping out with the annual Open Gardens weekend and the village fete.

Having the time to be able to welcome people to their home was a great joy: lunch parties round the kitchen table, monthly meetings of the local book club and charity coffee mornings.

The house itself, with its uneven floors, twelve-inch thick walls, noisy plumbing and low ceilings was the perfect place for Sir Norman to slop about in his favourite old cardigan, baggy corduroys and carpet slippers. His study housed all his books, files and electronics. Meg got on happily with her life whenever he told her he was 'a bit tied up'. She had learned never to enquire.

It all looked so peaceful and orderly, far away from the world of political manipulation, deceit and infighting that had continually hampered Sir Norman's attempts to protect the integrity of the nation's defences, trying to make sense of Britain's intrusions into conflicts around the world that were none of its business. And yet now, as chairman of The Last Resort Squad, he was arguably more involved in the intrigues of world affairs than ever.

The conversation he had just overheard between Hong and Marksworth had been, at the same time, revealing, confirming and hugely frustrating. He looked at the jotted notes on his pad. They were in two columns: years earlier, he'd found that, if he started by separating what he called 'the dross from the nuggets', the interesting from the important, the urgent from the rest of the in-tray, on one sheet of paper, the result was a far clearer, uncomplicated day. This time, one column was a great deal longer than the other.

Distracted for a moment, as the family cat tried to escape a dive-bombing mother blackbird on the lawn, he smiled and re-concentrated his thoughts.

Let's start with the dross. The Chinese are in trouble. We knew that. Yes, they did that huge gas deal with Russia back in 2014. But they hate being in hock to the Russians; they don't trust them an inch and the feeling's mutual. We guessed correctly that they would want to get more resources from somewhere and that would almost certainly include a few Commonwealth countries. So far, so good, but none of that takes us any further forward.

So now then, let's look at what's new? – the nuggets: number one has to be an almost off-the-cuff remark that Hong slipped in late in the briefing session:

'It will only take a few to announce they are leaving, for the others to join the rush.'

What was he talking about? thought Sir Norman. I can understand why the Chinese might want to grab a chunk of places like India, Pakistan, and Bangladesh: they could easily pipe their energy straight across their common borders. But it sounds as though he has something a lot bigger in mind. What and why? How could a mass defection away from Britain and the Commonwealth get China out of this mess?

His private phone rang. Andy Fields.

'Sir Norman,' said Fields. 'Good afternoon. Did you hear all that clearly enough?'

'Yes, thank you, Commissioner Fields. I cleaned the wax out of my hearing aids only this morning,' replied Sir Norman, a touch of humour in his voice. 'What did you make of all that, young man?'

'Much as you, I should think. On the plus side, we're on the right track; on the minus side, we can't use any of it as evidence – hacked telephone conversations aren't admissible in court. And somewhere in the middle, we have no idea whether Hong was giving Marksworth the true story, we haven't a clue what they are actually planning to do and we don't have any new agents' names. Except for that one Hong mentioned – Jeanne Devereaux. To me, that sounds uncannily close to Jenna Dobrosova. So I'm having it checked. Anyway, all in all, a mixed report – as my old form master used to say, could do so much better with a little more effort.'

Sir Norman nodded. 'I agree with you entirely. Hong was clever enough to keep the details of the plan unspoken; did he suspect someone could be listening? But one thing I can't understand, Andrew, is why on earth they didn't talk more about Marksworth's work for the Prime Minister. Could it be that the whole thing is just a charade?'

He paused. 'So where do we go from here, Andrew? Even if it was all genuine, Hong would only have told Marksworth the absolute minimum he wants him to know. So that's all we have to work with too.'

'You're right,' said Andy. 'Too many questions still unanswered.'

'Hmm. Those names – the other spies. Who knows? People who occupy positions of extreme influence, Hong said. Where do we start looking for these sleepers? After all, everyone missed Kim Philby in the fifties. Nobody could believe he was a spy, even when he came under suspicion. My guess is that this lot are just as plausible as he was. We need a lucky break or . . .' He paused, unsure of what to say.

Fields helped out. 'Or we need to dig a great deal deeper, or just hope one of them makes a slip. OK, sir, I'll get a debrief from Patrick Cameron when he's free to talk, check out this woman Jeanne Devereaux and put someone on Hong Jintao's tail. Which won't be easy: the Chinese are as good as we are at spotting watchers.'

'Thank you, Andrew,' said Sir Norman and rang off.

He sat down and turned to his laptop. Opening a heavily encrypted set of files, he located a name and began to type a message which, when it was received in Beijing, would be utterly untraceable.

In the embassy car on the way into central London, Hong Jintao made a number of calls, two to fix meetings and the third to send a photograph of David Marksworth's shaven-headed bodyguard to the Chinese secret service HQ in London, asking for the man to be identified and security checked. The shades he'd worn throughout Hong's meeting with David Marksworth would make the task more difficult but the men doing the analysis were reckoned to be world class operators.

There was something about that man which rang a bell with him. Was it his walk? Or his voice?

The meeting had passed off as well as he'd hoped. Marksworth now had sufficient information to feel trusted and to get on with the job but it would have been a mistake to let him in on the most brutal fact: that, if he failed, if Hong himself failed, China could well unleash its massive military strength and plunge the world into war once more.

He closed his eyes and began a silent prayer. Some years earlier, Hong Jintao had converted to Christianity – a fact he kept hidden from all but a close coterie of fellow believers. Every so often, the Chinese authorities, while overtly welcoming the rapid expansion of the Christian faith, would develop an attack of nerves about what they called "overly popular" religious activities and introduce a couple of new laws to keep them under control, to discourage over-zealous worship. If his faith were to be discovered, Hong's career could well be finished. It was not the done thing to talk about Jesus inside the Forbidden City.

Heavenly Father, give me the strength and wisdom to serve my country, to help it in its hour of need, and the resourcefulness to ensure a successful outcome without the need for human bloodshed. In the name of your Son, our Saviour. Amen.

David Marksworth was unusually quiet as Patrick drove him back into the city. A brief phone call to the Permanent Under-Secretary at the Ministry of Defence appeared to free him to take up his duties inside 10 Downing Street right away; all his responsibilities at the Ministry were being reallocated and his files were up-to-date. Patrick did his best to appear impressed when Marksworth informed him, in his most pompous tone of voice, that 'From now on, Monks, you and the others will have the honour of protecting one of the Prime Minister's closest aides'.

'Well, done, sir,' said Patrick. 'So we'll still be needed when you move across?'

'Even more so, Monks,' replied Marksworth. 'My work will all be top secret. It is imperative, for the safety of the nation, that my security is guaranteed.'

'You can count on us, sir,' said Patrick. 'No worries. Here, you couldn't get me her autograph, by any chance? My kids would be really chuffed.'

'The PM's autograph? I'm not sure that would be appropriate for an official of my senior rank but I'll see what I can do,' came the patronising reply.

Marksworth's phone buzzed – the private one in his inside pocket - and he answered it.

'Yes?'

He listened.

'Tomorrow, ten p.m.,' he said. 'My flat.' He closed the call. Patrick made a mental note to check whether Julian had picked up the call. They drove directly to Downing Street where David Marksworth made something of a show of getting out of – 'alighting from' - the car. As Patrick held the door open, Marksworth waved and smiled at the gaggle of bored press photographers on duty on the opposite pavement. Not one of them looked up from his newspaper.

Patrick met Julian in Downing Street's underground car park. An armed security guard strolled up, stopped and asked to see their passes. Patrick watched him carefully.

'Haven't seen you two around here before,' he said, handing the passes back.

'Boss has just got a job in the big lady's office. Starts today,' said Patrick, pointing to the new windscreen sticker he'd collected a couple of minutes earlier.

'Good luck to him,' said the guard. 'Funny woman. She can change with the wind: nice as pie one day and the bat out of hell the next. Never used to be like that. I reckon she's got stuff on her mind she's not talking about.'

Patrick grunted. He looked at the man's badge and noted his name – Neville Baker. Known in the Tradesmen's Entrance tea room as "Nasal Neville". Apparently, the last question one should ever ask him was 'How are you?' He was convinced he'd been suffering from a heavy cold since the age of seven. For the last fifteen years, he'd been working underground and some people thought 'it was beginning to tell'.

'Anyway, nice to meet you, Neville,' said Patrick. 'We must catch up some time. Keep your nose clean.' He shook the man's hand and headed for a distant staircase, Julian in tow. Baker stayed a moment longer, looking puzzled, then strolled away shaking his head.

Once they were alone again, Patrick briefed Julian on the Hong-Marksworth conversation at the airport. 'I'll need to talk to Andy Fields but you and I are going to have to be in two places at once for a while,' he said. 'I'll carry on keeping tabs on Marksworth; watch his every move, who he contacts.'

'Can you cover me while I'm away?' said Julian.

'We'll have to come up with some acceptable excuse why you're not around and you'll need to keep us briefed on Marksworth's phone calls as well. By the way, did you pick up that call he took about twenty minutes ago?'

'Yes,' said Julian. 'Strange. The line was a bit fuzzy. No voice, just a snatch of music. Too short for me. I never was any good at Spot That Tune. They'd blanked the number the call was coming from.'

'Marksworth obviously recognised the signal. He's meeting him or her at ten tomorrow evening, right?'

'Yes, at his flat.'

'OK. We'll have the flat watched. Julian, your number one priority now is to track down this woman, Jenna Dobrosova. She's bloody dangerous, and clever. And you can bet your boots she's acquired some nasty new kit. We have to intercept her before she has a chance to commit whatever dirty deed she's planning next. That call may have been her. Even if she's not in London already, she's on her way, under an assumed name. I've arranged for all the shots we have of her to be sent to your phone. But remember, she can change her appearance in no time.'

'Look who's talking,' said Julian, looking pointedly at Patrick's shiny pate and the gaudy tattoos sprouting above the collar of his chauffeur's white shirt.

Patrick laughed. 'Anyway, is that OK with you?'

Julian grinned. 'You mean tracking down one of the sexiest assassins in the world? I think I can handle that.'

'Your mission, young man is to find her and follow her – not to handle her! Just for once, keep your hands to yourself, unless it's absolutely necessary. Oh God, why did I say that?'

'You're no fun anymore, boss,' said Julian. As he turned to go, he looked back and stuck his tongue out.

At that very moment, a woman was approaching the Avis desk at Heathrow airport, trailing two rather battered suitcases. Struggling to keep the cases under control, she looked tired and nervous in the hustle of the huge crowded terminal, constantly looking around and stopping to adjust her spectacles.

The reception clerk smiled as she arrived.

'How can I help you, madam?' she asked.

The woman let go of her cases, one of which toppled over, and pulled her heavy handbag around her body.

'Umm, I reserved a car for a few days,' she said, her voice almost too soft for the clerk to hear. The accent hard to place, perhaps a touch of Irish, or Scots. 'I think I have the paperwork here somewhere.' She started to delve into her bag, planting handfuls of clutter on the counter.

'That's all right,' the clerk reassured her. 'I'm sure we can find your reservation, if I could just have your name.'

'My name? Oh, it's Donnelly, Jasmine Donnelly. Here's my passport.'

The clerk took the well-used Irish passport, opened it, looked at the blurred photograph and hit a few keys. 'Ah, yes. Here we are. Oh, are you sure I've got the right booking? It says here you've asked for a four-wheel drive goods van.'

'Yes, but a fairly small one, please. I'm not very good at parking big cars.' She tittered.

'I do apologise,' said the clerk. 'It's just that you don't look . . .'

The woman looked down at her aging chain-store belted coat and clumpy shoes. She pushed a lock of her mousey pudding-basin hair away from her face.

'Not like a typical van driver?' she asked. 'No, I don't suppose I do. Actually, if you promise not to tell anyone . . .' She leaned forward confidentially. 'I've come over here to collect my mother's coffin. She stipulated in her will that she wanted to be laid to rest in the Scottish coal mine where my Dad worked until he died. It's closed now. And I'd rather not let people see I've got a coffin in the back on the journey up there. That's why I need a van.' She smiled winningly.

The clerk coughed, trying not to laugh.

Fifteen minutes later, Jenna Dobrosova, assassin, now minus the spectacles and brown wig, was on her way to a secret location, a farmhouse in Buckinghamshire, for intensive training on the equipment she would be using to put the final nail in the coffin of the British Empire.

CHAPTER 18

Julian was on his way too. This was the chance he'd been waiting for, to prove once and for all to his boss Patrick that he was not just the office nerd. He loved playing with technology, making it turn somersaults for him, revealing information that it had never been designed to do.

But, now that he was working at Patrick's side on a second undercover case, this time in much closer contact with the "enemy", he was itching to go out into the field alone and feel trusted enough to do things his way.

First, however, he needed to check a few things, using his own computer set-up, back at the lab in Oxford. Tracking down this woman was not going to be easy: he had little to go on – just a few old photographs, which only served to prove how adept she was at altering her appearance, plus her real name and one alias.

Riding north-west along the M40 towards Oxford, taking care to stay just below the speed limit, he felt his special phone buzz once inside his jacket. He'd have to wait before picking up Marksworth's call and sending anything interesting back to Patrick in London.

Parking his bike behind the lab, he removed his helmet, shook his unruly hair and bounded up the steps.

'Morning all,' he said as he pushed open the laboratory doors, to be greeted by one 'Morning, Jules,' and a chorus of grunts. Every one of his white-coated colleagues was either staring intently at a screen or bent over a microscope, absorbed as usual.

'Please yourselves,' he muttered and headed for the drinks machine.

As he settled into his chair, Patrick's PA Rowena sidled over and grabbed his shoulder in a bone-crunching grip. Today's outfit comprised a black pill-box hat with veil, a plunging purple silk blouse, a black leather pencil skirt, fishnet stockings and high heels. The long cigarette holder, complete with electronic cigarette, did not look out of place.

'Hello, my darling,' she proclaimed in a husky mid-European accent. 'Can I interest you in something chewy?' She held out a bag of sweets.

'Hi, Rowena. Another humdrum day at the office, I see,' he said and laughed. If she hadn't been such a brilliant PA, with an uncanny knack of anticipating his next request before he had thought of it, she would not have lasted twenty-four hours in this intense research establishment.

Rowena ignored him, leaned close to his ear and asked, 'Will you be staying long, my dear? Because I can only spare you ten minutes behind the filing cabinets, I'm afraid. So many men; so little time.'

'Patrick sends his regards to you all.' Julian raised his voice for everyone to hear. 'He's a bit tied up on government stuff for a few days.'

'He's called in every other day,' said Rowena in her normal voice. 'So he knows what's happening here.' She smooched away.

'Right, I'll need to crack on,' said Julian, and opened up his system.

Within five minutes, he had accessed the airline passenger lists for the previous week. Neither Jenna Dobrosova nor Jeanne Devereaux was registered. He tried something else.

J D, J D. Surely that doesn't make sense; far too risky, to carry on using her own initials for her cover name.

Then he recalled reading somewhere about how certain criminal minds got a kick out of covering their tracks while, at the same time, laying a series of seemingly obvious clues to their identity, just for the thrill of nonplussing their pursuers. Vanity.

Well, it's worth a try, if only to eliminate it, Julian thought and ran a filter through the database, looking for female passengers arriving in London with the initials "J D", aged between thirty and forty. Despite the vast number of passengers – around a hundred thousand a day at Heathrow alone – the list for each day was relatively short.

By concentrating just on white-skinned passengers travelling alone, he managed to reduce the numbers even further. Each one had been routinely photographed as they presented their passport at the desk. Julian already knew Dobrosova's vital statistics, at least her height and weight, from the short time she had been held in custody a couple of years previously, before being released without charge. And that was where he hoped to make progress: one of her distinguishing features was that she was unusually tall for a woman, just under six feet.

Was it possible that all of the cameras were mounted in the same position behind the passport desks? A long shot – he smiled at his own joke – but again, it was worth a try.

When he put all of the mug shots into a gallery on his screen, he breathed a sigh of relief. The heads appeared in different positions in the frame depending on the woman's height. Clearly the cameras had been set up to cope with a wide range of heights without having to be adjusted.

Now he had only three tall "J.D." women from last week's arrivals. He leaned back and stretched, looking intently at the three faces. None of them resembled any of the photographs Patrick had passed on to him but one had a long narrow face. The other two faces had a similar bone structure to that of Dobrosova: an American named Juanita Davila and Jasmine Donnelly from Ireland. Both were tall, both had large blue eyes, regular features and . . . quite different ears. The American woman's ears were clearly visible as her hair was swept behind her ears, while only the other woman's lobes could be distinguished below her pudding basin haircut. He checked the Dobrosova shots once more.

Her ears. I'd never noticed them before. One's bigger than the other. The lobes.

The more he studied the photographs, he saw that Jenna's left lobe was a good deal smaller in relation to the rest of the ear; as though part of it had been removed, or chopped off, at some time in her life. That was probably why she always wore large earrings, in an attempt to disguise this tiny deformity. The left ear-lobe of the Irish woman, who wore no earrings at passport control, was identical: same size, same shape.

Despite himself, Julian leapt from his chair and whooped for joy.

'Yessss!'

The whole lab stopped in its tracks. Everyone was staring at him. Some had left their post and were heading his way.

He quickly hit the keys to turn the screen blank and stood there looking sheepish.

'Sorry about that,' he said. 'I've just found a file I thought I'd lost.

The guv'nor would have killed me if I hadn't tracked it down.' He grinned innocently, knowing perfectly well that nobody believed a word he was saying.

As they all drifted back to work, he settled down to find out everything he could about Jasmine Theresa Donnelly, born in Limerick in 1982, who'd arrived at Heathrow the day before from San Francisco and . . . where was she now?

When he fished out his phone to call Patrick, he noticed the flashing symbol – Marksworth's call. He played it back. It was a voicemail message:

'*Landfall*,' was all the male voice said.

Julian made a note and smiled. He was on track.

The Buckinghamshire farmhouse was certainly in Buckinghamshire but it had not been a working farmhouse for some years. Set in the middle of a hundred and twenty acres of fields and woods, the registered owner was a Cayman-based property conglomerate working on behalf of a Malaysian multi-millionaire. Its true owners, the Chinese Security Service, had bought the house and land both as an investment and as a technology training centre, a euphemism for espionage and weaponry development.

To the locals, it was now a rich man's country residence that the owner had extended beautifully but rarely visited, leaving his staff, most of whom were Asian men with perfect manners, to run the estate and look after the occasional visitors. Vans came and went but they were assumed to be the kind of craftsmen and contractors that any property of that size would always employ. The villagers' only regret was that nobody from the surrounding villages had been offered work there. None of them had even been inside.

Jenna Dobrosova felt a tingle of excitement as she announced her arrival on the gate intercom. It was that feeling she sensed every time she was about to get her hands on some new technology – the nervous thrill of a child unwrapping a new Christmas toy blended with awe at the prospect of spending time in the presence of brilliant engineers and psychologists.

This time however, there was something else. The equipment she was about to encounter was revolutionary. The call for her to fly to England and head for the farmhouse had been in code, yet she still sensed excitement in the way it was worded; they had discovered something that would "interest her professionally", they said. She was an assassin by profession, so it could be a new means of killing people. Or a new form of mind control? If she had the time to reflect, she would have to admit she was also just a little scared.

As she approached the main building along the long narrow drive, through parkland scattered with browsing sheep and goats, she spotted two men in suits, guards, waiting to guide her to a parking place. She switched off the engine and stepped down onto the immaculate gravel. The men, well built, European, grasped her by the arms, turned her to face the van and frisked her thoroughly but professionally. She did not resist.

Neither spoke as they ushered her out of the sunlight through the main farmhouse door. Removing her sunglasses, her eyes became accustomed to the well-lit room. There was nothing remotely rustic about this farmhouse's interior: she was standing in the reception area of an ultra-modern hi-tech research establishment. The upper floors of the house had been cut away to create an impressive atrium, beyond which dozens of glass-fronted rooms housed men and women, mostly Asian, some working in teams on unrecognisable pieces of equipment while others scurried along corridors, stopping only to bow as they greeted a colleague *en passant*.

The whole effect reminded her of the Tardis – the interior of the house appeared to be at least twice as large as its exterior, the ultimate fantasy of a science fiction movie set-builder.

A figure emerged from the depths of the atrium and walked towards her. She gasped. She had been told to expect to meet a few senior people but she had never expected the top dog to be there. She had met Hong Jintao once before, years ago; since then all communications had been conducted online. And yet here he was, one of the most recognisable faces in the diplomatic world, here to brief her in person.

He smiled and held out his hand. She gathered her wits, smiled and shook it.

'Good morning, Miss Donnelly. Thank you so much for agreeing to be our guest here.' Using her alias rather than her real name made sense as they could be overheard by others in this public area. She would have to remember to use her Irish intonation when she spoke.

'Would you like some coffee or tea?' asked Hong. 'I have arranged a room where we can talk. And there's someone I'd like you to meet before your training begins.'

He turned and she followed him to a lift which sped them to the top floor. The room was designed for a relaxed discussion, tastefully furnished with comfortable chairs. Coffee and tea were laid out on a sideboard alongside a well-stocked drinks tray.

Two men were already there – a uniformed Chinese waiter with military flashes on his shoulders and a tall English-looking middle-aged man with a neatly trimmed moustache.

'May I introduce a close friend of mine? John, this is the woman I told you about. Jasmine Donnelly, this is John.' No surname and John was probably not his real name.

'Delighted to meet you,' the man said, shaking her hand, which she acknowledged with a smile. There was something distinctive about "John"; distinguished certainly, strange eyes, interesting. She felt a tiny spontaneous stir.

'Now, let's settle down and talk,' said Hong Jintao, indicating three armchairs as the waiter left the room.

'I need to give you a little more background on your mission,' he continued.

For the next twenty minutes Hong, with occasional interjections from John, went into detail about Jenna's target, the time schedule, the security arrangements and how "our people" would help her to circumvent them, and her escape route. By the time they had finished, as far as she could see, they had thought of almost everything. The only missing elements were the nature of the "weapon" she would be using, whatever form that would take, and the purpose of the mission.

She had no need to take notes; everything was being recorded by the tiny device installed in the ring on the second finger of her left hand, which had not been detected by Hong's security guards. But she seemed to have convinced these two men that she possessed the audio version of a photographic memory, which was true.

'Do you have any questions for us?' asked Hong.

'Yes, several, as you'd expect,' she replied. 'I assume I will be allowed to suggest adjustments to the equipment I'll be using when I see it later.'

'Yes, naturally,' said Hong, smiling.

'And I will be given the names of your people on the inside and their cover jobs?'

'On a need-to-know basis, Miss Donnelly.' No smile this time. 'However, John here occupies a position of considerable responsibility in London, so you can be reassured that everything will be taken care of.'

John's contributions to the briefing had been relatively short; he seemed far more interested in her – as a colleague, or as a woman?

'Please call me Jasmine,' she said to Hong. 'One final question - I'm intrigued to know why you have selected this target.'

Hong's smile had returned. He passed a piece of paper across the table. Jenna picked it up and scanned the text. She was none the wiser.

'And the purpose of all this?' she asked.

'Regrettably . . .' Hong spread his hands. 'National security. I'm sure you understand.'

Jenna looked him straight in the eyes. He returned her stare. There was little point in pursuing the matter; she would just have to find out for herself.

After John left, Hong led Jenna downstairs past groups of men and women in white coats, each of whom looked up from their work with a courteous smile, towards a large room at the back of the house.

Jenna asked Hong, 'Now do tell me about all these people.'

'As you can see, nearly all of them are from China. Most were sent over here on a short-term secondment by our Ministry of Science and Technology, while we also recruited a few of our best post-graduates studying at British universities.'

'Do they all have a particular speciality?'

'Yes. They all work in the field of microwaves.'

'Microwaves?' she asked. That was a surprise.

'The British are delighted that we have chosen their country to develop a far more efficient technology here which will give their home appliance manufacturers a global competitive advantage. And to that extent, they are right. But only to that extent.' Hong laughed out loud. It was the first time she had ever seen him do that. He would have seemed genuinely happy if it hadn't been for the faint trace of nervousness in his eyes.

As she drove away the following day, knowing what she had stashed away in her head and in the rear of the van, she knew she should be feeling exhilarated. But her nagging annoyance at Hong's reticence to put her fully in picture was still bothering her. So was the intriguing John.

Hong's parting remark had been, 'By the way, as far as Marksworth is concerned, you have never heard of John. Is that understood?'

That bothered her too. There was more to John.

If she'd known how much Julian had managed to learn from hacking into the Avis database, she'd have been even more bothered.

CHAPTER 19

It took Julian longer than he'd anticipated to ascertain that the address Jasmine Donnelly had given to the Avis clerk was either false or a poste restante. The house in Highgate certainly existed - a three storey 1920's terraced dwelling with a long front garden in a quiet street – but, for the last few years, its only resident had been a British Airways pilot, John Griffiths, who lived there alone during his breaks from long-haul flights.

The cellphone number she gave diverted all incoming calls to an anonymous answering service. The phone had been acquired on a pay-as-you-go basis – no name was listed against the number and, when Julian accessed its voicemail, no calls had been recorded.

At least he still had the photograph taken when she checked in her passport and the van's licence plate number. And the possibility that it was Jenna / Jasmine who would be calling at Marksworth's flat at ten the following evening. He mulled over what he'd discovered.

I need to be sure that Jasmine Donnelly is Jenna Dobrosova. Apart from the funny ear and a similar bone construction, the woman who hired the van looks nothing like her. I guess all I can do is keep going until we can "eliminate her from our enquiries", as the saying goes. I've no other threads to follow up right now. Or have I?

On a hunch, he decided to run a search on Jeanne Devereaux, Dobrosova's previous alias. This proved rather more fruitful: according to the records, Jeanne had entered the country two and a half months earlier, rented a studio flat and a high-powered motorbike. A credit card in her name had been used profusely to buy groceries, restaurant meals, beauty treatments, short-term membership of a fitness club and of a private club in the St James area. A quick Google check revealed what kind of club she had joined. The website was clearly addressed to those who preferred their evening entertainment discreet and indulgent.

Julian smiled, for more than one reason.

Now he had an address and a list of "Jeanne's" favourite haunts to explore. Things were looking up. He clicked to the gallery of mug shots of the lady in question, then back to the private club's website.

'Mmm,' he muttered. 'Things are definitely looking up.'

North London

It was gone five o'clock by the time Andy Fields pulled up outside the house.

His first action was to double-check he was in the right place. This street wasn't what he had expected. In truth, it was more of an avenue – detached double-fronted houses with well-kept front gardens and white pseudo-Roman porches, with nearly-new, freshly washed cars sitting on the paved drive in front of the garage. Each house was virtually identical but, in an area like this, they would have still set you back the wrong side of half a million before the property price crash.

It was hard to believe that the man he had come to see was in that league; most police patrol drivers who took early retirement would find it difficult to make ends meet in a house half that size.

He got out and walked up to the front door. It opened before he had a chance to ring the bell.

'Yes?' The man who filled the door frame was in his early fifties, dressed in what Andy presumed was the appropriate style for the local golf club, and holding a cut-glass tumbler of whiskey. The sound of an over-excited horse racing commentator blared from somewhere behind him.

'I've come to see Jack Davidson,' said Andy.

'Do you have an appointment?' Hostile.

Fields took out his wallet and showed his warrant card. Without even looking at it, the man's expression changed, first to one of panic then to resignation.

'Come on in.'

He led the way into the spacious lounge, turned off the sound on the TV and slumped into an armchair, staring into his glass. Fields parked himself on one of the settees.

The room was expensively furnished, but lacked any warmth - it could have been lifted, lock stock and barrel, from a store showroom.

The TV screen filled almost one entire wall. A flight of porcelain geese, twelve strong, filled another and a gold framed aerial shot of Manhattan a third.

Fields waited for Davidson to begin. Then after two minutes, he said softly, 'Do you want to tell me what happened?'

As he drove away, Andy could foresee the poor man refilling his glass and staring out of the picture window at the leafy avenue he knew he would have to abandon before long. His fantasy life was finally over.

It wasn't really his fault. He and his two colleagues had just attended the wrong motorway accident. Except that it wasn't an accident, nor was it suicide: Alistair Thomas had been murdered and Jack Davidson's crew had guessed the truth.

It was Jack who'd spotted the small black box attached to the steering rods of the overturned car. A tiny red light was still blinking. Somebody had taken control of the vehicle using a remote transmitter.

When the crew returned to the station to write their report, they had been intercepted by a man who described himself as a "Security officer – Scotland Yard" and guided them to a car parked nearby. The man made it very clear that, because the accident victim was a national political figure, this was a Security matter and any report or investigation would be handled by the Metropolitan Police. The three officers were ordered not to discuss the case with anyone, on pain of dismissal.

Within weeks, each one had received a home visit from this same man who informed them that they had all been recommended for a special award that none of them had ever heard of before. As all three were in their fifties, they would be eligible for immediate early retirement. The award, he was delighted to say, entitled each one of them to a considerable lump sum on top of a handsome pension and a Scotland Yard-owned house, rent-free.

Jack knew full well that the whole affair had been hushed up but, with an offer like that, what was he to do?

'It feels good to be able to tell the whole story to someone.' He stood up and stretched, turning away from Andy. There was no anger, more an overwhelming sadness in his manner.

Driving back to London, Andy Fields' mind was buzzing. Who was the mysterious Scotland Yard security man? According to Jack, he had never shown his warrant card and had refused to give them his real name. He always referred to himself as simply "Adrian". From his description – middle-aged, clean-shaven, well-spoken – there was nothing in particular that Andy could use to identify him. He had a thin moustache, according to Jack, but that was all.

Did he have anything to do with the Security Services? Andy had met pretty well every officer in the branch and none of them sprang to mind. None of the crew's senior officers had asked them for their report. Clearly, they had been warned off too, by somebody in authority.

From somewhere, at high level, the order had gone out for everyone to leave the whole affair alone.

Fields decided to call off interviewing the other two officers. Jack had been the senior man in the car that night and he was the kind of copper who inspired respect, Andy reckoned. The others would have told him about anything else they'd spotted.

A couple of miles down the road, he pulled over and called Sir Norman at his home.

Jenna Dobrosova was finally getting used to her new identity. The quiet, shy Irish Jasmine was in such contrast to her real self that, for once, she found she could move around London without attracting attention. By choosing her outfits carefully so that they masked her figure, she could walk along the crowded pavements unnoticed, particularly by all the men who would normally have snatched a lustful glance as she passed by.

Parking the van two streets away from her first floor flat, she hoisted the heavy bag onto her shoulder, set her suitcase on the ground, extended the handle and set off to walk the two hundred yards. The weather was mild and she took the time to enjoy the bustle and rumble of this wonderful city.

She had almost reached her front door when a biker pulled up to the kerb a few doors further down the street. The rider dismounted, removed his helmet and shook his mop of curly hair free. He looked her way and muttered a polite 'Afternoon'.

Without thinking, Jenna smiled and responded in kind. As the young man smiled back at her, she caught her breath and stared for a moment before lowering her eyes and scuttling up to her door.

As she put the key in the lock, she couldn't help glancing round. He was bending over by his bike, searching for something in a pannier. He turned his head for a moment, smiled at her and returned to his search.

Arriving in the flat, she dumped her bags, walked into the kitchen and poured herself a large glass of water.

She was angry with herself for dropping her professional guard. *But he's so beautiful. Those eyes, the hair, the slim leather-clad body . . . What is he? Fifteen years younger than me? But who cares? That young man is distinctly fuckable.*

She walked across to the front window and looked down. The bike was still there but there was no sign of the young man. She went to unpack.

In a café around the corner, Julian smiled to himself. He had found her. She was back in the Jeanne Devereaux flat. That figured: if Jenna Dobrosova got a kick from dangerously using her own initials for her aliases, she would adopt the same logic by returning to the same old address. It appealed to her sense of fun.

He knew he had taken a huge risk turning up in her street just at the moment she arrived. Patrick would certainly not approve. But Julian had put his trust in what he'd come to recognise as his special talent. For years now, whenever he met an attractive older woman, it would only be a matter of time – in some cases less than a minute – before she would start making it abundantly clear that they should find a quiet corner together, now or sooner. It had started with his mother's friends, then his friends' mothers . . . He had never really understood it; he had given up trying.

Taking a swig from his latte, he sent an SMS message to Patrick. Within minutes, he had the reply:

Well done. Now stay on watch. Don't get too close. She's a pro. And so are you, remember. P

Patrick put his phone away and returned to join Mike Challoner in the official car. They had delivered Marksworth to a meeting at the offices of MI6, the Secret Intelligence Service, on the South bank of the Thames, and they had nothing to do but sit and wait.

'I'm on Downing Street business,' Marksworth had said as he alighted. 'You do realise that I'm one of the Prime Minister's closest advisers, don't you?'

Both Mike and Patrick decided that, if Marksworth saw fit to remind them one more time, they would probably both throw up. The pompous git.

What they were more interested in now was who their boss was seeing at MI6 and why. They decided to get some fresh air with a stroll along the embankment, making sure they kept their car in sight in case Marksworth re-appeared.

Leaning over the wall, watching the mighty river flow past, it was Mike who opened the discussion.

'If the rumours are true, that Marksworth's been taken on as the PM's Bullshit Buster, what on earth is he doing in MI6? I can think of plenty of other government departments he should be tackling before them.'

Patrick nodded. 'On the other hand, we know he's a spy – a double agent. So he could be doing one of two things in there: digging for secret info he can pass on to his controller or . . .'

Mike's eyes lit up. 'Or touching base with another double agent! Right under their noses.'

'Keep your voice down, mate,' said Patrick.

Mike didn't reply. He was looking past Patrick along the footpath. Without warning, he slammed his hand down on Patrick's head and shoved downwards. Patrick, totally off guard, lost his balance and crashed down onto his knees by the low wall.

'What the fuck?' he cried, just as a bullet screeched past his ear and gouged a chunk out of the wall's parapet.

'Stay down,' urged Mike, crouching alongside him. Slowly, he raised his head and took a look in the direction of the gunman. Patrick did the same. Seventy or eighty yards downstream, a man, who looked like a typical young Chinese tourist, was struggling to break away from the grip of a man and woman wearing white medic-style coats. Seconds later, the man ceased to struggle and calmly allowed them to usher him into the back seat of a white saloon with paramedic markings. The two white coats jumped in and the car drove away unhurriedly into the traffic.

Patrick and Mike stood up, shook the dust from their clothes and both took a deep breath. Looking towards the MI6 building, they spied two armed security guards who had clearly heard the shot and emerged, weapons at the ready, to check it out. One of them was on the phone, while the other watched as the paramedic car disappeared into the traffic. The two guards looked back at Mike and Patrick, gave them a synchronised thumbs-up and turned away towards the door.

Patrick's phone buzzed. Sir Norman. He spoke briefly.

'That man has been following you for the last few hours. Don't worry; we'll look after him now. But you'll need to watch your back until we find out who he was working for and why. Talk later.' He hung up.

Hong Jintao told the man to leave his office. He stood and walked to the bureau, poured himself a glass of water and stared out at the London skyline. Heavy black clouds were dumping a lot of water on the suburbs to the North but it looked as though the central areas would be spared.

The report from the embassy's technical staff had identified several possible identities from the photograph of David Marksworth's shaven-headed bodyguard. The most convincing was a man named John Monks, currently employed on security duties in Whitehall. Every identity check - passport, driving licence, bank account - showed that Monks was genuine but Hong knew, from long experience, how competent the British were at setting up fake records.

There was one name that caught Hong's attention, near the foot of the list – a name that brought with it enough memories to put the Chinese Foreign Minister on red alert:

- Patrick Cameron, 38, medical research scientist, resident of Oxford, married, no children.

And one of the most dangerous, intelligent agents I've ever encountered, thought Hong.

Immediately, Hong had ordered his people to put a discreet tail on Johnny Monks and, at the first clean opportunity, to put him out of action.

If that man is Cameron, and he's working close to David Marksworth, that means Marksworth has been compromised. I'll need to bring the plan forward, before the British get too close, or the whole mission could be threatened.

And for Hong, disposing of Patrick Cameron would be immensely satisfying. The man had proved, time and again, to be a formidable foe.

The embassy had assigned their most accomplished killer to the task. Now, not only had he failed to kill Cameron but he had been captured.

The man won't talk: even if he did, he knows nothing that could lead him back to me. Someone must have spotted him. He must have got too close.

Or . . .

We've been infiltrated.

Sitting down, he waited a minute for his hands to stop shaking and began to type.

CHAPTER 20

The meeting had gone well; at least David Marksworth thought so. His excuse for asking to see a senior MI6 officer – that he had the authority of the Prime Minister - had been accepted without question.

As soon as he arrived, he explained that it was 'all just routine' and duly went through his standard spiel about the priority the Prime Minister placed on 'retaining and enhancing the Government's credibility at all times' and the need for all communications to be in 'plain English' rather than hiding behind traditional Civil Service jargon – 'otherwise known as bullshit'. He always seemed to gain his audience's full attention when he said that.

'As MI6 rarely, if ever, communicates via the public media, I entirely accept that much of what I'm saying is irrelevant in your case,' he told the man, who had introduced himself as Peter Deamer, Deputy Director, Strategy. His easy-going manner went well with the slight stoop, full head of white hair, elderly suit and brogues – the sort of chap for whom you'd give up your seat on the bus, Marksworth thought.

He continued: 'I suppose the only exception would be when you need to put out a cover story after the press gets wind of one of your more clandestine operations.' He smiled winningly at the MI6 man.

'For example?' asked Deamer blandly.

Marksworth hesitated, trying hard to look as though he hadn't anything particular in mind.

'Well, let me see. For example, what if a journalist ran a story about foreign spies in Government circles?'

'Oh, you mean moles.'

'Yes. Like, what were their names? Ah, yes, Burgess and MacLean in the fifties. And Kim Philby. But I suppose they'd all be working for the Chinese these days, rather than the Soviets.' Marksworth laughed without humour.

The man looked at him hard. 'Not entirely. And, of course you're right: we'd have to issue a credible denial. Thankfully, between you and me, that situation's most unlikely to arise. We and our friends in MI5 run a pretty thorough mole-watching programme, you know. The fact is we always have question marks about a few individuals but, usually, we keep an eye on them for a while and, when nothing iffy crops up, we lose interest. I know you're the sort of chap that I can trust to keep everything I say off the record, Marksworth, by the way,' Deamer said, leaning forward as a gesture of comradeship.

'Of course, old chap,' Marksworth replied, nodding. 'You can trust me.'

As he left the building and looked for his car, he retrieved his official phone from an inside pocket. Among all the emails in his Inbox, he noticed one from the PM's private secretary headed "Security". He opened it.

Dear David

Regret we're having to cut back your bodyguard detail to one officer. Neal and Monks will be re-deployed elsewhere. The size of your detail has put a few noses out of joint at Number Ten and Audit say they can't justify so many for a communications officer.

Sorry about this. I feel sure you'll be safe as houses with just Challoner looking after you.

Best,

Paddy

'Bollocks,' said Marksworth, just loud enough for the two MI6 armed guards to hear. They turned away, hands covering their mouths.

Sure enough, Mike Challoner was alone when Marksworth reached the car.

'Looks like it's just you and me now, guv,' he said cheerfully as they set off.

'Would you mind if I asked you kindly to shut up and drive, Challoner?' came the reply from the back seat, his voice fading away at the end.

Mike looked in the rear view mirror. Marksworth was reading something on his "other" phone. His face had turned a very strange colour.

Back in MI6, Peter Deamer waited until he was certain that Marksworth had left the building before picking up the phone and reporting back to Sir Norman.

Red alert. J intercepted message from HJ to DM. Imperative you go underground NOW. We've released you both from your DM duties. AF alerted, on his way.

Patrick Cameron was already on his way underground. The message from Sir Norman moments earlier gave him no other option.

Andy Fields was thankful he had completed the emergency high speed driving course earlier in his career. In recent times, the blue light had gathered dust in a dashboard compartment but right now it was on the roof making its presence felt and the unmarked car's siren was blaring its way through the city's traffic.

As he zigzagged around a series of traffic islands along the Thames Embankment, heading for Vauxhall Bridge, vehicles pulled aside to let him pass. The call from Sir Norman had made him drop everything and grab his keys. And a gun. Cameron was in serious danger and had to disappear fast.

Sir Norman had sounded calm on the phone but Andy could still detect the sense of urgency in his voice:

'We were only just close enough to the agent who was tracking Cameron and Challoner to prevent him firing a second shot. We have the man in a safe place now. You can see him later but I very much doubt whether he'll talk. They rarely do. Now we've picked up a second man close by and . . . my contact in Beijing tells me an order has gone out from on high that Johnny Monks has to be eliminated today. They think he may be Cameron so, just in case . . .'

Andy knew Sir Norman had his people covering Patrick Cameron everywhere he went. So it was no surprise they had managed to grab the first assassin. But how the Last Resort Squad had succeeded in having the fake email from Downing Street prepared and routed through to Marksworth so quickly, Fields had absolutely no idea.

That's why they call them the Last Resort Squad, I suppose, he mused as he swung the wheel left onto the bridge, searching for Patrick among the crowds of tourists.

As usual, at least half of them looked Chinese, their baseball caps, sneakers and expensive cameras at the ready as their guides pointed out London's famous landmarks on both sides of the river. Every one of them was either engrossed in a guide book or glued to a viewfinder.

Halfway across the bridge, Andy spotted Patrick weaving through and around the tourist groups. He'd managed to conceal his shiny pate under a woolly hat but Andy knew it was him: they had gone through so much together over the years, he'd know that gait anywhere.

He sounded the car's siren once and Patrick looked around, spotted him, gave a discreet thumbs-up and set off at a trot to cross the road, dodging vehicles. Andy's police pistol sat on the passenger seat, cocked, silencer fitted, his hand poised.

Cameron had reached the centre of the road. He stopped to allow a bus to trundle past, then waited before setting off again, thanking the driver of the next vehicle with a wave of his hand. Suddenly, he appeared to stumble and grab his arm, as if he was in pain.

As Andy Fields looked further up the road, he spied a burly Oriental man in a black leather biker's jacket sprinting down the middle of the road towards Patrick, trying to steady a gun on his prey with both hands as Cameron staggered forward towards Fields' car, clutching his wrist.

Andy raised his pistol, took careful aim, and fired. He missed because, twenty yards away, a car door was suddenly flung open and the gunman crashed into it full tilt. The force of the collision knocked him backwards so hard he was now lying motionless on the road surface.

Within moments, Patrick reached Andy's car, yanked open the rear door and threw himself headlong onto the back seat.

'Bastard got me,' he shouted, holding his bleeding hand up for Andy to see. But Andy wasn't there; he was kneeling beside the fallen man, his gun already tucked away in his pocket. A uniformed policeman had appeared from nowhere, accompanied by a middle-aged man in a raincoat.

'Don't worry, sir,' said the officer. 'We'll take care of him. This gent's a doctor. I've already radioed for an ambulance. Looks like a nasty gash he's got there. Idiots like him get some sorta kick from playing dodgems with London traffic. Deserve all they get, if you ask me.' He turned away and set about getting the streams of vehicles moving again.

Andy looked at the 'doctor' who winked at him, very discreetly, as he kneeled to examine the fallen man, whose eyes were quite lifeless. Andy stood, walked calmly back to his car and got in. As he thanked the 'policeman' for holding up the traffic and for waving him through a U-turn, he turned to Patrick.

'That's not the hand you count your cash with, is it? You owe me a pint, mate.'

Patrick's 'Ha, bloody ha,' sounded rather less than sincere.

Hong received news of the latest non-developments and shivered. He knew full well that the same information was being monitored in Beijing, by some very pragmatic people.

He could have assigned Jenna Dobrosova to kill Cameron but he needed to save her for the main event. Thankfully, he'd made the right decision or she would have been arrested or even worse.

There were only two possible explanations: either David Marksworth's double life had been discovered: what other reason could there be for keeping that damned man Cameron – Hong was now convinced that it was he – under protective surveillance? Or, and he could hardly bear the thought, the British had somehow stumbled upon his so-called brilliant plan and were waiting to make their move when they felt the time was right.

If they are onto us, how much do they know?

The men who would have prevented us taking control of the media and the banking system, the blogger who was getting far too close to our strategy or, Heaven forbid (excuse me, Lord), the next British Prime Minister. Every one of them eliminated brilliantly by Jenna Dobrosova; every killing so far undetected.

I've been so careful: each operative only knows what he or she needs to know. Not even Marksworth knows about those killings. So why would the British suspect our involvement?

Another thought screamed into his consciousness. He slumped forward, holding his head in both hands.

If they suspect Marksworth is a spy, they could have connected him to Gregory Bellingham. They were friends for years. And if they have got that far, they could find the Paris link and connect them to me.

Somebody, somewhere must have leaked information, even inadvertently, or even worse, one of my people has been turned by the British.

Hong spent the next hour deep in meditation, willing his mind to relax, not to rush to conclusions. Then he began calmly combing through his entire network of espionage agents in the UK – commercial, military and diplomatic. The vast majority could be discounted; in each case, their sphere of operation would never have brought them into contact with this action.

By the end, he had narrowed the possible sources of the leak down to three names – David Marksworth, the man he always referred to as the Locksmith, and Jenna Dobrosova.

There was one other, but only he and Guo Dalong, not even the President, knew who that was. Nobody else could possibly understand the common bond that had brought this person into their fold many years earlier. The two of them had watched with pleasure as their "Sleeping Beauty" rose to positions of great power and respect in the country. The time would come one day, but not quite yet.

As he stared at the other three names on his pad, over and over again, he kept coming back to the same question:

Which of them, if any, can I trust?

CHAPTER 21

Once everything was unpacked and stashed away in her favourite flat, Jenna opened the bottle of Prosecco she had picked up en route and sat down at the kitchen table. She needed to draw up her plan for the next few days.

In less than a week's time, she would be on her way to what the British, amusingly, referred to as "foreign parts", an expression which, when literally translated into a number of other languages, could mean something altogether different.

First things first. She was determined that not even the huge fee she would earn for committing the deadly deed would stop her from discovering the true objective of her mission. There was nothing more irritating than to be treated as a simple contractor. She had reached the top of her profession because her clients had taken her into their total confidence; they knew she would deliver. Yet this time, the Chinese were keeping her out of the picture and that was just not acceptable. She still had enough time to put things right.

She decided to begin by doing some research online. Hong had mentioned a name. When she read the man's biography, she was surprised that she hadn't heard of him before: perhaps because Vanmali Mehta had made his fortune primarily in Africa and the Indian sub-continent before turning his attention to training the inexperienced leaders of newly independent states.

Each country had gained its independence from Britain in the last thirty years. In every case, a new president had been thrust onto the world stage, attempting to run a country that, for the large part, had to fend for itself for the first time, in fierce competition, not only with its own neighbours but also with the far more sophisticated, giant economies of the West, Japan, China and Russia.

As if that weren't enough, the short-term temptation for ministers to line their own pockets from the myriad of commercial "incentive programmes" and international aid grants was too much for many to resist.

Most of the new leaders soon realised that their first challenge was to win the cooperation of the people: to earn the respect of the different tribes and cultures and to persuade historically hostile groups to live, work and learn together. In every case, their first attempts quickly failed. Corruption and inter-group rivalry were too deeply entrenched. What was needed was a crash course in multi-cultural leadership skills and this man offered to provide them with the answers.

Over the years, he'd worked closely with peaceful democrats, autocratic dictators, scholars and religious leaders, earning an extraordinary reputation and a Nobel Peace Prize. Many of the places where he'd worked, not all, were countries which had been all but written off by the Western media before they started. Now they had begun to flourish, both socially and economically. Today, Africa, in particular, was truly "on the march".

For an ethnic Indian to be voted "African Man of the Year" was unheard of but Mehta was regarded there as something of a miracle worker. Many commentators expressed surprise that he had never sought a more public profile but, in his rare interviews, he had always expressed a preference for the quiet private life. The Western media all but ignored him. There had been some minor speculation that this was about to change but nothing concrete had emerged.

Until now.

Jenna opened a recent newspaper report announcing that he would be coming to London the following week as part of a regular Commonwealth delegation. She read on and made detailed notes.

Aha! Now I know his schedule and why he will be here. But I still don't know why he is important. Why him?

She sat back in her chair and stared thoughtfully into her Prosecco. Checking her watch, she shrugged, stood, removed her clothes and headed for the bathroom.

As the steam rose, she admired herself in the mirror before easing down into the water. Work could wait. Her focus was now on other things: a visit later to her "special" club and . . . that young man on the motorbike. What was it about him?

Mmm. Those eyes. So beautiful. So sensual. So bewitching.

Jenna closed her eyes and allowed her mind, and her fingers, to drift. The hedonic pleasures that awaited her that evening were quickly replaced by a series of remarkably vivid images of being in that young man's hands, if the occasion arose. She could see, feel the intensity, the sheer power of their shared passion, deep inside.

Minutes later, as her body regained its composure, the images were still there.

What is it about that guy? Why can't I get him out of my mind?

At last, Patrick began to sense his pulse returning to normal. Every time he was shot at, even after all these years, it was a while before he could feel calm enough to think clearly. His wrist had been bandaged; no serious damage but still bloody painful. Thankfully, he was right-handed and even his wounded left hand could still grip a mug of tea.

'What the hell do we do now, Andy?' he asked.

They were ensconced in a safe house in Battersea, a faceless, bog-standard London semi in an anonymous street. Fields was slumped in the armchair on the other side of the gas fire.

'Well, my friend, you're going to have to disappear from view. From here on, we'll have to rely on Julian tracking Dobrosova and Mike Challoner covering Marksworth. You're far too dangerous to let loose until all this is over.'

Patrick reacted angrily. 'Oh, bloody hell, Andy. I was getting so close. I can't duck out now. We need every bit of manpower we can muster if we're going to have a chance of stopping this. Surely . . .'

Fields put up a warning hand. 'You stay right where you are, Patrick. Every Chinese killer in London will be out looking for you now. And there are plenty of those, believe me. I wouldn't be at all surprised if Hong has pulled in some of the Chinatown Triads for this job. The moment you set foot in central London, you'll be a dead man.'

'How did they track me down this time? Did they run a check on Marksworth's bodyguards and get lucky?'

'Yes, I reckon so. My mistake. I never expected that.'

'Well, at least I can still help from behind the scenes,' said Patrick wistfully. His mind was already working on ways of getting back on centre stage but he kept his thoughts to himself. He changed the subject.

'So, OK. What's next? Why don't we just pull Marksworth and Dobrosova in now and make them talk?' he asked.

'Because, as you know very well, we need to flush out the entire network, otherwise they'll just drop Marksworth or get rid of him and leave the others to carrying on spying.'

'Yes, I can see that. You're sure there are others but, so far, no suspects?'

'Yes, I'm certain. And I fear one or two of them are in very high places. Very high indeed. Think about it, mate. Otherwise, why would they have killed Alistair Thomas?'

Patrick nodded. 'A future Prime Minister. And, on top of that, if Jenna Dobrosova's in town, they must be planning another big-time assassination.'

'Speaking of Jenna,' said Fields, 'have you heard from Julian?'

'Only to say that he'd found the woman and was staying close to her. Julian has his own peculiar way with women.'

'That's what worries me. But I guess we just have to trust him not to blow the job, if you'll excuse the expression.'

Cameron laughed out loud. It helped to ease the tension. In the past, his relationship with Andy Fields had often been stormy. This time, they were colleagues, partners. Friends?

'Any clues on who they're going to try to hit?' he asked.

'We've considered all the usual targets – the Royal family, the PM, etcetera, etcetera. But none of them makes any sense. What would they have to gain by killing them?'

He opened a page on his tablet. 'I checked through what's coming up in London,' Andy continued. 'Any big names in town, for example. Apart from a Commonwealth delegation next week, it's just the usual selection of oligarchs, actors and gangsters. Anyway, those Commonwealth get-togethers are usually no more than a mutual back-slapping session and a chance for their wives to do a bit of shopping.'

'Hey, come on, you're not being fair. There are some serious statesmen in the Commonwealth. Are they all coming? That's more than fifty nations. Including some real heavyweights like Australia, Canada, Singapore . . .'

'No, this time they're mainly from Africa,' said Fields.

'Will you have people covering it?'

'Of course. We have to be seen to be providing a certain level of security. But it will be minimal – more a show of strength. In global terms, there are a lot of much bigger fish. No reason for these guys to be on our A-list, Patrick.'

Patrick nodded but something was telling him Andy was being a bit too dismissive.

'What's the latest on Marksworth?' he asked.

'According to Mike, he didn't say a word on the way back to the office. Just sat staring at his phone, looking quite pale.'

'Good. The cocky bastard needed pulling down a few pegs. To discover that one of his own bodyguards was an undercover agent and then that the Chinese had failed to kill me won't have done much for his confidence. With any luck, he'll start making a few mistakes now. Meanwhile, it's over to Julian.'

'I think I've just had an idea,' said Fields.

Julian strolled past a small white van parked two streets from Jenna Dobrosova's flat. Having established that it was the one rented by Jasmine Donnelly, this was his third attempt to check out the vehicle, without attracting attention, in the last hour. On the first pass, he had stopped to retie his shoe laces; on the second, he had to keep moving as a couple of mothers with baby-walkers were chatting and laughing only ten yards away.

This time, the street was quiet. Pausing to answer an apparent phone call should seem fairly natural. Two minutes would give him enough time to scan the van with the self-designed gadget he was carrying in his rucksack. He had pre-set it to spot any electronic devices and, in particular, any weaponry.

He began an inane conversation, speaking just loud enough to ward off any passers-by.

'Hello, George. What? You're joking. Tell me more.'

The machine picked up a couple of buzzes near the engine compartment: in common with every modern vehicle, it was the automatic locking system and the on-board computer emitting the signals. The front seats and the rear compartment appeared to be empty.

'Hold on, George,' he said to his imaginary caller. 'I'll need to see if I'm free.'

He crouched down and unzipped the bag. That was when he heard another vibration: it was coming from near ground level, close to the rear chassis.

Whatever was emitting a standby signal, it appeared to be located beneath the van, hidden from view, and stretched several feet forward from the rear axle.

A car had stopped close by. He would have to wait until he could examine the reading in private before he could make any attempt to identify the mysterious item. He stood up, finished the "call", checked his watch and hurried back towards the street where Jenna's apartment was located. He slipped into the tiny alley where he had parked his bike.

A taxi was drawing up outside the house. Jenna, looking utterly different from the meek and mild, rather dowdy Irish woman he had encountered earlier, was emerging from the garden gate and climbing aboard.

This time, she was dressed entirely in black - a stylish sombrero covering her hair, leather jacket, half unzipped, skin-tight pants and knee-high boots. From the brief glimpse he had of her, she appeared to be wearing heavy gold ear-rings and jewellery around her neck and wrists.

Julian checked the licence plate before turning back into the alley as the taxi passed, hoping against hope that he hadn't been spotted. He fired up the engine, swung into the street and set off, headlight blazing so that the woman would not be able to identify him if she looked back.

Checking the street names as he passed, he suddenly revved the bike, slipped the clutch and screeched forward, sliding sideways towards the taxi's rear end. The skid was hard enough to floor both bike and rider, where he lay still, holding his head and moaning with pain.

CHAPTER 22

'Will somebody please switch those sodding lights off?'

'Sorry, sir. Let's get this helmet off you. There, is that better, young man?'

Julian laid back down. He had a slight headache and one arm and leg felt sore. A cold breeze was making him shiver. At least those nightmarish flashing lights had moved away.

A man's voice again. 'Lie still, please, sir. We just need to check a few more things.'

Julian did as he was told. The man shone a bright light in his eyes.

'What do you think, Lee? Apart from grazes on his arm and leg, no more than a bang on the head, I reckon. Concussion? Nah, that's my opinion too. No need for an ambulance; they're all busy this time of night with serious stuff. If you feel any weird symptoms tomorrow, sir, I should get a doctor to look at you.'

Slowly but surely, Julian's eyes were adjusting to the lights, and he was thinking clearly.

'Right, let's get you on your feet.' The man helped him up and handed Julian his gear.

He stood up and lurched, grabbing the man's arm. Instinctively, he checked the pocket where he always kept his phone. Nothing.

Shit! If I've lost that, I'm sunk. So much stuff on it. I can wipe it clean but I'd need another phone to do that. Damn!

'You'll be OK,' the police sergeant was saying. 'Still a bit wobbly but no great harm done. You were lucky Constable Lee and I were just around the corner.'

Another voice. 'Excuse me, officer. I think I know this man.'

There, dressed all in black, a look of deep concern on her face, stood none other than Jenna Dobrosova. Julian gaped.

'Hello. Well, well, it's you. What a coincidence,' she said, smiling at Julian. 'Are you sure you're all right? I was in the taxi you nearly crashed into. The driver asked me to find out how you are.'

The soft Irish accent was still there.

'Hello,' he mumbled, thinking fast. 'Yes, thank you. Just a bit bruised.'

This was the moment. He had to be convincing. She was too clever.

She looked at Julian long and hard, then at the policemen, then back at the taxi, before she spoke.

'I say, why don't you come home with me and rest? It's only a few streets away,' the velvety voice was saying. 'Is that acceptable, officer?'

'Well, yes, I suppose so, Miss. What about you, sir?'

Julian opened his mouth. Nothing emerged so he nodded. He looked down the road where queues of cars were being directed around the police car by another yellow-jacketed officer. Jenna took his arm.

'Right,' said the police driver, handing Julian his slightly battered helmet. 'We'd better get this lot out of the way. Traffic's getting a tad impatient. Would you mind checking out with that officer over there before you go, sir.'

Across the street, another uniformed figure was standing beside the slightly bent taxi. An overweight man, who Julian assumed was its driver, wearing a quilted jacket, a black and white striped Beanie hat, scarf and gloves, looked less than happy.

Jenna walked Julian across, chatting cheerfully 'The driver was afraid that, if you were badly hurt, he would have his licence suspended. He wanted to inspect the damage; that is why he asked me to see you. Wasn't that lucky?' She grinned.

The officer was scribbling in his notebook. The taxi driver was muttering into his scarf.

'Bleeding idiot. This could have cost me serious money. Kids like him shouldn't be allowed out.'

The policeman interrupted him without looking up. 'It's all right, sir. We found all your details, insurance and stuff, on your bike. No need to detain you now. More important you get yourself home and have a nice rest. The bike's a bit knackered; the garage will give you a call tomorrow once they've assessed the damage. Here's their card. Your bag's by the wall.' He pointed to the place where Julian's rucksack lay.

Julian slipped the card into his pocket, picked up the bag and nodded his thanks. As Jenna guided him towards another cab which was waiting close by with its motor running, he sensed something in the back pocket of his trousers. His phone. Had it been there all the time?

Looking back, he couldn't be entirely sure but he could have sworn he saw the policeman and the taxi driver wink in his direction.

David Markswoth was back in his office in Downing Street, trying to write up his new "bullshit-busting" progress report. A knock on his door made him look up. A uniformed messenger entered and silently handed him a sealed envelope.

It read:

From the Office of the Prime Minister of Great Britain and Northern Ireland

Confidential: For the personal attention of Mr David Markswoth.

His hand trembled slightly as he picked up a paper knife and slit the envelope open. It contained a gold-edged card.

Your presence is formally requested at a Reception at Lancaster House to honour a delegation of Commonwealth leaders. In the presence of His Royal Highness the Prince of Wales.

The reception was fixed for 11am the following Tuesday. The card carried no RSVP. It was clearly a command rather than an invitation. Markswoth placed it on his desk and read it once more. This was highly unusual. Only senior ministers and officials from the Foreign and Commonwealth Office were ever invited to an event of this status.

At that moment, his "other" phone buzzed in his pocket. A message.

"We seek not to be born on the same day, in the same month and in the same year. We merely hope to die on the same day, in the same month and in the same year."

Markswoth's breath stuck in his throat. This was the oath of brotherhood. Sworn by Hong Jintao, Greg Bellingham and himself all those years ago in a Parisian garden. The message could only have come from one source.

Hong Jintao.

What does he mean?

What am I, David Marksworth, being called upon to do?

And if Hong has such strong connections that he can engineer an invitation to a royal reception . . .

. . .Who else is he working with?

Only one answer made any sense.

There is someone here, in this building, 10 Downing Street, with access to the Prime Minister's files, who is also an undercover Chinese agent.

Patrick was back in the safe house, a large mug of tea and a bacon sandwich at his side. The taxi strategy had been put together in no time but had been carefully executed: in the fading light, his disguise had worked too – even Julian hadn't recognised him with all that padding and the hat pulled down to his eyebrows.

Staging an accident was definitely not the way he liked to work and it had taken a lot of persuading to convince Andy Fields to let him take part in the operation. At least, Julian had gone along with the plan and he wasn't badly hurt. Plus, Patrick had had a chance to re-acquaint himself, albeit silently, with Jenna Dobrosova. But that was that, for now. He was back in his box.

He and Andy knew full well they were taking a big risk putting Julian and Jenna together – the woman was a heartless killer. But the stakes were so high, what was the phrase?

"Desperate times call for desperate measures."

And they were certainly in desperate need of a breakthrough: right now, everything they had learned amounted to nothing more than a rudimentary sketch-plan. Yes, Jenna Dobrosova, David Marksworth and Hong Jintao were planning to execute something, or somebody, that would shake the world and that thing, whatever it was, had to be intercepted. They could do that now, by taking out all three.

But, if they missed the opportunity to land the bigger fish, the network of traitors, they would be closing one door only to leave another unlocked for the rest of them to march through.

Patrick was very worried. Would his young friend and colleague come out of this safely or had he and Andy Fields placed him in mortal danger?

He just had to trust in Julian's extraordinary powers of persuasion. Patrick tried to picture what was going on back in Jenna's flat.

Jenna was pacing up and down the kitchen. She had made the young man, the *gorgeous* young man, comfortable on her settee, lying prostrate with a rug and a large glass of brandy.

Deep down, she knew it was unprofessional to start a physical relationship in the middle of an operation, but she'd decided, out there on the street, that just this once it couldn't do any harm, could it?

She had been tempted to get him to strip off his damaged trousers but she honestly didn't trust herself to keep her hands off him. The bang on the head was still affecting his balance and he hadn't uttered a word since they arrived. Now he was asleep.

Yes, she had to take her time, she knew that. But the longer she had to wait, she knew the more intense the itch would become.

She checked the sleeping Adonis once more. Flat out. She would use the time to nip down to the local store for some food.

Julian was far from asleep but his head was still throbbing a bit and the scrapes on his thigh were stinging. As soon as he heard the door close, he threw off the blanket and found his bag, apparently untouched. Inside, the scanner he'd used on the white van was bruised but mercifully unbroken. He started it up, keeping an eye on the street through the curtains.

Within seconds, he was looking at the scans of the white van. The one showing the lower rear of the vehicle was the one he needed. And there it was – a long slender object, bolted to the underside of the chassis. For all the world, it was the ordinary kind of elbow crutch used everywhere by people who had hurt their ankle: an open padded cuff, grip handle and a ferrule at the foot. The only thing odd was an illuminated electronic light close to the handle. That was what his scanner had picked up.

Julian enlarged the image, concentrating on the handle. Now he could see that it was unusually large – almost too fat for a hand to grip it in the normal way.

He switched off the scanner and stood thinking for a moment. He had to get his hands on this thing and discover what it was. A night sight? A transmitter? A weapon of some kind? It could be almost anything but it certainly wasn't a crutch.

Returning the scanner to his bag, he checked the window again. No sign of the Russian woman. He took a quick look around the living room. All neat and tidy except for a few papers on the table. Papers!

He picked up the top sheet. Detailed directions to some farm in Buckinghamshire.

He remembered his phone and fished it out of his trouser pocket. Quickly, he typed a message to Patrick, asking him to check out the Buckinghamshire farm. He decided not to spell out the events of the last couple of hours; that could wait.

He flicked through the other papers – printouts of online recipes. Except that, on one of them she had scribbled what appeared to be a flight number, a time and terminal number. She was planning to leave from Heathrow on Tuesday night, bound for Nice.

Why would such an experienced operator leave papers like these lying around?

He checked the doors and windows. High security electronic locks everywhere.

Good ones too. She wasn't anticipating anyone in here.

Next, he accessed David Marksworth's phone. There were no voicemails but there was one text message that intrigued him. Some kind of quotation: an oath of allegiance? He read it through twice, shrugged and forwarded it to Patrick.

Hong Jintao went about his duties at the embassy, discussing UK-China trade relations, greeting ambassadors and trade commissioners. He was feeling more relaxed than earlier. Two matters had been satisfactorily concluded. He had ensured that Marksworth would be where he wanted him and his deep cover agent in Downing Street was fully prepared.

Tuesday could well be the last day of his life, and Marksworth's. That didn't concern him: he had never expected to die of old age. But at least, this way, he would die knowing that he had prevented his government from launching an armed attack on Africa – the opening phase of a possible world war.

CHAPTER 23

When the messages from Julian came through, Patrick was in the safe house working. Andy Fields had put his research team onto looking for clues: sweeping through the most recent intelligence on China, its long term international strategy and its government's current "big issues": at any given moment, every government had to focus its attention on today's pressing matters.

Patrick had chosen to concentrate his own research far more narrowly. Ever since his last brainstorm with Fields, something had been nagging away in the back of his mind - Africa. It was widely acknowledged that the Chinese saw Africa as a huge economic opportunity. For many decades, they had been buying friends there, investing billions in infrastructure projects in return for influence and first call on the vast quantities of minerals and raw materials it needed to feed its industries – seventy-five billion dollars in aid projects between 2000 and 2011 alone; far, far more than the Americans.

But, as he read online from a respected journalist:

China's strategic investments are often poor quality, aimed at short-term gains of keeping non-democratic regimes in power, particularly those that are unfriendly to the United States.

Patrick sat back, ignoring his bleeping phone for the moment. He picked up a one-page note from Andy's researchers and read it aloud:

'There has been much recent speculation that China's current sphere of influence in Africa is proving inadequate to supply it with the resources it requires.'

He made a note to follow that up later and opened his phone. Two messages from Julian. He opened each one in turn.

A farm in Buckinghamshire?

He Googled the farm's name while he read the second message. That one stopped him dead in his tracks.

We seek not to be born on the same day, in the same month and in the same year. We merely hope to die on the same day, in the same month and in the same year.

An oath. Blood brothers. The sender of the message had hidden his number but Patrick guessed Fields' team had ways of decrypting that. He called one of the men who were guarding the safe house and briefed him to get someone working on it.

Turning back to his screen, he scrolled through the many references to Middlecroft Farm. Several reports of local authority planning agreements to extend the buildings, but nothing specific about the occupants until a cutting from the local newspaper's letters column from the previous year:

Dear Editor

I would like to express my grateful thanks to the nice Chinese gentlemen from Middlecroft Farm for returning my cat Fraggles to me after she strayed off her usual night-time prowling route. As I told them, it's a blessing that Mr Butcher the vet persuaded me to have her micro-waved (sic) otherwise I'd have probably lost my dearest friend for ever. The nice gentlemen told me they made microwaves too. Wasn't that a coincidence? Anyway, I mustn't keep you.

Miss Edith Dyke

'Yessss!' cried Patrick, leaping out of his chair, which toppled to the ground. He strode across the room to a flip chart and grabbed a marker. He wrote:

CHINA AFRICA
INFLUENCE / RESOURCES –
Need more? Of what? Where from?
LONDON CONFERENCE - African leaders
"We hope to die on the same day"
MICROWAVES?

He stood back and looked at what he had written, stroking his chin. So far, so good. Somewhere on that chart lay the key to unravelling the mystery, he felt quite sure. And - he checked his notes - time was short. He wrote the word "Tuesday" next to the London Conference line. Today was Friday.

Or, on the other hand, he could be barking up a totally irrelevant tree.

He looked at the flip chart again. He made his decision. Picking up the phone, he composed an SMS message to Julian:

Could be something to do with microwaves

That brought back his deep underlying fear for Julian's safety. He closed his eyes for a minute, heaved a big sigh and went back to work. Now, he needed to find out everything he could about microwaves.

But first, what about that strange oath?

She was back. As she climbed the stairs, she heard a gentle rumble coming from inside the flat. And there he was, the beauty, exactly as she had left him, spark out on the settee, snoring gently. Jenna set down her shopping, removed her boots and tiptoed across the carpet. Lifting the blanket, she allowed herself the luxury of inspecting every ripple of the boy's tee-shirted torso. In his sleep, the shirt had been pulled clear of his waistband, revealing an expanse of soft skin. A wispy trail of fair hair ran from his navel, in a southerly direction, under the belt . . .

What had just been an annoying itch of erotic frustration as she walked back from the store was now a churning ball of desire. She knew full well she was doing the wrong thing, but it was irresistible. When she felt this way, it was no good trying to fight it.

She reached forward, touched his stomach, caressed it and then watched as her fingers found their own way along the wispy trail, down under the belt, onwards, closer . . .

'What???'

He woke with a start. He didn't need to say 'What the fuck?'. His face said it for him.

He looked down and saw the woman's hand trapped inside his trousers. She was desperately trying to retrieve it but to no avail. It was stuck.

Julian started to laugh – a snigger that grew into a bellow. Her expression advanced from confusion to embarrassment to sheer joy. Within seconds, they were both collapsed on the settee, his arms around her body, her hand firmly gripping his erection.

An hour later, she stood and walked, naked, towards the kitchen area.

'What would you like for supper?' she asked, as she looked for an apron. 'By the way, my name's Jasmine. I forgot to ask yours.'

More laughter.

'I'm Sebastian,' he said, using his bodyguard alias. 'Actually, I'm bloody starving, so anything meaty will suit me.'

'You've had that already. That was the first course. But I bought some fillet steak, salad and a bottle of Burgundy. OK?'

'Suits me. Medium rare, please.'

When she turned her back to open the fridge, Julian sneaked a quick look at his phone.

Could be something to do with microwaves

He scowled as he blanked the screen.

Microwaves? Microwaves? What the hell did Patrick mean?

He grabbed a pair of old jeans that Jenna – oops, Jasmine - had found in a cupboard – 'The owner's kit. He's a long distance pilot, you know,' she'd told him – picked up his bag and headed for the bathroom.

'Shower. Shan't be long,' he called.

'OK, I'll use the one in the bedroom,' she called back.

As soon as the door was locked, he turned on the shower full blast. Sitting on the lavatory, he connected his phone to the Web and began to search recent headlines on developments in microwave power.

The first one that caught his eye was not recent at all. Julian speed-read the opening paragraphs. Back in the 1980's, the Canadian Communications Research Centre had created a small unmanned plane that could run off power beamed to it from Earth. They discovered that the plane could be guided at an altitude of up to thirteen miles and run for months using only a large ground-based microwave transmitter. A disc-shaped rectifying antenna, or rectenna, just behind the plane's wings, changed the microwave energy from the transmitter into direct-current electricity – a constant supply of power.

Since then, multi-national companies and government agencies were reported to be working on a whole range of applications where microwave technology could be used to transmit power, wirelessly.

Whatever was happening behind the scenes, the only tangible product to hit the streets so far had been the development of wireless home networks to power all the property's electrical appliances.

Knowing he was running out of time, Julian flicked back to the search list and stopped on something entitled Active Denial System.

'Hey, what are you doing in there? Supper's ready in two minutes! Clothing optional.'

'On my way,' he called.

He copied the articles' hyperlinks to Patrick, shut down the phone, stashed it in one of the bag's padded pockets to nullify the signal and jumped in the shower for the fastest strip-wash of the year. When he was dry, he pulled on the jeans, leaned over the basin and looked in the mirror. He needed to think, clearly.

Here he was, after a bout of wild sex, about to eat dinner – and surely have more wild sex - with one of the world's most deadly assassins: by reputation, a killer who, very soon, was going to execute some terrible crime. And he, Julian, expert lab researcher but apprentice secret agent, was the one person who could scupper the whole plan . . . or he could completely blow it and have to bear the consequences.

I have to get out of here and back to that van, fast.

'Sorry I was so long . . . I borrowed your shampoo . . .'

When he opened the door, she was facing him, still wearing her apron but now dressed in a black silk dressing gown. In her right hand, she held a long-bladed knife. Her eyes were steady, emotionless.

'Now, Mr Sebastian, we need to have a chat,' she said. 'Drop the bag and walk over there, very slowly.'

Julian did as he was told. Very scared, he tried to make light of it. 'Hey, Jasmine . . . don't let the steaks go . . .'

'Shut up! A little bit further. Now stop.'

He was up against the island that separated the living room from the kitchen, his back towards the assassin. Not daring to look around, he sensed the woman approach. The tip of her knife touched the side of his neck. He could hear her breathing.

By now, he was shaking with terror.

'What is your real name?' she whispered into his right ear.

'Sebastian,' he mumbled.

'No! Your *real* name. Julian!'

Panic. 'How . . .?'

'Your key ring, you idiot.' She waved the bunch of keys in front of his eyes. There it was: the cheap key fob he'd picked at a motorway service station months previously. *Julian* in sparkly silver lettering.

Shit! Andy Fields' people had been so meticulous when they gave him his new identity of Sebastian Neal, bodyguard. Everything - driver's licence, travel card, bank card . . . They'd even changed the plates on his bike. In a flash, it dawned.

I attached the keys they gave me to my own key ring! I can't believe it – what a stupid, stupid mistake. Think, you idiot, THINK!

'No, honestly, I am Sebastian,' he pleaded. 'Sebastian Crispin Merryweather, born . . .'

'I'm not interested in where you were born, young man.'

'But the keyring – it came with the bike when I bought it. I can show you the receipt. It's in the pannier . . .' He was burbling now.

'Oh, forget it,' she said. 'I don't give a shit what your name is. In truth, it adds an extra sense of mystery to tonight.'

He looked round and saw her eyes gleam as the knife broke the skin of his neck. The woman was having fun: all this knife stuff was her idea of a dark sex game. He'd heard about knife play somewhere. Sometimes it went horribly wrong.

And now the voice was menacing, the accent guttural.

The accent – what happened to the sweet Irish girl?

Julian gripped the counter, waiting for the next, inevitable, decisive move. Tears sprang to his eyes.

The woman laughed, a cruel, humourless laugh.

'Which, for me, makes fucking you again even more intense. After that, we'll have to see.'

She released him, pulled the knife away,

'Now, open that bottle and I'll get the food.'

As he twisted the corkscrew, an old saying he'd heard somewhere suddenly came to mind:

The condemned man ate a hearty supper.

As she dished up the meal, she smiled quietly to herself.

He's so sweet, so innocent.

She was always so careful; in her line of work, it paid to

be constantly on the alert. Once before, she had allowed her overwhelming sex drive to ignore warning signals. On that occasion, her intended lover dropped his guard and lost his life. But this man, just a lad really – had passed that test.

I adore this game: that extra element of fear is so damned spicy.

She decided to add an extra slug of Balsamic vinegar to the sauce.

High over North Africa

He usually preferred not to fly first class but, in this case, the presidents had insisted. And he had to admit that the food was a lot better. The Vankaya Pulusu, a traditional Andhra stew, made with aubergines, chilli, garlic, coconut and tamarind, had been cooked to perfection and the rice was light and fluffy. The people at Kenya Airways were clearly making extra efforts to attract the travelling Indian elite away from British Airways.

At the age of seventy-three, Vanmali Mehta's month had been more strenuous than he would have liked. Not that he didn't adore his work but, as he had discovered throughout his career in business, and latterly while working with African leaders, the oldest rule in life, the Eighty-Twenty rule, still applied. This month, eighty percent of his exasperation had been caused by twenty percent of his current clients – to be precise, one national president who, having declared his firm intention to crack down on moral and ethical misbehaviour in his regime, had been discovered using the nation's uncut diamonds to pay for the murder of two rival leaders in a motor "accident".

Mehta's disappointment had been somewhat tempered when the presidents of three neighbouring countries, each of whom was also his client, had jointly expressed their disapproval by cancelling a symbolic visit to the offending leader's capital city.

Tonight, he felt tired; he would have loved to be heading home to his wife, daughters and grandchildren, to play tennis with his friends and go for a long walk. But, he'd had no choice but to agree to make this short trip to London, as strategic adviser to a group of African Commonwealth country presidents.

He had detected that some of them were becoming increasingly dubious about the true value of Commonwealth membership. The balance of world power continued to shift east and south and what was once known as Great Britain had begun to loosen its links with mainland Europe in favour of its fantasy "special relationship" with a fast-declining America. International aid budgets to the Commonwealth had been slashed and Britain seemed to speak out less and less against those who equated the very word "Islam" with extremism, danger and disruption.

While Vanmali Mehta understood their fears, he had continuously warned the presidents against the temptation to cosy up to the alternative great powers, whether it be China or Russia - "Better the devil you know than the devil you don't" - or indeed the United States, where the new regime was becoming increasingly introspective and desperate.

In the end, he had persuaded them to go with him to London to discuss their concerns face to face with the British government.

He said, 'When they hear how serious your doubts are, direct from your own lips, you never know what the British may offer to persuade you to stick around. It's worth a try, at the very least. But leave most of the talking to me,' he told them. 'I know these people better than you do.'

Indeed he did, having studied at Brasenose College Oxford and gained his MBA from the London School of Economics, along with a large percentage of the British meritocracy. Mehta held an impressive number of keys to the most influential doors.

He had to admit he liked these presidents, with all their faults, and it appeared that they trusted him. They had all agreed to join him on the trip.

He hailed a flight attendant.

'Do you think I could have a little more tea, please?'

Then I'll sleep. Mmm, I love London. While I'm there, I must remember that promise my wife made me make, to look up - what was his name? Ah yes, Sir Norman Tudway and Meg, his wonderful wife.

CHAPTER 24

Microwaves, microwaves. Patrick Cameron was already building up a small library of research material. Over the years, engineers and scientists had discovered a wide variety of applications for the technology. The more he had learned over the last hour, the longer the list grew as each new option emerged as a possible motive for the Chinese to use microwave power to achieve, or perhaps defend, their strategic dominance.

Patrick knew it had to be something vital to their national welfare – survival? - for them to deploy Jenna Dobrosova on active service in England.

That was enough reading; it was time to select the most likely and to concentrate his search on the short list. But which to choose? He leaned back in his chair and saw his phone blinking on the table by the window. He had become so absorbed in his work, he had not checked it for half an hour.

Another message from Julian. Two hyperlinks, that was all.

Copying the first onto his laptop, he began to read. At first, he was puzzled.

Why has the lad sent me a story from the 1980's?

He had scanned the article earlier, but now the relevance started to dawn on him:

If it can power an aircraft thirteen miles away, just how powerful could a microwave beam become if the juice was turned up sufficiently high? Is there any limit to its power?

He glanced at the phone screen again and answered the call.

The steak was undoubtedly delicious and he was very hungry but Julian hadn't tasted a thing. The woman appeared utterly relaxed, chatting away happily about everything and nothing, offering to top up his glass and only pausing occasionally to push one side of her gown aside and casually caress one perfect breast. She was clearly enjoying her little game, whatever that was. Now her eyes had changed again: he had often wondered what a psychopath looked like. The long-bladed knife sat on the table, close to her right hand.

Julian knew he was failing to respond as she wanted, to appear excited at the prospect of more uninhibited sex. Libido couldn't have been further from his mind. He was far too scared for that. He had never felt fear like it.

What surprised him was that he was, also, excited: the fear was making him excited. He would never have believed it but his mind was as sharp as ever. For the first time in his short existence, he knew his life was in danger. Somehow he had to save two lives – the assassination target's, of course, but first his own. And all he could see was a challenge.

As he nibbled at his food, nodding and answering her with monosyllabic grunts, he waited. He had no idea how much time he had.

He had done his bit; he just had to trust the others to do theirs. It had worked every time in training, after all.

Once again, Fields had insisted he stay in the safe house. Once again, Patrick had flatly refused and had donned his cab driver fat-man disguise. As the yellow van, complete with local authority markings, was driven expertly towards its destination, he watched the GPS screen's constantly updated estimate of their time of arrival. He was tense; it was taking too long and his man was in grave danger. Arriving too late to save him was unthinkable.

On a professional level, everyone knew that casualties were inevitable in this "business", but this was his boy, the scruffy young man who had turned up one day at his lab, without an appointment, and in whom Patrick had detected something very special – a judgement that had since proved hopelessly inadequate. Now that Andy Fields had seen the same qualities in Julian, it was, he reminded himself, partly so that he could carry on working with the young maverick that Patrick had agreed to sign up for this assignment.

Come on, come on . . . he silently urged the driver. Come ON.

Julian didn't dare look at his watch as she finished her meal. He had long since given up trying to force food down his throat. Breaking off from a long, highly erotic tale of how she had seduced a woman and her mother on the same day in Madrid, Jenna leaned back and stretched, causing her gown to fall further open. She left it there.

'Well, though I say it myself,' she said, 'that was wonderful. What a shame you were not hungry. More wine?' She picked up the bottle. Julian's glass was still almost full. He picked it up and took a tiny sip.

'No thanks.'

'Now, as I recall, just before we sat down,' she said picking up the long-bladed knife, 'we were discussing how we might spend the rest of the evening. Tell me, Julian, have you ever experienced the joys of bondage?' She chuckled.

Julian shrugged and shook his head. He didn't like the sound of this one bit.

'Ah, you are so young; there are so many wonderful, exciting things I could teach you, if only we had the time. But this evening, let me tell you what is going to happen. I can see that you are dying to know,' she said picking up the knife.

Laughing at a private joke, she stood and walked over to his side of the table, holding the knife in front of her.

Julian gripped the edge of the table.

'The bedroom is over there. I want you to go in and lie down on the bed, on your back. Keep your jeans on.'

He had no choice and at least this was using up time. The fear had gone up a couple of notches now but he was still thinking clearly. He did as he was told once more.

Jenna entered the bedroom carrying a bunch of beautifully crafted short ropes, each with its own silk tassel, and proceeded to fasten his wrists and ankles tightly to the four corners of the bed.

When she was done, she climbed onto the bed, knelt between his outstretched legs and released the button on his jeans. The zip she left halfway down. Then she pointed her knife at his groin. Julian looked at the ceiling; he felt the knife penetrate his jeans and start to cut downwards. So far it hadn't touched the skin but he knew it was only a matter of time.

'Ah, your little man is sleeping,' she said, patting him with her other hand. 'But I'm sure we can do something about that later.'

The knife was obviously razor sharp as she easily cut open the whole of the left leg; then she worked her way slowly up the right, humming quietly to herself all the time. This time, he felt the tip touch him twice and he jumped.

He could feel the air on his skin as the denim parted and the knife edged closer to his crutch. Every fibre of his lower body was now hyper-sensitive, waiting for the next piece of cruel teasing. He pulled and pulled at his bonds but it was useless.

'Perfect,' she said, sitting back on her knees. 'So that only leaves the part in the middle, the important part.'

From where he was lying, Julian could only imagine what the bitch was doing now. How much longer would this ridiculous game go on before the pain began? The pain and the blood.

Jenna's grinning face came into view, the knife clearly visible now. The tip touched his throat.

'Now, Master Julian. Before we fuck – and I assure you that you will be - how do you say? – up for it, you are going to tell me who you really are and the real reason why you are here in my apartment. After all, when your friends find you dead, nobody will accuse you of betraying them.'

That was the point at which Julian, for the first time in years, began to pray.

And that was the moment when all the lights went out.

It had hardly taken the team a minute to unload the van, set up the red and white barriers, access the distribution transformer and cut off the power to the house, its immediate neighbours and the street lights.

Within a couple of minutes, people were emerging from their doors onto the street, chatting and pointing out to each other how many properties had been blacked out.

By then, the "power workers" had spread out, each taking up a hidden position that gave him a good line of sight of the house, front and rear. They were all armed.

As Patrick watched the house from the alley that ran behind the rear gardens of the terrace, he gripped his gun.

It had taken too long to assemble the required skills after Julian pressed the panic button on his phone. They all knew the plan, so why had it taken so long?

Had they arrived in time to save Julian's life?

He was almost frantic.

Time slipped by. Nobody reported seeing anything.

Then he heard a creak. He lifted his night sight and focused on the back door. A black-clad silhouette emerged, ran along the garden wall, crouching military-style, stopped and looked around. Then the gate into the alley opened slowly, a head, black woollen hat pulled down over its ears, looked both ways and the shadow turned left, ran silently past Patrick and disappeared down the alley. From its shape and movements, it could only have been a woman, with a heavy bag slung across her shoulders.

Patrick, as agreed, didn't follow. He whispered into his radio,

'Target has left the premises. Heading for Prospect Road. OK to enter now. You're electricians, remember.'

He pocketed his weapon, ran through the gate, in through the back door, and located the stairs where he bumped into a confused elderly couple, standing by a door.

'London Electric. Sorry about the lights, love,' he said in his best London electrician voice. 'We think it's a problem on the first floor. We'll sort it out in a jiffy.'

As he vaulted up the stairs, he heard a man's voice, muffled, close by. No distinguishable words, just a series of grunts and whimpers. Patrick feared the worst.

Luckily, Jenna had left the door to her flat unlocked in her haste to get away.

Shining his torch as he entered, gun in hand, he swiftly recce'd the main room to ensure it was empty and headed in the direction of the noises.

The lights came back on just as he walked into the bedroom, giving him a floodlit view of his young colleague, looking pale and rather embarrassed, spread-eagled almost naked across the bed. A sharp knife lay beside him.

Patrick stood at the door, taking in the entire scene, unsure whether to laugh or cry with relief.

'For God's sake, Patrick, What are you doing? Don't just stand there,' said Julian. 'Get someone to Kilmington Road, small white Peugeot van. Fast, man.'

Patrick relayed the message and listened for the acknowledgement. 'Now, Julian,' he said. 'Do you want me to untie those knots or had you something else in mind?'

The amusement of the other team members, now gathered behind Patrick, was not shared by Julian.

David Marksworth straightened the papers on his dining table for the fourth or fifth time, then looked in the mirror, brushed the shoulder of his new sweater with his hand and checked his watch. Two minutes to ten.

His cleaner had come in specially that afternoon, polished the silver and cleaned the glass in the doors of the illuminated display cabinet. His collections of Delft Blue seventeenth century pottery and Waterford decanters were his pride and joy – a silent demonstration of their owner's impeccable taste.

He had chosen the contents of the drinks tray with care: Talisker 10 Year Old Single Malt, Absolut Elyx vodka, Veuve-Clicquot Champagne, Crème de Cassis, and a 2004 Chateau Lynch-Bages, decanted.

At precisely ten o'clock, the front door buzzer sounded. Marksworth let the visitor in and waited by his door.

To his consternation, the figure who emerged from the stairs was a slim young man in a dark suit, white shirt and tie. In his hand he held an envelope.

'Message for you, sir.'

He handed the envelope to Marksworth who took it. It was blank. He looked up at the man who was standing quietly, as if waiting for a response.

Marksworth obediently opened the envelope and withdrew a single sheet of paper, hand written. He recognised the script instantly. Something made him look up again. Someone else had appeared in the doorway. This time it was a face he recognised.

'What on earth are you doing here?' Marksworth asked, astonished.

'I have been here longer than you will ever know,' said the newcomer. 'At the beginning and now at the end. I think you ought to read it, David'.

David Marksworth turned around, knowing the two visitors would follow him into the apartment. The first words he read were all he needed. He didn't have to read the rest.

"It is with great regret . . ."

When he turned back to face his killers, his face was calm, resigned. He was ready.

CHAPTER 25

China

Although he spoke Mandarin fluently, Guo Dalong's English butler announced his arrival in English; Guo encouraged Harrison to surprise him from time to time by challenging his command of the old colonial power's mother tongue.

The weather was hot so the sixty year-old former Marine commando wore a simple white tunic suit instead of his usual white tie and tails. The outfit did little to disguise his well-toned body, maintained by hours in the gym while his employer slept.

'A message from London for you, Master,' he said as he approached Guo's wicker peacock throne chair on the terrace.

'Ah, Harrison.' Guo did not look round, continuing to gaze upon the formal gardens outside his home and the pale blue hills beyond. 'I know you mean well, but you really should refrain from calling me *Master*. I am but my country's servant, my people's servant. If I were their Master, they would speak my name in whispers or shout it aloud, in awe or in hatred, and yet only a tiny selected few even know that I am still alive. So, tell me, Harrison, what does the message say?'

With the onset of chronic dry macular degeneration, Guo had virtually no clear vision in the centre of his retina, so that, while the misty hills in the distance were quite sharp, everything within a short distance was now so blurred that faces, pictures and words, even food, were almost indistinguishable. Harrison's eyes were now his eyes and even he needed stronger lenses these days. He squinted at his tablet's screen.

'The message reads: *Project 49B accomplished securely. No complications*. So it would seem that our concerns about Marksworth being compromised are no longer, Master – ahem, sir.'

'Such a shame.' The old man appeared genuinely sad.

'A shame that he had to be eliminated? Do you mourn his death?'

Guo reverted to English. 'No, it is a shame that it was his one character flaw which brought my plan to the brink of failure. He was a loyal servant of China; within his limited sphere, he accomplished much that was of value to us. But he was a self-important little . . . what is the word I am looking for?'

'Prig, sir.'

Guo smiled. 'Yes, prig. Such a delightful English word. Now, my friend, to what should I be turning my attention next?'

As he scrolled through his notes on the tablet, Harrison allowed himself a fleeting smile too, in his case at his employer's impeccable English grammar.

'May I sit down, sir?'

'Of course, of course. How rude of me. Please sit here.'

He settled himself into one of the more simple chairs adjacent to Guo Dalong. Harrison was not just the obedient butler: he was also Guo Dalong's director of operations. It was his role to ensure that instructions were carried out to the letter, to take care of the details and of any dirty work – in particular, the removal of any obstacles from the track of Guo's great plan.

Hong Jintao, ostensibly one of the most influential men in China, its Foreign Minister no less, was in truth but a puppet dancing on Harrison's strings. Harrison handled all communications, both with Hong and with the two figures who would shortly emerge in England to play their central roles: the Locksmith and Sleeping Beauty.

'I have been working on the minutiae of the final phase, sir. Hong informs me that his Russian woman has safely evaded capture; she has retrieved her equipment and her transport and is already installed in the operations centre we have set up for her in central London, this time under a new identity. I am satisfied that we should retain her services: her career record persuades me that, even now, she is sufficiently resourceful to delude the opposition and do what must be done.'

Guo sighed. 'Do what must be done,' he repeated. 'How I wish that it was not necessary for so many fine, decent people to lose their lives. They say that revenge is sweet but I have to tell you I feel no sweetness in bringing about the downfall of a nation that has made such enormous contributions to the way the world's people live their lives today. But they have to be made to pay.'

'Sir,' said Harrison. 'I share your sentiments. As an Englishman by birth, I look back on Great Britain with a mixture of pride and shame. But for all their achievements in science, literature, medicine and the law, we cannot forgive their rampant exploitation of what they arrogantly refer to as "The Third World".'

'Nor indeed what they did to my family.' Guo growled, turned his head and spat on the ground.

Harrison simply nodded. Neither of them needed to recount how Guo's grandfather, father and two brothers, the prosperous owners of a business in Malaya that gave employment and dignity to hundreds of poor villagers, had perished at the hands of a British firing squad in the nineteen-fifties, accused, wrongly as it turned out, of harbouring Communist guerrillas.

Guo looked long and hard into the distance, then clapped his hands, turned to his man and smiled.

'And tell me, what of our two prize exhibits?'

'Ready to play their part as required, sir. They have both been subjected to intensive briefing but we really have no need to be concerned. As the drama unfolds,' he looked at his watch, 'starting very soon now, every member of our cast will play their part, scene by scene, well-rehearsed word for word, to inflict maximum disgrace on the British government.'

'And on their Establishment?'

'And on their Establishment,' Harrison confirmed. 'The next few days will bring about the inevitable collapse of the Commonwealth, a run on the pound Sterling and mass withdrawals of capital from the London Stock Exchange. Britain will be bankrupt, friendless and powerless.'

Harrison could see that Guo was becoming weary. He decided to close the discussion and fetch his employer some of the special tea which always helped him sleep.

Once he was happy that the old man was dozing off, he slipped back to his rooms and opened up his computer.

A military base close to London

The seven men inside the closely guarded communications room were hard at work. The Last Resort Squad had never before allowed anyone but their most trusted associates to attend one of their meetings but, in view of the exceptional nature of the crisis they faced, Sir Norman had taken the executive decision to relax their rules on this occasion.

Information had reached them that there was a direct threat to the stability, not only of the UK, but of much of the Western world. So Patrick Cameron and Andy Fields had been joined by Julian at the meeting.

Looking round the table, Patrick couldn't help but feel a little upstaged by the array of wisdom, experience and brain power assembled there.

Andy Fields and Julian sat either side of him – Fields, without question the brightest copper in the land and Julian, who more than made up for his short career with an innate ability to spot things of which nobody else had even dreamt. The four LRS members, with a combined age of around three hundred, seemed an unlikely group to be charged with such weighty matters, but beneath their aging pates and straggling white hair, Patrick immediately discerned what writers meant when they talked about "a fierce intelligence" and absolute integrity.

'So, gentlemen,' said Sir Norman, looking up from Fields' handwritten report, 'we have a Russian assassin on the run *somewhere,* a *suspected* double agent committing *apparent* suicide, a *theory* about microwave weapons, an as yet undefined Chinese connection, and an *apparently unconnected* meeting of Commonwealth heads of state in London.'

'Sounds like a bugger's muddle to me,' grunted the portly Lord Harptree. 'Is there any decent wine in this place?' He got up, walked to the door and had a brief word with the soldier outside before resuming his seat.

Sir Norman ignored him. Clearly this was quite normal.

'Our task this afternoon, gentlemen, is to assemble this unlikely set of pieces of information into something that makes concrete sense, and then to form a plan. Agreed?'

Everyone nodded.

He continued. 'Oh, before I forget, one of the Commonwealth delegates is a friend – Vanmali Mehta, the African arbitrator chap, although he's Indian by birth. Long career in business. Nobel prize for something. We had a long natter when we met at Wimbledon a few years ago and we've stayed in touch. Fascinating man. I'm hoping to meet him while he's here. Now, I suggest I go round the table, ask each of you for your thoughts, and then I'll sum up.'

'Excuse me, Sir Norman,' a timid voice piped up. It was Julian. Patrick glared at him. This boy needed a few lessons in etiquette.

Sir Norman smiled kindly at the young man. 'May I call you Julian? Thank you. Is there something I've missed?'

'No sir, but I think I may be able to save us all a lot of time.'

There was a tap on the door. Jonty Harptree leapt to his feet and returned with three open bottles of decent claret and a tray of glasses.

Heathrow airport, London

Vanmali Mehta was met at the aircraft door by two officials, each brandishing a warrant card, who introduced themselves as John, a senior official from the Foreign and Commonwealth Office and a security officer from the Diplomatic Corps. He was escorted to one of the airport's private VIP lounges.

John said, 'Before we take you to your hotel, sir, we'd like to spend a few minutes with you here, to give you an up-to-date briefing on the arrangements for the next few days. By the way, you'll be pleased to hear that the aircraft carrying the presidents and their staff landed safely an hour ago. Each group is being driven to their respective High Commission. You'll be staying at The Savoy, as usual.'

'Very well,' said Mehta, 'but could you please make it brief? I need to get to my room to take a rest before we all meet for dinner later.'

He put his cabin bag on his lap and unzipped a compartment, revealing his laptop and a file of papers.

'Now, here is my schedule,' he said, lifting out the file and opening it. 'Tell me what has changed in the last few hours.'

John stood up. 'We'll have those, please, Mr Mehta. And the laptop.'

'Why?'

'Security.' The man reached out to take the items from Mehta, who instinctively gripped hold of them.

'Oh, by the way, sir, we've just heard that your wife and grandchild were delayed on their way home from school this afternoon. Something about a traffic hold-up. I'm sure it's nothing to worry about. They will be back safely in the house in no time, I understand.'

'Now, if I could have the file and laptop for safe keeping, sir. Just security, you understand.'

Mehta let go of the laptop and file, feeling confused. The grandchild they were referring to was eight years old and had been born with a damaged brain. His wife was always accompanied by a trusted driver who would not normally report such a trivial matter, especially when Mehta was away on business.

This time, it wasn't the FCO official who had asked him to hand over: it was the security officer, a tall, fit-looking woman with short, spiked black hair, heavy eye makeup, wearing a brown leather jerkin, combat trousers and boots.

The name on her warrant card read *Juliana "Jules" Dabrowski.*

CHAPTER 26

'Forgive me, Sir Norman, for going into so much technical detail. I suppose it's my science training: formulate a hypothesis, test its validity against all available data, and then compare its robustness against other possible hypotheses.'

He needn't have worried. Looking round the table while Julian explained his thinking, using a series of hand-drawn graphics and charts, Patrick saw nothing but fascination. To watch a group of the country's most eminent men enthralled by a scruffy, jeans-clad "boy" in his early twenties would have been a delight in itself, if his topic were not so disturbing.

'So, I suppose I'd better sum up,' Julian said, looking at his watch.

Sir Norman smiled and nodded.

'Right.' Julian took a deep breath. 'Chinese industry has expanded faster than the state's ability to supply sufficient power. So they embarked on a massive power station construction programme, almost all of them coal-fired.

'China has vast reserves of coal so it's they're cheapest option. However, coal mining and coal-fired power stations use huge amounts of water to wash the coal and cool the generators. But China's water resources are already at crisis point – in addition to agriculture and industry, economic growth has brought more and more people to the cities, now earning enough money to buy washing machines, dishwashers, etcetera. Fifty-one major rivers in China have disappeared in the last ten years. In some regions, particularly in the coal-rich North, agriculture is running dangerously dry.

'My hypothesis was that, in order to arrest the water depletion, China would, among other things, need to source its energy from elsewhere. However, their immediate neighbours are either facing similar difficulties or are politically unstable.

'So, my next stop was Africa. But how do you transmit massive amounts of energy across huge distances, quickly and efficiently without laying thousands of miles of cable? That's when Patrick happened to discover that the Buckinghamshire farm visited by Jenna Dobrosova specialised in microwave technology.

'From there it was a simple matter of following published research to figure out what the Chinese are up to, at least in my opinion: they have to stop building power stations at home so they've decided to generate energy in Africa instead and send it, using vastly enhanced microwave transmitters, to China via relay stations in space.'

He sat down, looking quite pale from all the effort. Patrick passed him a glass of water.

'Thank you, young man,' said Sir Norman to Julian. 'Thank you very much. Now, I would be most interested to know what everyone else thinks about what you've just heard.' He looked round the table. 'For my part, I find Julian's theory both plausible and profoundly worrying.'

The man who was only ever addressed as George was the first to speak. Patrick had been told little about the former Special Branch man, except that, at some considerable risk to his own personal safety, he had once exposed a plan by senior police officers to sabotage a Home Secretary's car. Rumour had it that the threats to George's life continued to this day.

'As you know, Norman, I'm just a simple copper; international politics are not really my thing. So I can only speak from a strict policing point of view. I would remind you all that we have a killer out there. While everything we've heard does give us a possible motive and a modus operandi, I would caution that it's still very thin in terms of hard evidence and, rather importantly, on the identity of the intended victim.'

Why do policemen always have to talk like policemen? wondered Patrick, before returning to listening mode.

'Thank you, George,' said Sir Norman. 'Now Gerald? You know China and Africa a great deal better than the rest of us.'

'I tend to agree with George,' said the former head of one of the world's leading international business schools and, reputedly, one of the sharpest brains in the country. 'As he says, we're all assuming that they intend to kill someone. Why else would they employ a world-class assassin? But until we know who the target is, there's little we can do. We may have to move in now and give up the chance of exposing the rest of the spy ring.

'As for China, would they kill to get their own way? The answer is most definitely yes. In a crisis, they will stop at nothing to protect themselves. And I have no doubt that, for them, this is a major crisis – unless they can source energy from new countries, their industry will grind to a halt or they'll run out of water.

'Until today, none of us could see how they could ever source energy from across oceans, from Africa, so we dismissed the whole idea. Now, thanks to Julian, we have the solution, or rather a solution to that. It's quite ingenious.

'But consider this, gentlemen: unless China can detach the leading African countries from the Commonwealth, they have no hope of erecting the dozens, perhaps hundreds, of power stations they need there. Britain and its friends would immediately intervene and put a stop to it. The western world simply can't contemplate vast swathes of Africa coming under Chinese control. But a mass exodus from the Commonwealth would play directly into China's hands – these countries would become free agents.'

'As you say, Gerald,' said Sir Norman, 'it goes without saying that, once China gets its teeth into those countries, their global power base will grow substantially. Which, I suppose, brings us back to this week's conference. I propose we examine that in great detail now. Bearing in mind our twin objectives, gentlemen – preventing any killing and apprehending all of the agents in our midst before they cause more trouble. Agreed?'

All four members of the Last Resort Squad nodded.

Andy Fields was staring at his phone.

'Excuse me, Sir Norman,' he said without looking up. 'I believe they've started already. Did you say earlier that you are friends with someone named Vanmali Mehta?'

'Mehta?' exclaimed Sir Norman. 'Yes, I know him. Quite well, actually. An extraordinary man. Don't tell me . . .'

'He's gone missing, sir. Arrived at Heathrow today on a scheduled flight and never emerged from the Arrivals lounge.'

'Tell us more about Mr Mehta, please, Norman,' said Lord Harptree, who seemed to have forgotten about the wine for the time being.

The woman kept the black Range Rover strictly to the speed limit all the way into central London. So far, the FCO man, seated next to Vanmali Mehta in the rear, had been on the phone throughout the journey.

'Yes, he's with us. All clear. OK. Talk later.'

He switched off and turned to Mehta smiling.

'Right, sir. Your wife and grandson are quite safe and on their way home. Our people explained that there was a road block – vehicle pile-up. Gave them a cup of tea. Apparently, they were most grateful.' He laughed.

Mehta said nothing. The man appeared perfectly genuine and, although his security officer colleague's appearance was rather weird, in particular when she needed an elbow crutch to walk to the car – *a one-armed security guard?* - she had behaved in a professional manner throughout.

But why bring my family into it? I am not under arrest, under caution. And I am hardly what anyone could call a high-profile political figure! So what's going on?

He had always been a good man in an emergency. Throughout his business career, he had a knack of assessing unexpected events and devising the right response strategy, quickly.

On the other hand, now that they had left the airport, everything seemed perfectly normal. His conference file and laptop were still sitting on the front seat, untouched.

'Do you mind telling me what's happening, please?' Mehta asked.

''What's happening, sir? Nothing unusual, I assure you. We're just making sure you arrive at your hotel safely. Orders from on high, you know. Can't be too careful. Oh, by the way, you don't mind if we make a brief detour, do you? Someone wants to meet you. Won't take us far out of our way.'

'Yes, I do mind, actually. And you can kindly pass me my file and laptop. I need to check a few things too.'

'Sorry, sir. We'll need to hold on to them until we arrive. Laptops send out GPS signals, like phones, these days. Security, you see. Dangerous place, London. And you're classified as a major potential target. Sir.'

'I find that hard to believe.'

'Sorry, sir. Only carrying out orders.'

Only carrying out orders. How often have I heard that before?

The woman swung the car south off Knightsbridge and negotiated her way through to Belgrave Square. She drew to a halt outside a private residence in a quiet mews, marked only by a plain white door and a brass knocker.

The door was opened from the inside before she had time to kill the engine and a young, well-groomed, anonymous-looking woman – as anonymous as the man from the FCO sitting beside him, Mehta thought – emerged and opened the car's rear door.

'Good afternoon, Mr Mehta. Welcome to London.' The accent was perfectly clipped, the smile appeared quite genuine.

'Good afternoon,' said Mehta and shook the proffered hand. 'Now do tell me, who you are and why am I here.' The tone of his voice was under control, just.

The smile did not change. 'If you would care to follow me.' She turned and walked ahead of him, just sexily enough to stay within the bounds of decency, till they reached a lift door.

All three of them stepped in. Somewhere along the way, John from the FCO had disappeared.

Silently, they ascended. When he emerged, Vanmali Mehta found himself in a spacious, elegant drawing room, large enough to accommodate a baby grand piano, a Georgian desk, a well-stocked drinks table and three settees positioned around an original Adam fireplace. While the entire room was immaculate, everything it contained was clearly old, beautiful but a little worn. It radiated comfort.

The man standing in front of the fireplace stepped forward. In his late fifties, his suit and tie more appropriate to a London gentlemen's club than the office, sandy hair going grey at the temples, his moustache neatly trimmed.

'My dear Mehta,' he said. 'How delightful to see you again. I do hope you remember me.'

Vanmali Mehta stopped in his tracks. Outwardly, he was his usual calm self but inside his mind was racing.

'Hello, Richard. What a nice surprise. How are you keeping? Now, tell me if I'm wrong but, when we last met, in Kampala, I think it was, you were chairing that Africa-Asia Business Partnership conference. Are you still racing all over the world charging outrageous fees or have you managed to settle down in London?'

He was playing for time, weighing up a number of possible scenarios. On the one hand, this could be a perfectly innocent welcoming gesture, from one international conference chairman to another, no more than that. On the other, Mehta knew that Richard Merriott never wasted time on perfectly innocent gestures, at least in his experience. There was something about the man that Vanmali Mehta had always found decidedly disturbing.

And besides, Richard Merriott was one of the very few people who knew of Vanmali Mehta's deepest secret. It all happened long ago and, as far as he knew, all of the others were already dead.

'No.' Merriott laughed. 'My chairing days are over. Downing Street, special projects now. You know what I mean.' He waggled his fingers. 'Can I offer you a drink, by the way?' He walked towards the display of bottles.

'Just a cup of tea, please,' replied Mehta. 'That sounds fascinating, Richard. Do tell me more.'

As he organised the tea, Merriott started to ramble at length about all the work he had been engaged in since they last met. Everything was made to sound frightfully important – lots of name-dropping mingled with words like strategic, global and pivotal - but Vanmali Mehta was only half listening. He was conducting a balanced risk assessment, reflecting on the events of the last couple of hours and what Merriott's true purpose might be.

Inevitably, his thoughts went back to October 31 1984.

Indira Ghandi, India's third Prime Minister, was on her way through the garden, on foot, from her residence to a nearby building for a television interview. It was 9.20 in the morning. Members of her personal bodyguard were posted in their usual places along the path.

As she was about to pass through a gate, two Sikh members of her guard opened fire with a handgun and a Sten gun, firing thirty-three bullets. One of the assassins was a favourite guard of Mrs Ghandi, who had worked for her for ten years.

The assault took place four months after the Indian Army had attacked the Golden Temple in Amritsar, the most holy Sikh place of worship, leaving it badly damaged.

Rumours of a high level conspiracy spread throughout India in the following weeks. Although none of them reached publication or resulted in arrests, the names of several notable figures in Indian society were suggested as possible plotters. There was no shortage of candidates.

Mrs Ghandi's time in office was characterised by political ruthlessness and centralisation of power. She had inherited an economy in tatters, rampant inflation, widespread corruption and class discrimination. Her solution was to attack the issues head-on. Her opponents were routinely removed, replaced by ministers loyal to her; privately-owned banks were nationalised; enemies were made.

At the time, Vanmali Mehta's business empire was just beginning to expand through a programme of aggressive acquisitions. Although he was less than forty years of age, his father had allowed him to take full control of the agricultural supplies company.

The decision to move into Africa was his. International aid programmes were pouring large sums into improving the crop growing efficiency of poor African countries and Vanmali found that he could not only undercut his European rivals but, through an innovative cross-funding system, he could also provide the farmers with health education and paid work for their families.

It was pure chance that led him to discover who had masterminded Indira Ghandi's assassination. He was talking with one of his managers, whose brother worked for a wealthy but notoriously corrupt hotel owner.

Over the following months, the brother fed Vanmali titbits he had picked up from being close to his employer and a clearer picture emerged: not only had he blackmailed the assassins into shooting Ghandi but now he was planning a military coup against the national government.

One afternoon, as he was leaving to attend a meeting, the hotel owner's car exploded, killing him and two Army generals who were with him.

Mehta was proud of what he had done: he had saved his nation from a corrupt dictatorship. But he knew the risk he had taken – murder was murder.

And somehow, Richard Merriott had found out about his involvement in the hotel owner's death. On three separate occasions, he had quietly reminded him of that fact.

They were now alone in the room. Merriott had completed his verbal autobiography. He offered Mehta more tea but he refused, looking at his watch.

That was when Merriott dropped his bomb.

'Just before you go, Vanmali. I have a proposition for you.'

'Thank you, Richard.'

Hong Jintao put down the phone. As each day passed, he could feel the tension getting to him. Everything had to work perfectly if he was to concoct an outcome that would satisfy everyone: Guo Dalong, the Politburo and his own determination to prevent an outbreak of war.

But at least he now had the reassurance of knowing that Richard Merriott, his Locksmith, had played his part to perfection. Hong had spotted him in Paris all those years ago: like so many of the others, he was a young man with a passion to save the world but, when it came to leadership potential, this one stood out above the likes of Bellingham and Marksworth. On the advice of Guo Dalong, Hong had kept Merriott's conversion to China secret from the others, preferring to ask him to keep a watch on the two Brits.

Since then, Hong had kept his key man under wraps – "asleep" - as he rose to the highest ranks of the British Civil Service – with a little help from Hong's friends, it had to be said.

Sending him to Delhi to deal with Gregory Bellingham, trusting him to liaise with the microwave specialists at Middlecroft Farm and to despatch David Marksworth had given Hong the opportunity to watch his performance in the field, at minimal risk, before letting him loose on Vanmali Mehta.

CHAPTER 27

'Found him!' Patrick looked round and beckoned the others over.

As soon as the news of Vanmali Mehta's disappearance came through, Sir Norman had suspended the meeting. Pulling rank with the base commander gave them access to the communications room, and they were each – Patrick, Julian and Andy – now seated at a terminal scanning CCTV recordings from Heathrow's international arrivals building.

Narrowing the search was the easy part: they knew the time and the gate where Mehta's plane had arrived. As the others clustered round, Patrick ran the tape again.

Although the picture quality was far from perfect, the man emerging from the plane door was certainly Mehta. The distinctive high brow, flowing grey hair and strong profile matched the shots they had pulled earlier from Google.

They watched as he was approached by two people before he could proceed to Passport Control. They both had their back to the CCTV camera so, apart from the fact that it was a man and a woman, there was no way of identifying them.

'Now, take a look at this,' said Patrick and switched to a shot of three people walking along a corridor, towards another camera. Now the faces of Mehta's companions were clearly visible – a man in his thirties, clean-shaven, unremarkable, wearing a dark suit, and a woman with black spiked hair wearing a jerkin and combat trousers, who appeared to be walking with the aid of an elbow crutch.

Julian and Andy exploded in unison. 'Look! Jenna Dobrosova. That must be her!'

'And that's the crutch I spotted under her van,' added Julian. 'It has to be some kind of weapon.'

'Not a trigger mechanism?' asked Andy Fields.

'No chance,' replied Julian. 'She could hide a remote control device in her pocket. To risk carrying something as noticeable as a crutch, it must be the weapon itself. I wonder . . .' He looked thoughtful and headed off to another terminal.

All three men went quiet as Patrick flicked through more CCTV footage, looking to follow his targets through the terminal and outside. Nothing. He tried accessing the private lounges but each attempt brought up a "No Entry – confidential site" banner. In frustration, he switched to the VIP car park.

Julian turned to Andy and pointed to the shot that Patrick had frozen on one of the screens.

'Who's that guy, Andy?'

'No idea.' He leaned forward and held the slow motion key. The man's face inched past the camera, allowing them a clear view of his profile.

'Can you ask one of the resident technicians to come in, Julian? I'll need help sending a few close-ups to my database people. They should be able to track him down quickly.'

Minutes later, the pictures were on their way and the uniformed technician, a quietly competent woman in her late thirties, had left. But not before she had slowed, taken a long look at Julian, shivered, and smiled to herself.

'All clear?' asked Patrick, suppressing a grin.

'Yep,' answered Fields, with a long-suffering look. 'Why? What have you come up with now?'

On Patrick's screen, three people were climbing into a Range Rover. The licence plate was clearly visible. Andy jotted it down, walked to the far side of the room to make a call, and returned.

'We'll know where the car's registered in a couple of ticks.'

'While we're waiting,' Julian intervened, 'I've a theory about Jenna's crutch I'd like to share with you.'

The two other men burst out laughing.

'I presume you're talking about her elbow crutch,' spluttered Andy.

Julian looked rather hurt.

'I'm trying to be serious here,' he insisted, and the others recovered their composure.

'The first time we located the elbow crutch was when I spotted it under her van in London. And where had she just been earlier that day? Middlecroft Farm, the Chinese microwave research establishment in Buckinghamshire. So, when I saw her on screen just now, I started thinking. Patrick, do you remember that link I sent you from Jenna's flat? Take a look at this.'

He tapped a screen and a page headed "Active Denial System (ADS)" was displayed.

'I remember you sending me two links but I never got round to looking at this one. Sorry,' confessed Patrick.

'Apparently,' Julian continued, 'the US military experimented with a vehicle-mounted, non-lethal weapon for use in . . .' he read from the screen, ' . . .*area denial, perimeter security and crowd control.* In 2010, they wanted to use it in the Afghanistan war but . . .,' he read again, ' . . .*it was withdrawn without seeing combat.*

'It was also known as the Heat Ray, since *it works by heating the surface of targets, such as the skin of targeted humans.* It was only powerful enough to penetrate the skin surface. *"For the first millisecond, it just felt like your skin was warming up. Then it got warmer and warmer and you felt like it was on fire.... But as soon as you're away from that beam your skin returns to normal and there is no pain."*

'Remember, it was purely developed to control crowds and to stop people entering secure areas. So, gentlemen, any guesses what kind of energy the Heat Ray uses?'

'Microwave,' they both whispered.

'But didn't you say it was vehicle-mounted?' asked Andy Fields.

'Yes, at that time, it was. However, the Americans, as well as the Russians and the Chinese, are reliably reported to have been working on a portable version,' said Julian. He was now wearing what Patrick called his "Eureka face", his arms spread wide in triumph.

Fields' phone rang and he retreated again to the corner of the room, muttering.

Patrick had another question for Julian:

'Could you kill someone with a microwave?'

'Let me read you this,' Julian replied. 'Critics cite that, although the stated intent of the ADS is to be a non-lethal device designed to temporarily incapacitate, modifications or incorrect use by the operator could turn the ADS into a more damaging weapon that could violate international conventions on warfare. So, while the correct answer to your question, Patrick, is "I don't know", my guess is that, if the frequency is high enough, the truth is "probably". It could kill or, at least, severely maim a target victim.'

Andy Fields had finished his call.

'Well, well, well. That is interesting. The man with Jenna is on temporary attachment to Cabinet Office security. His name is John Ingleby.'

'On attachment?' said Patrick. 'Who does he work for?'

'Special Branch. VIP protection and counter terrorism unit.'

'So he's a copper, like you.'

'Yes. We're both responsible for national security. My lot, the Security Service, or MI5 as it's known, do the undercover work, while Special Branch make the arrests. We often work closely together but, thank God, as this operation is a Last Resort Squad job, they know nothing about it. Blanket security.

'Problem: this man Ingleby is working alongside Jenna Dobrosova. Let's assume he's not just an innocent spook following orders. So my question is this: if a relatively junior Special Branch Officer like Ingleby is in on the game, who else, further up the chain, are we looking for now?''

'And the Range Rover?' asked Julian.

'That's what makes it worse. They're using an authorised SO1 vehicle.'

'SO1?'

'The Specialist Protection Branch. It's part of the Metropolitan Police. Responsible for protecting current and former prime ministers and other government ministers. They also protect ambassadors, visiting dignitaries and others who are deemed to be under some kind of threat.'

'Somebody, or several somebodies, has been pulling strings on behalf of Jenna's controllers,' said Patrick.

'You haven't heard the best part yet,' said Fields, his face set grimly. 'We hacked the car's GPS signal and it appears they stopped off in Belgravia for half an hour before delivering Mr Mehta to The Savoy.'

'Where in Belgravia?'

'In one of my own department's fucking safe houses!'

In all the time he had known him, Patrick had only seen Andy Fields lose his temper once. It didn't last long but the effect on those within range had been devastating.

The Savoy Hotel, central London

For such a seasoned traveller, the way Vanmali Mehta had unpacked his cases and scattered his clothes, shoes and wash things around the bedroom floor was very odd. But his mind was elsewhere and his body was only just beginning to recover.

He had no recollection of the short trip from Belgravia to The Savoy; his last clear memory was of Richard Merriott asking the spiky-haired security officer if she would 'Help Mr Mehta relax'. What happened after that was a jumble of sensations, heat, pain and then . . . nothing.

He was seated in an armchair facing Merriott at the time. As he turned to look at the woman, he saw her raise her elbow crutch and point it in his direction. He could recall the back of his neck starting to feel warm, then an intense burning sensation, after which he assumed he must have blacked out.

The pain had gone now and, when he touched his neck, it felt fine. He just felt dizzy and confused. The air in the room felt stuffy too.

Sitting on the bed, he removed his jacket and rolled up his shirt sleeves. There was a tiny sticking plaster on his inner arm, the kind nurses used to cover the skin puncture after an injection. Mehta stared at it: he couldn't remember having an injection recently, but then he couldn't remember much at all. It was as if someone else had taken hold of his steering wheel.

The room phone was ringing. Irritated, he picked up the handset.

'Vanmali Mehta?' said a voice.

'Yes, who is it?'

'It's me, Vanmali. Your old friend Norman.'

'Norman? Norman who?'

'Sir Norman Tudway. You remember, Meg's husband.'

'Oh . . . yes. How are you, umm . . . Norman?' He was struggling to focus.

'I'm very well, thank you. I heard you were in London. So am I; just round the corner, as a matter of fact. Wondered if I might drop in and say hello. Sample a drop of that excellent single malt The Savoy put in their guest rooms. That's if you have the time, of course.'

'Ah, yes. Wait a minute, would you?'

With the sound of a friendly voice, his brain was beginning

to clear. He looked round the room, at the chaos, and spotted his electronic diary lying in a pile of socks on the floor. He bent down to retrieve it and almost toppled over. Grabbing the bed cover, he steadied himself and sat down again.

'What time is it now . . . err?' he said into the phone.

'Norman. It's almost eighteen hundred hours, old boy. Sun's slipping over the yard-arm and all that stuff.'

Mehta felt as though he should laugh. Something was telling him to laugh.

He could hear his own voice replying, strangely wooden. 'Well, I don't have to leave the hotel until seven-thirty – sorry, nineteen-thirty. So, if you don't mind me changing into something more suitable for a formal dinner, I would be delighted to see you. I'll have the glasses ready, umm.'

'Norman. Splendid. I'll make sure you're wearing matching socks and your tie's straight. But don't ask me to scrub your back. Haha. I'm on my way.'

The Savoy American Bar

'Who is Sir Norman Tudway?'

Jenna Dobrosova, alias Jules Dabrowski, now dressed in a simple black jacket and skirt, modest blouse and high heels, had remodelled her black hair and donned black heavy rimmed glasses. The elbow crutch had been stashed away in favour of a Gucci bag. She was every inch the successful executive, formidable and self-confident, expensive but tasteful, and the man in the other chair matched her well, although he was rather older.

'Tudway? Rings a bell,' he replied, his manner so relaxed that anyone glancing in his direction would never guess that how nervous he was feeling. Flicking at his phone, he had the answer in seconds.

'Here we are. Sir Norman Tudway GCB, former Chief of the Defence Staff. Now retired, living in the New Forest, with his wife of forty-five years, Meg. Two sons, three dogs . . .'

'Yes, thank you. I understand. Is he involved in anything, shall I say, official these days?'

He looked at his phone once more, tapped the screen a few

times and waited for it to react. 'Nothing listed on the government's private database, Miss Dabrowski. But he is chairman of the village flower show committee and, look here, he sponsors a local theatre group . . .'

Jenna was beginning to find the man irritating. This was the UK's most senior banker, the new head of the Basel Committee on Banking Supervision, appointed at the last minute after the prime candidate vanished from a train in North-West England, with a little help from Jenna Dobrosova. On first meeting, he had impressed her: the kind of man who would turn heads when he arrived in a room, radiating a very British style. Yet he was turning out to be as boring and pompous as most bankers, and he was blatantly checking out her hemline every minute or so. "All breeding, no brain", as she'd once heard someone say.

If he were ever to be exposed as one of China's key agents in the West, he would certainly need to be taken out of circulation.

Until now, his duties had been confined to passing on financial intelligence but Hong had insisted on her introducing him to Vanmali Mehta. It was to be a surprise visit but this damned man Tudway had sneaked in before them. So she smiled her patient smile and discreetly adjusted the invisible radio receiver in her right ear, and her skirt.

'Norman, how delightful to see you again.'

Mehta was wearing a bath-robe as he greeted Sir Norman at the door. His hair was wet.

The two men shook hands, exchanged greetings and embraced briefly.

'You look well, my friend,' said Mehta. 'Come in. The Scotch is over here.' The words were in the right order but the voice was quite flat.

Sir Norman stood back and watched as the habitually fit-looking Asian shuffled slowly across the room and poured whiskey into two tumblers. This was far from the Vanmali Mehta he remembered.

'Now tell me, how are your family?' Sir Norman took his glass, then turned, picked up a remote control and made a selection on the hotel iPod. In seconds, the room was filled with the sound of Sir Simon Rattle and the Berlin Philharmonic's rendition of Brahms' *Requiem*.

'One of my favourites, you know,' he said as he saw Mehta smile nervously. 'And yours too, I seem to remember.'

Mehta used a table to steady himself, pointing to an armchair. 'Come and sit over here. We don't have much time.'

Downstairs in the bar, Jenna tried one last time to distinguish the conversation through the blare of the music in the room upstairs and gave up. She decided to wait until Sir Norman left the hotel and have him followed.

Sir Norman left The Savoy by the same route he'd used to get in: via the service lift and out through a tiny rear entrance where Patrick was waiting with the engine running. The hotel's security officer, a man well accustomed to guests' cloak-and-dagger antics, handled things perfectly.

Juliana Dabrowski had watched the MI5 agents move in on the banker as she returned from the Ladies' room. The whole matter was over in a few seconds, with no fuss – she was impressed. Fortunately, she had a clear line of sight and her aim was true. No need for an elbow crutch this time: the button on her key fob sealed the man's fate, making the arrest swift and barely noticeable.

In her ear-piece the music had stopped and Mehta was humming to himself. No sign of Sir Norman Tudway: he had left the hotel by another door, she assumed. As she hailed her waiting cab, she was already running through a mental checklist of developments she would now have to report to Hong Jintao. On this occasion, she would give him her version of the facts.

The following morning, the press reported that Britain's most senior banker, the new Head of the Basel Committee on Banking Supervision, had resigned with immediate effect after receiving the results of a routine medical check. His interrogation by Andy Fields had lasted less than an hour before he collapsed in a deep coma.

CHAPTER 28

Hong Jintao had little choice. He had to report the arrest of one of China's most important agents to each of his masters, Guo Dalong and the President, before they heard of the banker's resignation on the newswires.

While his loss was certainly a blow to the People's Republic's growing influence over European financial affairs, they could all take some solace that the Dobrosova woman had the presence of mind to put him out of action quickly.

Under the strict rules of informer management, no one agent knew more than was absolutely necessary about the others. So, even if the British had managed to get anything useful from him before he collapsed, it would be of limited value.

Hong told Jenna to go as soon as she completed her report. He needed to be left alone to work on the text of the two messages. It was vital that his President didn't overreact to the news that the British authorities now knew enough to have identified and arrested one of their leading agents.

Hong would reassure him that none of their other moles, in particular Merriott the Locksmith and Sleeping Beauty, was under suspicion and that Mehta was now so severely compromised that he could be relied upon to do as he was told. The plan to dislocate the African countries from Britain should still go ahead; there was no need for the President to even consider implementing Plan B, the military option.

He turned to his keyboard and had just begun to type when an alert flashed up on the screen: an ancient Chinese hieroglyphic. Hong waited a second before deciding to accept the call. Guo Dalong was on the line.

Was it a coincidence that he should call right now or, if not, how had the old man learned about the events at The Savoy so quickly? Hong accepted the call. As usual, it was Harrison's face that appeared on the screen. Hong had never been quite sure about the taciturn Englishman. Loyal but lethal best described him.

'Good day, Harrison,' he said, in Mandarin.

'Good day, minister. I trust you are well and in good spirits.' Harrison began every conversation in this formal way, by showing respect for Hong's seniority.

'To what . . .?' Hong stopped in mid-sentence, guessing that Harrison had no intention of dragging out the niceties. He was right.

'My master is curious to know your views on recent events, minister.'

'Ah, yes . . .'

'In particular, he is anxious? yes, anxious to hear how you explain your failure to prevent the series of lapses in security.'

Hong reached for a handkerchief from his pocket and blew his nose, hoping the slight delay would conceal the sight of the blood draining from his face. In formal Chinese discussion, the word "failure", with its implications of ignominy, betrayal and dishonour, was rarely heard. Its use by Harrison could not be attributed to his limited Mandarin: this was Guo Dalong speaking.

Hong did his best to compose himself before returning his eyes to the screen. Harrison had gone and it was Guo Dalong himself who was now staring at him, seeming less world-weary than the last time he saw him, his expression enigmatic. On the occasions they had met, he had rarely looked directly at Hong, preferring to stare into the distance as he extemporised around whatever philosophical point he was making. Today his eyes were focused straight at the camera, right at Hong; and Hong felt the full force of the old man's innate power.

'Good day, Master,' he mumbled. Then, try as he might, as he proceeded to articulate the list of mitigating factors, those parts of the operation that were moving forward as planned, everything he said felt wholly inadequate the moment it left his mouth.

Guo's expression never changed: he just listened. Without uttering a word, he was making it perfectly clear that he had lost faith in Hong Jintao, his protégé. And that could only lead to one thing.

Hong thought he was prepared for this: he had already accepted the inevitability of his own demise, sooner or later. The British security services had got wind that an attack was being planned but he hoped that, by disposing of David Marksworth and the banker before they could be interrogated, he was still far enough ahead of them to pull off the final act. But he also knew that the established Chinese protocol in affairs of espionage ruled that any mistake which resulted in the loss of a key agent was to be punished. Hong had lost two. The right of reply did not apply in such cases.

Hong was a wealthy man; as he rose through the ranks, he had carefully accumulated sufficient capital to provide for himself in old age and for those family members who would need his support to live comfortably. Today, he was facing the sickening thought that, as a disgraced party official, his assets would almost certainly be confiscated after his death.

As if he was reading Hong's mind, Guo's expression finally changed to one of gentle sympathy.

'I have been giving the situation much thought, Hong Jintao,' he said. 'We are old friends, after all. As we both know, whatever you have been ordered to accomplish by that idiot of a President in Beijing, your mission from me is to bring about the disgrace of Britain and its arrogant "Establishment"' – he used the English word. 'If you succeed in achieving that, I will ensure that your reputation as a faithful servant of the state remains intact after . . .' He had no need to complete the sentence.

The journey from The Savoy to their rendezvous with Andy Fields and Julian at Scotland Yard was so short, it would have been quicker to walk. Patrick, realising that Sir Norman was in no mood for small talk, kept quiet. The guard waved the driver through to the underground car park and, minutes later, they were all seated in a small meeting room with no windows or telephones.

'Is this place secure?' Sir Norman asked Andy. 'No cameras or mikes?'

'I swept it myself, Sir Norman,' Fields replied.

'Right. We have a problem,' the old man announced, helping himself to water. 'I saw Vanmali Mehta as planned. We had not met in three years. The moment I walked in, I knew something was wrong. It was as though he was in a state of shock – physically and mentally, the man was all at sea, bewildered, unable to focus, a bundle of nerves.

'I was unsure how to approach him, to help him relax. Then, for some reason, don't ask me why, I remembered how much he loves the great choral classics. Fortunately, his hotel room has the same sound system as the one I used when I was staying there last month with my wife. We were guests at the opening night of some ghastly ballet or other - can't recall its name. Anyway, it worked: as soon as I found the right track, Brahms, and the music began, he started to calm down. I gave him a glass of Scotch and slowly, he began to talk.' He took a long sip of his water.

Patrick was feeling increasingly impatient. Looking at them, he could tell Julian and Andy too were wishing Sir Norman would come to the point.

'We have a problem,' you said. Come on. Let's have it, now, please.

But this was Sir Norman's way. He always liked things to be seen in their full context.

'We talked briefly about old times. Laughed, recalled people we both knew. Then Vanmali looked at his watch and stopped. "Norman, my dear friend," he said. "As I'm sure you've already noticed, I'm not feeling quite right. I'm so sorry."

'He then proceeded to tell me the story of how he had been picked up at Heathrow and driven to a house in central London. Naturally, I didn't reveal what I already knew. I asked him why he was telling me all this.

'"Because I thought you would like to know," he said, almost like a child. Who had he seen at the house, I asked. He only met one man. However, that's why we have a problem - the man he met, gentlemen, was a certain Richard Merriott.' His voice conveyed only too clearly the importance.

Andy Fields looked horrified. 'What? Richard Merriott? You mean the Prime Minister's watchdog?' Patrick was none the wiser.

'Precisely. His official title is Special Tactical Adviser but he is commonly known in government circles as Oddjob. This PM likes to have someone who can bang heads together, persuade people to toe the line for her, here or abroad, with the minimum of fuss and without any public involvement on her part, while she sails serenely onwards.'

'Excuse me, Sir Norman,' Julian piped up, 'What's so strange about a representative of the Prime Minister meeting the head of a Commonwealth delegation for an off-the-record chat?'

While Sir Norman peered at the young man over his glasses, Andy replied on his behalf. 'Except, Julian, that my watchers, the British Security Service's best, were told Mr Mehta would leave Heathrow by another route and . . .'

'His driver was Jenna Dobrosova,' added Patrick.

'Ah.' Julian looked sheepish. 'I really do have a lot to learn, don't I?'

'And, she was driving a Special Branch motor,' Fields added sourly.

'And,' Julian perked up, 'they met in one of your safe houses.'

'Without my . . . king knowledge,' Andy confirmed. 'I'm trying to get to the bottom of that one. I want to know who asked to use the house and who authorised it.'

Sir Norman held up one finger to silence the conversation.

'There are two other pieces of information of which I should make you all aware. Let me warn you that, if you disclose any of this outside this room, I shall see to it that some quite sensitive parts of your anatomy are removed, one by one, with a rusty knife.'

Patrick had never heard Sir Norman speak like that before. He had made a joke but his face was deadly serious.

Sir Norman cleared his throat. 'Firstly, I'm embarrassed to have to tell you that Richard Merriott was, for some time, a confidential associate of the Last Resort Squad.'

The silence lasted a full ten seconds. Julian stood and withdrew to a corner of the room to consult his tablet.

'What exactly do you mean by associate, Sir Norman?' asked Patrick.

'As a senior civil servant, he was excluded from full membership. Our whole *raison d'être* is that we are free to go beyond and behind official Downing Street lines. But, and this is where it gets damned tricky, over recent times, we have been consulting with him regularly. We held him in high regard. Not only does he know who I am, on occasion he has been privy to some of our more sensitive discussions.'

Patrick said, 'But, Sir Norman, you're assuming that Merriott is a traitor. We can't be sure yet, can we? He could have been duped into meeting Mehta.'

'I fear not. It seems the Chinese have even infiltrated my own group.' He looked desperately sad.

'Did anyone see you at The Savoy? Could you have been recognised?'

'I don't believe so. I used a back entrance when I arrived and when I left.'

Julian had reappeared. He placed his tablet on the table and pointed urgently at the screen, demanding attention. He spoke slowly:

'Richard Merriott was on assignment in Paris at precisely the time when we believe Gregory Bellingham and David Marksworth were recruited as agents for China.'

Patrick put his pen down and sat back. Sir Norman nodded, sighed, deep in thought.

Andy Fields left it a few seconds before saying, 'You told us there were two other things you wanted to talk about, sir.'

Sir Norman had apparently come to a conclusion. 'Yes. Vanmali Mehta didn't tell me much about their discussion. He was clearly unwell so what he said to me was quite muddled. All he kept repeating, over and over again, was that he had been offered a job – he couldn't remember what kind of a job - and how much he loved his family. Then he stopped, began to sob quietly, apologised and indicated that he would like me to leave, immediately.'

Julian broke the silence. 'Sir Norman, you described Mr Mehta earlier as a calm, well-balanced, immensely likeable man. In the hotel room this afternoon, however, he was confused, shaky and weepy – almost as if he was having a breakdown. Yes?'

'Yes, why?'

'Anything else you noticed? His eyes, for example?''

'Actually, I did notice his eyes looked quite strange. Pale, almost blank.'

Julian nodded. 'Patrick, do you recall the work I was doing in the lab on the early signs of dementia? That man Alistair Thomas, the politician who killed himself on the motorway. I showed you his brain scan, remember?'

'Yes, I do,' said Patrick. 'He had been perfectly normal earlier in the day but his brain scan after he crashed his car showed all the signs of active dementia. So?'

Julian had seemed to gain in stature. He was the authority now. He turned his tablet round so that everyone could see the screen.

'This is another shot from Alistair Thomas' file. Taken at the autopsy. How do these eyes compare with Vanmali Mehta's, Sir Norman?'

Sir Norman took a good look. 'Yes,' he said. 'Just like that. Really quite disturbing.'

Julian addressed the whole table. 'I've never seen anything remotely similar. It's almost as if both men, Vanmali Mehta and the man widely tipped to be our next Prime Minister, were "got at" by the same people in the same way.'

CHAPTER 29

Back in her apartment, it was time for Jenna to run a check over her equipment. She was well into the final twenty-four hours and everything had to undergo its last thorough examination. With the exception of the microwave "crutch", each piece had been tested in action on several occasions, so the routine was familiar.

Her newest weapon had come through its final trial run well. Not quite its ultimate challenge – so far she had not used microwaves to kill – but the power level she had selected had proved to be just enough to weaken Vanmali Mehta's defences and to allow the hypnotic messages to be implanted in his subconscious. She felt confident that, when the moment arrived for her to destroy a target, it would not let her down.

What continued to amaze her was why it had taken so long for the tech people to realise the full potential of a range of weapons, silent, lightweight, infinitely adjustable and very concealable, using microwave power. After all, it had been around since the Second World War. The people at Middlecroft Farm had done their best to explain how the development of the appropriate delivery module was a highly complex task but she had switched off halfway through the presentation. To her, it just seemed such a simple, obvious piece of technology.

A thought drifted into her mind as she examined her other weapons for the second time that evening:

If I'm right, and it is so simple, why has nobody else developed this kind of weapon? Or have they?

There was little point in worrying about that now. She needed to concentrate on committing the layout of Lancaster House and the surrounding streets to memory before setting off for Belgravia.

Two hours later

The Dorchester Hotel in Park Lane is known as one of the most secure in London, hosting regular conferences and dinners for "the Great and the Good". It is also handily situated within a short walk, or at most a ten minute drive, from most of the foreign embassies and high commissions in London.

In deference to the age of many of those attending and the long journeys they had all undertaken that day, dinner for the Presidents of the African Commonwealth delegation countries had been relatively brief and simple. The media had been asked to stay away, enabling the guests to dress more casually on this occasion and, as coffee was served, the atmosphere was relaxed and friendly. While they always appeared fiercely patriotic and competitive on television, these men had the wisdom to recognise that, as Africa's economic power grew, there was much to be gained from quietly working together, in partnership, and close personal friendships had been forged.

Vanmali Mehta, as group co-ordinator, had been assured by the hotel's security team that the room had been swept for bugs and that everyone could speak freely once the serving staff had left.

He tapped gently on his glass with his cheese knife, calling the group to order.

'Gentlemen, your Excellencies, I trust you have eaten well. I know you are all keen to get back to your high commission and to whatever comforts await you in the presidential bedroom . . .' He paused until the laughter had died down.

Mehta coughed and hesitated while he caught his breath. 'So I won't keep you long, long, long . . .' He gripped the table edge as a wave of giddiness swept through him.

'My apologies, a touch of London flu, perhaps.' He smiled weakly and continued, staring straight ahead at a point on the far wall.

'We should remind ourselves that, together, your countries account for over fifty percent of the economy of the Commonwealth's African bloc. And that strength grows every year as your global trade increases. You can no longer be called developing countries; you all have real power these days.'

The murmur of agreement assured him that he had their attention.

'So I am delighted to inform you that tomorrow, following a slight change of plan, you are going to have the opportunity to use that power to change history.'

Mehta was feeling happier now; he seemed to have recovered his composure. Although he felt detached, floating, looking down on himself and the rest of the group from above, he was enjoying the ride: this was fun - he was heading in the right direction, but someone else was doing the driving.

He didn't know it but his voice sounded as if he was reading from a script. The Africans had begun to look at each other, shifting uncomfortably in their seats.

'Mr Mehta, are you . . .?' one of the more senior Presidents interjected. But Mehta continued as if he hadn't heard. Reaching for a folder, he withdrew a small sheaf of papers and passed one sheet to each President. It only took seconds before the mumbling started.

'Tonight . . .' Mehta needed to raise his voice now. 'Tonight, I ask you all to memorise this statement, which I shall read out on your behalf when I address Britain's Prime Minister and the monarch's representative, the Prince of Wales, at Lancaster House tomorrow.'

'What the hell is this all about, Mehta?' The speaker slammed his paper on the table.

'We know nothing about this! Have you gone mad?' exclaimed another.

Mehta continued his monotone discourse through a growing storm of protest. 'As you can see, with effect from tomorrow, the world will at last know the despicable truth about the British Empire; each of your countries will finally be liberated from the indignities of your colonial subjugation, from the vile rape of your land and your women. You will be able to hold your heads aloft with pride, not just among your own people, but all around the world, as the champions of a new African freedom.

'And,' his voice changed tone, 'you will be free, free to make new alliances, but this time, not with yesterday's tyrants but with the truly great powers of today.' He was unstoppable now.

'You will take the lead, giving all the other former colonies the confidence to throw off the stigma of so-called benign British imperialism . . .'

Men were standing now, waving their arms and thumping the table.

Mehta's final words were lost in the din. He flopped back in his chair, exhausted, but oblivious to the mayhem in the room.

For the paper they were all reading bore no heading, no signature, no provenance, no supporting evidence.

The text was simple but devastating: it simply informed the British monarchy and its government that,

" . . . in view of our recent discovery of a number of incriminating files, which you, the British monarchy and government, have kept hidden for years, without our knowledge or permission, we regret to inform you that we, the undersigned, are compelled to withdraw our nations from all trading, financial, diplomatic, and cultural arrangements with the United Kingdom monarchy, its government and its banking system, together with the Commonwealth of Nations, with immediate effect."

'A summary of the contents of these files, together with lengthy extracts, will be distributed to the media shortly after I speak,' Mehta muttered but nobody was listening. He threw a thick dossier on the table.

Mehta took a series of deep breaths, knowing he had one more important duty to perform. He sat forward and reached for a second folder.

'I would also draw your attention to this second document,' he said, in the same monotone voice. He pushed a sealed envelope towards each President and waited.

'While I feel sure that you will all welcome the statement and realise the enormous benefits of lending your support, for the avoidance of doubt, the document before you spells out, in the simplest of terms, the consequences for you, your family, and for your nation if any of you should choose, foolishly, not to lend the statement your unequivocal support.'

The shouting had stopped. The gasps around the table were a clear indication of how the second paper was being received. For, in addition to phrases such as "support for armed insurrection", "revolution", and "summary execution", each one contained an individual list showing precise details of that particular President's overseas "investments", his sexual indiscretions and the more sensitive details of his medical record.

In the house in Belgravia, two people stood up and took a breather.

It had been a tense time as the almost undetectable bug that Jenna Dobrosova had planted earlier in Vanmali Mehta's elbow relayed the "discussion" from the Dorchester.

Jenna had left the listening to Richard Merriott. After all, it was he who had orchestrated the removal of the necessary files from the so-called "Migrated" section of the National Archives at Kew in South-West London. Until a national newspaper had leaked news of their existence in 2014, twenty thousand files, relating to thirty-seven former British colonies, all deemed too embarrassing for public consumption, but only a tiny proportion of a much larger hoard of documents, had been secretly, and illegally, stored in a country house outside London while successive UK governments strenuously denied that anything of that nature existed.

Once discovery of the files had been exposed, they had all been moved to the National Archive, where access was again strictly controlled. Anything labelled "Extremely sensitive material: not for public disclosure" required the highest security clearance. Richard Merriott, as a member of the Prime Minister's closest staff, had that clearance. Copying the files had been straightforward; reading the contents took much longer. For even Merriott, a seasoned double agent, had been appalled by much of what he read.

In addition to confirmation of stories and rumours that had been circulating for years, here was enough documented evidence to incriminate, for the first time, hundreds of named members of former British governments, colonial authorities and the armed forces in assassinations, massacres, torture, embezzlement and worse. Merriott recognised many of the names: former ministers, members of Britain's aristocratic families, chairmen of large corporations. Those who were still alive were almost all members of that most exclusive club - the British Establishment.

All that was needed was a little judicious doctoring, adding a name here, exaggerating the truth there, and the bombshell that would blow away every vestige of Britain's reputation was primed.

Merriott turned to Jenna. 'I think that went rather well. For a novice, Mehta did a remarkable job. Oh, I know it wasn't really him speaking but . . .'

'I agree. Mr Merriott, should I contact Hong Jintao now? I know he's anxious for an update.'

'Yes, get him on the phone. You know which parts to leave out, don't you?'

They both knew who their ultimate masters were. Hong Jintao was not among them.

CHAPTER 30

Patrick and Julian were on their way. Their instructions from Sir Norman and Andy Fields were crystal clear:

'Do whatever it takes to find out exactly what they are up to and intercept it, with a minimum of collateral damage.'

'You mean physical damage?' Patrick had asked.

'Any kind of damage,' Sir Norman had been quite firm. 'It would be better for all concerned if the public hear nothing. Life must be seen to go on in its own sweet way, unruffled, *status quo intactus*. Do we understand one another, Patrick?'

'We'll do our best, sir.'

'That's all I ask. Go with my good wishes, chaps. Your country relies on you.' He shook hands with both of them.

Patrick knew why Sir Norman winked at him as he left the room. His Churchillian "frightfully British" script had been for Julian's benefit.

Julian was now en route back to the lab in Oxford, on his high-powered bike. He'd persuaded Patrick he needed swift access to his own IT set-up for what he needed to create.

Patrick decided to check out the safe house. There was no sign of life: only one security light over the front door and no response when he remotely accessed the alarm system. Inside, it was immediately apparent that Merriott and Dobrosova had "spring-cleaned" the place before they left.

As he was closing up, Andy Fields called.

'I've established that Merriott simply pulled rank when he commandeered the Range Rover from SO1: the desk officer leapt into action as soon as he heard the magic words "Downing Street". Now for the bad news: as for who let Merriott use one of my safe houses, according to the records, it was a call from one of my people to central bookings desk. The caller used the correct security passwords, sounded completely genuine.'

'And?'

'And that agent died from a sudden heart attack six weeks ago. I went to the poor bloke's funeral. They used the oldest trick in the book. And we bloody well fell for it.'

'How come he was still on the database?'

'Have you ever tried getting your name removed from a government file, Patrick?'

'Point taken. Hey, any luck with John Ingleby, the Special Branch guy who met Mehta at Heathrow with Jenna D?'

'Disappeared. Hasn't been seen since he left the safe house. My guess is they've squirreled him away out of sight, now that he's done his dirty work.'

'So we stick with the strategy we agreed with Sir Norman. He keeps out of the way in case Merriott is tracking him, and I go underground, with Julian's help.'

Fields interrupted. 'Patrick. A question. Does the name Sleeping Beauty mean anything to you?'

'Only the old fairy tale. Why?'

'A message has just been forwarded to me from our watchers at GCHQ. Strictly off the record, these people monitor certain Internet traffic, including some, but not all, of the Chinese London embassy's communications to and from Beijing. Most of it's routine stuff but they've sent this one on to me in case I could understand it. They thought it was a bit odd.'

'What does it say?'

'"Sleeping Beauty reactivation authorised."'

'Doesn't mean a thing to me. What do you think? Who was it addressed to?'

'Hong Jintao.'

'But they would never send anything sensitive over an unencrypted channel, surely.'

'I didn't say the channel was unencrypted, did I? Anyway, we all make mistakes, Patrick. If I told you how often people press the wrong key here, you'd be horrified.'

'Ah, I see. So where does that take us?'

'I'm still not convinced that Merriott's their top dog in London. Someone else sent him in to deal with Vanmali Mehta. I've met Merriott – he's a doer, not a top flight strategic thinker.'

'And Sleeping Beauty?'

'I'm paid to think the unthinkable, aren't I? Hold on a second,' said Fields.

Patrick waited. He heard a voice. He couldn't be sure if it was a man or a woman.

'Commissioner Fields?'

Andy replied, 'Yes? Look, I'm rather tied up. Wait outside, would you mind?'

'Sorry about this, sir.'

'Oh, sweet Jesus.' Andy's voice again.

Patrick listened in horror to the unmistakeable sounds of a man crashing off his chair, struggling to escape his attacker, then gasping his final words on this Earth as he gradually choked to death. The phone went dead.

Patrick sat in his car, his beloved classic MGB, unable to move. He'd just heard one of his closest friends, a man with whom he'd gone to hell and back any number of times, die. He felt helpless, hopeless, angry, sad, confused.

What to do now? A hundred thoughts raced through his mind as he gripped the wheel, shouting, swearing at the world.

Instinctively, he started the engine. At that very moment a black car swept into the mews, lights blazing and headed towards him at speed. A hundred yards away, Patrick slammed his car into gear, released the clutch and felt the tyres gain a grip on the cobbles.

Thanking his stars that he had reversed into the parking space, he saw he had a clear straight run to the far end of the street. Except that the exit onto the main road was a former porter's gate, wide enough for a handcart but hardly enough for an MGB – in fact, as he crashed out into the street, minus one wing mirror, not wide enough at all.

As he swung in front of a delivery truck, ignoring the loud blast on the horn, he began to think clearly again. Whoever had assassinated Andy Fields must have monitored their phone call. That was how these people had found him so quickly.

He zigzagged through a dozen residential streets before finding a quiet place to park. Jumping out, he slammed the door, paused to look at the car's wrecked wing and ran towards the nearest shopping street. It was a risk in the bright street lights but he had to dump the phone fast. He stopped, managed to remove the SIM card and dropped it into a roadside drain.

He knew many shops stayed open late in this part of London, manned by entrepreneurial Asian families. Within a couple of minutes, he spotted a typical general store and walked in.

'Good evening, sir,' said the smiling owner, a man in his forties, dressed in a loud, cheerful tropical shirt. 'What can I do for you?'

'My SIM card's packed up,' he said, waving the handset. 'Any chance you could let me have a new one, if I give you the number?'

'I can't do that, sir. Against the law. You'll have to have a new number.'

Patrick looked at him, fished his wallet out of his jacket and waved his Security Service ID at the man.

'Ah, I've just remembered. I've taken delivery of a new kind of SIM card that you can programme yourself,' said the shop-keeper, smiling, as he reached under the counter. 'Rather expensive, I'm afraid, the very latest thing, though.'

Patrick forced a smile and sighed. 'OK, let's get on with it. Here's the number, I'll be back in five minutes. I'll pay you for your time, of course.'

'Delighted to be of service, sir.'

At the shop door, Patrick paused and checked the street before slipping outside.

A small non-conformist chapel was tucked between two banks of shops. Patrick entered the tiny garden and began to study the notices pinned to the door. Just in time, as three large men in suits were making their way along the street behind him, checking every shop and alleyway.

He held his breath, dropped to his knees and began to pray as they approached the chapel. They hurried straight past and continued on down the street.

Five minutes later, armed with a working phone that now carried his emergency number, and more than a hundred pounds short on his expenses float, he was on his way, this time in a faceless taxi.

He made two calls – first to the phone company to have his old SIM card wiped and the number blocked and then to Sir Norman to give him the news about Andy Fields and to relay the contents of their final conversation. He tried to control his emotions but, by the end, he was almost sobbing. Images of Andy's face were kaleidoscoping through his brain - Andy friendly, Andy angry, Andy brave, Andy nervous, Andy human.

The veteran head of the Last Resort Squad was remarkably calm. Once Patrick had finished speaking, he stayed thoughtfully silent for a few moments and then said,

'Sleeping Beauty? A person or a plan, I wonder? Could it be a woman?' He was thinking aloud. 'I was going to have Merriott arrested and interrogated but this news has made me change my mind. I need to contact a few people I can trust first. I'll be in touch.' They agreed quickly on Patrick's next moves. Sir Norman gave him an address which Patrick passed on to the cab driver.

'Change of plan, my friend,' he said cheerily. 'Wife's changed her mind. Bloody women.'

The driver laughed and launched into a lengthy tale of a friend whose wife had decided she'd rather go to Clacton-on-Sea just as they were about to board a flight to Barbados.

'True story, as I live and breathe, mate.'

Patrick wasn't listening. He was thinking about Andy Fields.

For Jenna Dobrosova, an early night meant bed, alone, before two a.m. She was having an early night. The rooms Merriott had found for her included a luxurious bath and she was taking full advantage. Lying in the sea of bubbles, she allowed her mind to wander. She always felt horny lying naked in warm soapy water; she'd shared so many baths with quite delightfully sexy men and women over the years.

It helped her erase the evil thrill of disposing of that police Commissioner. It had taken all her ingenuity to gain access to the building, dressed as a tea lady. She knew where to find his office – the plans had been forwarded to her and memorised.

It was a pity she hadn't been able to use her new toy again but a tea lady on crutches was a touch too memorable. Still, the old rope trick had worked for her once again. By the time she left, it was a perfectly plausible suicide scene.

Tonight, her sexual filing system had selected that young man from the other day – what was his name? Sebastian? Julian?

Oh, yes. He was a natural. How could one so young know so much, know exactly where and how hard I like it? I wonder where he is now.

He was approaching the outskirts of London on an empty motorway, his destination the address Sir Norman had given him over the phone, his "special" phone, newly adapted, tucked away in his jacket. If he was called upon, Julian was confident that he had mastered the technology well enough to handle the situation.

At eight next morning, two men emerged from a door in West London: a man in his sixties, the image of the "ancient retainer", white cropped hair, dressed in a black suit, black tie, white shirt and highly polished shoes, and a tall, slim younger man, a natural exhibitionist by the look of him, just a few notches short of outrageous, with a simply *gorgeous* haircut.

Patrick and Julian were dressed to kill, or rather to prevent a killing.

CHAPTER 31

Sir Norman Tudway knew it was time to get a grip on himself.

As early as his student days, he had learned hard lessons about the value of self-awareness, about recognising his own weaknesses. A lively, impulsive lad with an acute sense of fun, he'd attracted attention and made friends easily but, among those friends, he'd found himself involved with some of the less scrupulous elements that hung around the student bars.

Fortunately, when the police and the university authorities broke up the drug ring, they took the lenient view of Norman's lack of judgement and he had escaped severe punishment.

Compulsory National Service conscription at the age of seventeen had been abolished at the end of 1960, so Norman missed it by a whisker. But joining the military had always been in his blood. When the RAF signed him up as a junior officer, the camaraderie he discovered there presented further opportunities for getting into trouble but the rigorous military training regime and the service's strict code of values instilled a newfound ability to spot the warning signs and pull back before he bumped up against the walls of authority. Not always, but most of the time.

Within a few months, Flying Officer Tudway was flying helicopter missions in the Malaysian conflict, demonstrating outstanding self-discipline to his fellow pilots and earning him swift promotion to the rank of Squadron Leader. His senior officers recognised that here was a talent for leading by example while making everyone else feel valued, and comforting those who found the stress of warfare hard to take.

In private, he too suffered periods when the weariness, loneliness – by now he had married Meg and become a father – and anguish at seeing so many body bags sent home became almost too much to bear. Until a colleague confided in him, it never occurred to Norman how much his inability to entirely conceal his pain endeared him to his men. They all felt they knew Norman the human being as much as Norman the officer – they were all in this together.

By the time of the Falklands war, about which he had mixed feelings, his leadership qualities had led to a rapid rise through the senior ranks. Later, it was he who supervised the establishment of the RAF Leadership Centre and drove the beginnings of a whole new culture in the service.

And yet, despite his widely praised ability to judge people, he had utterly failed to spot that Richard Merriott was a traitor. And now, his failure to act sooner had contributed to the death of one of the security services' most able officers, not just a trusted colleague – a friend.

True, his fellow members of the Last Resort Squad had backed his every decision and none of them had ever questioned Merriott's loyalty either, but Sir Norman still felt a deep sense of mortification. He had let his country and his friend down.

But now, he had to pull himself together.

Get a grip, man. Andy Fields has gone. Nothing you can do about that. Your job is to save your country. Get on with it.

Meg had gone out for the day, sensing her husband's need to be left alone. Sir Norman picked up the list he had made earlier and embarked on a series of phone calls.

In his hotel room, Vanmali Mehta opened the file for the third time and began to read. He knew the report's summary and its key conclusions by heart; he was certain he could quote the important passages from memory as and when he was called upon to do so. The language the author used was formal, dispassionate: not so much the case for the prosecution, more the judge's verdict – guilty on all counts.

Merriott had marked the pages that covered each grisly episode with adhesive tabs. Mehta flipped to one at random. It concerned a detention camp in Kenya during the Mau Mau uprising of the 1950's – the militant rebellion culminating years of oppressive colonial rule. Following a series of violent attacks on settlers, more than three hundred thousand tribesmen were transported and imprisoned in appalling conditions. The camps were often manned by white settlers who had been conscripted into the British forces and there were those who sought revenge. Many thousands died from illness, starvation, systematic torture, or the brutality of the camp guards. Still more were murdered by their own people, suspected of spying for the British.

Up to that point, there was nothing new about this report. In 2012, the UK government had admitted that they had been concealing many incriminating files on the Mau Mau uprising. What was entirely new was the devastating evidence of the complicity of 10 Downing Street, the ruling political party's grandees and the heads of several of Britain's wealthy aristocratic families. Some had only been kept informed, some had explicitly authorised, while others had actually taken part in the atrocities.

Mehta reread the footnote:

Paragraphs 23 to 30 are summaries of files contained in the thirteen boxes of documents related to this subject, the existence of which the Government still chooses to deny.

He could not have known that these paragraphs were entirely the work of Richard Merriott – pure fiction.

Mehta stood and walked to the window. Far below, the river Thames, London's serene focal point, witness to countless political crises over the years, flowed past as if this was just another day. The television in the room was showing the BBC's twenty-four hour news channel – no mention of the Commonwealth leaders' visit, no inkling of the storm that was about to break.

Ever since meeting Merriott in the house in Belgravia, he had felt different. For years, he had become accustomed to success, in business and, more recently, working behind the diplomatic scenes. But today he felt utterly convinced of his own invulnerability, his right to overcome the fiercest foe, and his certainty that he was on God's side, the chosen agent of profound global change, sent to release the afflicted from captivity. It was a wonderful sense of impending glory.

And yet, at the same time, there was something very faint at the back of his mind: something worrying. He couldn't quite recall what it was: did it concern his family?

He'd had a strange dream in the night – there he was, franticly searching, in a dense jungle, for his wife and children. He could hear their voices. They had to be somewhere close by but every turn he took only led him further from their cries. Then, suddenly, they were all standing there in front of him, covered in mud, dressed in rags, shrieking. But they were not calling to him for help – they were shouting at him, telling him to go away, to get out of their sight, hatred burning in their eyes.

Mehta shrugged the images away; it was only a dream, after all. Whatever it was that was worrying him could not be so important, otherwise he'd have remembered. He turned back to the desk and picked up the phone.

Within a minute, he was talking with his wife. She sounded perfectly happy, relating a funny story about a friend's dog and some local news, before checking when he expected to be home again.

Before signing off, she said,

'Are you alright, darling?'

'Fine, thanks. Never better. Why do you ask?'

'Oh, nothing. You sound a bit odd, that's all.'

'It's probably a bad line.'

She didn't sound convinced.

He looked at his watch. He needed to gather his things together, put on a tie and go downstairs to meet the presidents for one final meeting before they headed off to Lancaster House.

Lancaster House, London

With only a couple of hours remaining before the guests arrived, members of staff were working flat out, directing the catering and broadcast crews with calm efficiency.

In the main hall, a long top table, dressed with name-plates and microphones, a chair bearing the Prince's coat of arms positioned at its centre, faced seating for more than a hundred guests and journalists. After the official welcome, exchange of formal gifts and speeches, lunch would be taken in the dining room next door.

The conference that followed would be in a room upstairs. It would begin that afternoon and continue for a further day.

All that was needed now was the arrival of the flowers for the tables, a couple of sound checks, and the final inspection by the Lancaster House chief steward, the Under-Secretary of State for African Affairs, and the Prince of Wales' private secretary.

Patrick Cameron stood quietly against a wall. His elderly appearance and demeanour explained why he was not involved with other duties, leaving him free to watch and memorise everything he saw; there was no shortage of younger, more agile staff to cope with the final tasks.

The same function management firm, whose owner was a good friend of Sir Norman, was regularly brought in to handle occasions like these. They knew the score so well, they were almost an automatic choice. It was not unheard of for a "new" man or woman to be inserted into the team working on any particular event. Nobody questioned who Patrick was – they simply assumed, as usual, that he had something to do with security.

So far, he'd spotted nothing suspicious but he was certain it was close. Somewhere, someone, here or not far away, was preparing to strike.

The noise in the kitchen was deafening: pans, bowls and dishes being moved on and off stainless steel worktops, a stream of orders and encouragement from the senior chefs.

In one corner, a group of waiters were giving a final polish to each pile of bone china plates as they arrived from the store room en route to the warming ovens. Julian had plenty of experience of this kind of work from his student days.

When he met his fellow waiters earlier, he soon realised why Sir Norman's people had chosen that particular way to alter his appearance. Doing his best to stay in character, he kept up with the steady stream of cheerful banter, adding an occasional "Ooh, really", "Over to you, dear", or "That's for me to know and you to find out".

Every minute or so, as he moved aside to collect the next batch, he would scratch his shoulder to activate his hidden camera phone. Before long, he would have picked up the face of every member of the kitchen staff and transmitted it automatically for checking against the national security database.

Would he be able to spot Jenna Dobrosova? Last time he'd seen her, she was very recognisable. Spiked hair, heavy make-up. That would surely be rather too noticeable in the hallowed grandeur of Lancaster House.

He smiled to himself, recalling the events of the other night in her flat. *There's one certain way of recognising her. There's no way she could hide that tattoo.*

He polished yet another plate, placed it on the appropriate pile and checked once again for new arrivals.

Richard Merriott was surprised at how calm he felt. After so many years of waiting, playing the game, building his network, as he was asked to take on more and more responsibilities for the British state, he had become accomplished at leading a double life.

He had never settled down with a long-term partner: too many risks, one layer of deception too many. The few affairs he had allowed himself had sufficed. In the community he frequented after dark, none of the men were interested in relationships, content to conduct a libidinous private lifestyle that belied their respectable public image. He had made a number of friends without ever sharing with them his hatred of Western society, his determination to destroy all that they held dear.

That was all about to come to an end. In a matter of hours, his life's work would be fulfilled. At last.

Everything was in place. Mehta was fully briefed, his brain programmed to do China's bidding. If he stepped out of line, his deep fear of losing his family would be reactivated. The Dobrosova woman and her weapon had been successfully embedded. And Sleeping Beauty, the star turn, would be brilliant, he had no doubt.

He, Merriott would follow the Prime Minister to Lancaster House in one of the back-up vehicles, as part of her entourage. That would place him in the ideal position to see and control everything that happened.

Within a few days, he would be relaxing in a villa in China, one of those reserved for Western heroes of the People's Republic, as he had been promised.

Sleeping Beauty, however, would remain in place. Merriott was finally about to pass the baton to the most important member of the team.

CHAPTER 32

'Excuse me, Prime Minister.'

'Yes, Richard? How can I help you?'

'You should be preparing for the Commonwealth leaders' reception, ma'am. We leave in ninety minutes' time.'

Jane Beaumont smiled.

'Don't alarm yourself, Richard. I won't have much to say there. His Royal Highness and that man Mehta will be doing most of the talking. I'll just smile sweetly, shake lots of hands and say a few words of welcome. Thanks for getting me out of the lunch, by the way. What excuse did you invent for my absence?'

'An urgent telephone call from the US President, madam. He asks for your advice more and more, so I'm told.' It was Merriott's turn to smile. 'But I gather the news of your absence was not well received.'

She sighed. 'On top of which we told them the Foreign Secretary would be chairing their meeting this afternoon rather than myself?'

'Precisely.'

'Well, Richard, we both know the real reason, don't we? Anything else?'

'Only that I understand the director of the National Archive has been trying to get a message to you. Something about a breach of security concerning some old files. Seems the old boy is in a bit of a state.'

'I presume you told him he'll have to wait,' she said firmly. 'We have bigger fish to fry.'

Merriott nodded, turned and left the office. Jane Beaumont swung her chair round to face the window.

Unlike most Prime Ministers, she was not a career politician, thanks to her predecessor's Act of Parliament declaring that senior government ministers no longer had to be current Members of Parliament.

Like many before him, he had become exasperated by the dearth of MPs who had ever done what the public called "a proper job"; far too many, including the PM himself, were professional politicians, products of the party's "central casting" recruitment programme: spotted at university, hired as parliamentary researchers, then injected into a safe constituency. All highly presentable and good speakers but without a grain of experience of the world of hard knocks.

His new bill, following the US government's example, allowed him to seek out the best person for the job, from business, public affairs or academia, which made good sense to the modernisers but drew predictable howls of outrage from traditionalists and MPs alike. It was passed by the slimmest of margins.

In Jane Beaumont's case, her credentials had been brought to his attention by a leading management consultancy. After gaining a First at Oxford, they had snapped her up to join the firm. On her return, she gained her MBA at INSEAD and was posted to their Asian operations to complete her training.

Her success when she was drafted in by the government to rescue a UK-based emergency aid agency brought her to Downing Street's attention. After copious discussions, the Prime Minister had appointed her to head up the struggling Ministry for Women, where her strategic ability and negotiation skills had been spotted by the media. Late night talk shows and televised political debates placed her in the public eye.

A leadership election in mid-term was almost unprecedented for a party in government, but became the inevitable consequence of the Prime Minister's inability to command the respect of the people, the media or even his own Cabinet. Jane, by now an MP of barely a year's standing, was seen as a refreshing, if quite unexpected candidate for the top job. Her backers knew they were taking a risk putting forward someone with such limited experience of the harsh world of politics and it required a considerable effort to sell her to the media. She was no Thatcher but her intelligence and easy charm eventually won them over.

So far, she had proved a success. Some of her decisions had been a little puzzling but she had always managed to couch them in ways that earned her increasingly positive approval ratings from the public.

Looking down on the garden, bright with fresh spring colours after a night of rain, she realised how tired she was. At home, she was finding the strain of selecting the few topics she could safely discuss with her husband more wearing than before. An accomplished author and counsellor, he was becoming quite concerned about her stress levels.

She closed her eyes and allowed her mind to embark onto the gentle ocean of meditation that had been her daily routine for as long as she could recall.

On this particular day, she needed to take herself back to days gone by, to experiences that became the catalyst for her life's journey; and to the extraordinary people who had selected her, inspired her with their wisdom, enhanced her education and brought her to the attention of the country's ruling elite.

They were older now but their continued support was still vital - a constant reassurance in her moments of self-doubt or fear.

She was going to need their help again.

Hong Jintao had not slept well. At 5am he was awake, drinking tea, before kneeling by the bed to pray. If this day were to signal the end of his career, his freedom or possibly his life, he needed to be sure that his God was at his side.

He had always thought of himself as a decent, loyal man. True, he had done things of which the Lord would disapprove but they were all for honourable reasons.

It was he, Hong Jintao, who recruited David Markswort‍h and Gregory Bellingham to become traitors to their motherland; it was he who created the Locksmith and Sleeping Beauty, both of whom would now be instrumental in wrecking their nation's future; it was he who had authorised the killing of Bellingham, Marksworth and the policeman Fields; and the use of hypnotic drugs on Vanmali Mehta. But, he thought to himself, everyone, including God, would surely understand that he had just been fulfilling his duties – duties to those in the highest authority.

The duty to prise a clutch of African nations from the Commonwealth family so that his own nation, China, would be spared an industrial and economic crisis of epic proportions, placed upon him by no less an authority than his President.

The duty to deliver the plan safely – avoiding a disastrous military conflict – Hong had placed upon himself, for humanitarian reasons, knowing that his God would approve.

Hiring Jenna Dobrosova, supervising her "removal" of the media watchdog on the French beach, the banker on the train and the corruption-buster on Clapham Common, and equipping her with the latest microwave weaponry had all been justifiable. He had to demonstrate to his President that he could be tough when needed. More recently, she had also been useful in disposing of David Marksworth and the banker at The Savoy but today she would not be required. Surely not.

As to his own fate, Guo Dalong had assured him that he would look kindly on the errors he had made along the way.

At least, that's the way I read what he said. And all that talk in the oath of brotherhood in Paris about everyone dying on the same day was just a bit of Chinese mumbo-jumbo, designed to impress Bellingham and Marksworth, wasn't it?

It had been relatively easy, courtesy of a bogus message from Beijing, to ensure the Chinese ambassador to London would be "indisposed" and that Hong would take his place with the other senior ambassadors at Lancaster House.

He looked at his watch. There was just time to check his mail before leaving.

Lancaster House was ready. Patrick Cameron, holding station against the far wall, watched as the final vase of flowers was positioned and arranged on a pedestal close to the top table.

In the last hour, the room had become a television studio: microphones, lights and cameras set in place, tested and approved by the BBC director for the day. A reception for a few African heads of state would hardly be riveting news that evening, but the same meticulous attention to detail had been applied as for any headline event.

Cameron's attention was on the people. The technicians, sound engineers and cameramen all appeared to know each other well, running through their regular routine, working smoothly as a team. A security detail, led by a man Patrick knew, one of Andy Fields' top operatives, had completed their sweep of the room and retired to the wings. Nobody noticed the leader's gentle nod in Patrick's direction as he left the room.

Sleeping Beauty activated. Time had run out. Patrick knew he had to solve this riddle in the next few minutes. Who or what was Sleeping Beauty? Assuming it was a person, was it Jenna Dobrosova? And, if so, where was she now, the mistress of disguise, the coolest of killers?

And who was her intended target? An African President? The Prime Minister? Cameron had run through the possibilities time and again and was still none the wiser.

Why would they want to kill one of these dignitaries? What on earth was their motive? What would it achieve?

If she was planning to employ her elbow crutch as a weapon today, that would surely be far too conspicuous. So why was she carrying it?

He could have arrested her and Merriott on several occasions, but Sir Norman had insisted on holding back: it was essential to unearth the final link in the Chinese spy chain, the ultimate traitor, he said. And Patrick accepted he was right. Now he was starting to believe this was a risk too far. As each hour passed, the likelihood of preventing the plot from reaching a horrific conclusion was diminishing.

The heavy brigade arrived together, each flanked by a young, immaculately dressed assistant: the Lancaster House chief steward, a distinguished looking former member of the Queen's household, the Under-Secretary of State for African Affairs, a black female MP being groomed for high office, and the ex-ambassador who was the Prince's current private secretary. As they ran through their checks, the staff stood to one side, ready to answer any questions. Everything seemed to be in order.

Patrick's eyes were on the Under-Secretary. Early forties, tall, poised, quietly confident, a kind of British Condoleezza Rice.

Could she be Sleeping Beauty? Come on, Patrick, you can't suspect every woman in the place. And whoever said Sleeping Beauty is a woman, anyway?

After a few minutes, the dignitaries, all appearing satisfied, left. Patrick touched his right ear. The check-in messages from Julian and Sir Norman conveyed no news. And there was no sign of either Merriott or Dobrosova. Yet.

Jenna Dobrosova was not in Lancaster House. Her time would come. The disguise she had demanded gave her just the degree of anonymity she needed. No security officer would ever suspect her when she appeared on the scene to fulfil her mission.

These were the moments she lived for – the simmering adrenalin that coursed through her veins, the rhythmic clenching of her fingers as she paced back and forth, forcing her brain to concentrate on the task in hand, rehearsing the sequence of actions she would soon undertake.

The one thought she *had* to eradicate from her mind was that, forever, she would be able to rejoice in the knowledge that she, Jenna Dobrosova, had been responsible for one of the most remarkable, unexplained deaths of the twenty-first century.

CHAPTER 33

'Patrick, is that you?'

Cameron had seen as much as he needed. He left quietly and slipped into what he assumed was a small ante-chamber. Just as he parked himself in a comfy chair – an old man taking a breather in the middle of a long day - his phone vibrated.

The caller's number was stored in the hidden directory where he kept the contact details of those few people who should always be treated as a priority. All it said on-screen was "X74".

He vaguely recognised the voice.

'Patrick, it's me, Jamie Daniel. You remember, the anti-corruption blogger. The scam on Clapham Common?'

'Oh, yes. Hi Jamie. I hope this isn't a social call. Bit tied up right now.'

'No, you told me only to use this line in an emergency. I'll make it as quick as I can.'

'You've got one minute, mate.'

'OK. Look, don't ask me how but I've discovered that the Chinese are planning something big in London today. They want to . . .'

'Sabotage the Commonwealth. Yes, we know all about that. We're onto it.'

'Is that what you think they're up to?'

'What do you mean?'

'Sorry. My minute's running out.'

'Jamie! Keep talking. I assume you're back in business, by the way.'

'You bet I am. I never lost touch with my best informants. One of them has – shall we say? – access to someone important in the Chinese hierarchy. She's been my best source about corruption there.'

Patrick didn't have time to enquire what Jamie meant precisely by "access".

'Is she trustworthy?' he asked.

'Implicitly.'

There were steps outside in the corridor. 'Wait,' said Patrick.

He only just had time to conceal the phone as the door to the room opened.

'Ah, there you are, Mr Walker,' said the security man, using Patrick's cover name for the day. 'Just to let you know, the guests are running late. Could be more than an hour. Bloody bad manners, if you ask me. Enjoy your break.'

Patrick smiled and waved in acknowledgement and the man left.

'Who was that?' Jamie Daniel sounded nervous.

'No worries. Go on, please.'

'She came online early this morning. I've been trying to get through to Andy Fields but his phone isn't taking calls.'

'Andy's not around. I'll explain another time. Now, come on, tell me what you've learned. We could be interrupted again at any time.'

'OK.' Jamie Daniel had become very business-like. 'She didn't have any detail. All her man told her was, and I quote, *"London, Tuesday, a remarkable day the world will never forget"*.

'What the hell did he mean by that? Was that all?'

The noise of several voices right outside the door distracted Patrick.

'Jamie, I have to go. Here's a number: write it down and tell the man who answers everything you've told me.' He read out Sir Norman's private line from memory and closed the call.

He walked to the window, deep in thought.

"A remarkable day the world will never forget"? A few African countries leaving the Commonwealth? I don't think so. There has to be more to it than that.

What in the name of God were they planning to do? Was that why they'd hired Jenna Dobrosova? One thing was for sure now, if this was going to be as big as he feared, there was no way he and Julian could stop it on their own.

We're counting on you, Sir Norman.

He checked his watch again and buzzed Julian. The last minute delay would help but time was still running frighteningly short.

Hong Jintao emerged from the embassy and climbed into the waiting car. He was feeling physically sick: the email he had just read confirmed his suspicions: he had been massively misled by his President and, quite possibly, by his mentor, Guo Dalong, as well.

All the while he had been engaged in activating the spy network, which had taken him twenty years to build, following orders to the letter, carefully putting every piece in place to ensure that today's events achieved the greatest possible impact, these men, whom he had always trusted and respected were hatching another strategy altogether. And he, Hong Jintao, Foreign Minister of the People's Republic of China had now received a curt instruction to back off and leave everything to Sleeping Beauty and the Locksmith.

Humiliation, anger, and a sense of profound sadness filled his mind as he stared out at the London traffic, close to tears. He'd always known that he had never been truly accepted within the inner circle of the Party's top ranks – he was neither sufficiently wealthy nor devious. It was his intellect that had marked him out, or so he was told. And he had given his all in the best interests of his nation.

The soundproof screen between him and the driver was thankfully closed when his fury overflowed and poured forth in the form of a stream of curses.

The sheer frustration that he could do nothing to prevent whatever was about to transpire made him clench his fists and hammer on the window.

The bastards! I'm completely powerless; castrated . . . Aargh!!

Or am I?

He took a deep breath and sat back. It was not far to Lancaster House. He reckoned he had a full five minutes to think.

A car and driver on demand were some of the very few assets afforded to the Last Resort Squad but, in an emergency, Sir Norman had only to say the word and an expert driver from the local military base was swinging into his home's gravel drive within ten minutes. Naturally, given that they did not exist in any official sense, the Club's expenses did not appear in any budget or audit report, so they relied upon their friends in high places to cover the resources they required.

Today, Sir Norman had also managed to secure a couple of motorcycle outriders who were now carving a channel through the suburban traffic. He had already sent an alarm call to the other Squad members who were all undoubtedly beetling their way towards Westminster, each in his own way.

From the moment his convoy set off, Sir Norman was constantly on the phone. His first call was to the Squad's "paterfamilias", as the man liked to be known. His wise advice, coupled with his ability to tap the occasional government minister or senior civil servant on the shoulder, had been of great value over recent years. Sir Norman was one of a select few who had been given his personal number, on the understanding that it would only be used at times of serious threat to the nation.

'Hello, Norman. What can I do for you?' The familiar cultured tones always sounded relaxed, no matter how busy he was at the time attending to his many interests.

Sir Norman kept it short. 'We're becoming rather concerned, sir, about a possible intervention at the Commonwealth leaders' conference in Lancaster House this morning.'

'Intervention? What kind of intervention? By whom?'

'The Chinese, sir. As you know from my last report, a number of their agents here have recently become active and everything points to an attempt to split up the Commonwealth in order for China to gain access to certain African countries' energy resources.'

'Yes, I read about that and I'm ready to do my bit to intercept the whole silly idea while you take care of this killer woman,' said the paterfamilias. 'But you wouldn't have phoned unless there was a more serious problem, would you?'

'No, sir. We intercepted a message a few minutes ago that's given us reason to believe their purposes may be rather more destructive. We're now expecting some kind of serious attack – world changing, they are calling it. So I would like your permission to respond in like manner.'

'I see,' the man replied. 'It's that difficult conundrum, is it not? As you and I have discussed before, the importance of exposing their entire spy ring balanced against the risk of allowing them to do us great harm. Before I give you my answer, will you give me your absolute assurance that your people will use only the appropriate amount of force, out of sight of the media, preferably.'

'You have my assurance, sir.'

'I don't wish to be flippant, but have you any idea how much it costs to clean those carpets at Lancaster House? Some of them are three hundred years old, you know.'

Sir Norman never ceased to be amazed at the man's ability to ease the tension with a dash of gentle humour.

'Thank you for your call, Norman. I shall observe with interest.'

The call ended. The Last Resort Squad had been given the green light.

Now, should he call the Prime Minister?

Vanmali Mehta was on great form. At least, he believed he was.

'Gentlemen, you are conscious of the time and so am I. Personally, I am not in the least concerned about keeping these people waiting: it only strengthens our position. But we really should be on our way shortly. So, for one final time - are we all agreed? Will we present a united front?'

Overnight, each President had had the opportunity to reread the paper Mehta gave him at their last gathering. This morning, they all looked haggard. The threats to sabotage their country's future stability and the accurate, detailed account of their own misdemeanours, both in private and while in office, had clearly kept most of them awake. It was most unlikely that any of them would have consulted the others: the accusations were far too embarrassing.

Indeed, at the start of the meeting, three of them were missing. Mehta had not expected this so, in just the same manner as before, he found himself on the phone to their rooms, reciting the necessary words and, within minutes, everyone was present.

Once they were all assembled, the discussion quickly descended into fierce argument as, one after the other, these powerful men challenged both the ethics of the situation and each other. Mehta was not surprised when the debate turned to the pros and cons of siding with China, free from British interference.

In recent years, their countries had all received tempting financial offers of aid and investment from China; some they had accepted but many they had been forced – in some cases paid - by the British to turn down.

Gradually, under the guidance of the oldest among them, tempers returned to normal, but the three doubting Thomases were still not fully convinced. One of them even started to walk out before being called back by his closest ally.

Mehta had allowed the argument to run its course without intervening. Now, the voice in his head told him that it was essential, the time had come, to establish unanimous agreement. As if from a remote point in the room, he again watched himself as he played his final card.

'Gentlemen, I have an apology to offer. There was one small piece of information that was, inexplicably, omitted from the document I gave to each of you yesterday.'

Silence. He cleared his throat, for effect.

'I refer to the number and location of your personal offshore bank account.'

Some gasped. Some simply stared into space.

Mehta continued. 'I am delighted to inform you that I have today authorised the transfer of four million dollars to each of you.'

Consternation takes many forms and they were all present in that room.

When he asked them once again for unanimity, every hand went up, slowly.

CHAPTER 34

Lancaster House

A busy catering kitchen was not unfamiliar to Julian. After leaving school, he had worked in plenty of restaurants and pubs, but this was something else. Every member of this team had been hired for their expertise in haute cuisine and, while the head chef looked on, a meal fit for royalty and presidents was taking shape: hors d'oeuvres plated up element by element, blemish-free, perfectly shaped vegetables selected and the rest discarded.

Each artist, for that was the only way to describe these people, was going about the allotted tasks almost instinctively, one minute hunched over a tray of portions, the next moving smoothly to check an oven or the flavour in a pan, calling a younger assistant to bring the next sauce, more fresh herbs, or to reposition a quail's egg.

Julian, along with the rest of the waiters, was now kitted out in his blue and gold uniform; each of them had been checked over by the head waiter and they were all now standing clear, ready to move into action as soon as they were called. The majority would wait until the reception proceedings were complete and the guests moved through to the banqueting room but Julian and four other staff had been detailed to do duty in the main room when the bigwigs arrived, ready to offer refreshments as needed. For the time being, they could relax; except for Julian. He had things to do.

There was no need to attract attention to himself by checking his phone. Every text message from Patrick was being relayed to the tiny invisible speaker in his left ear via a voice translation programme. Not that there was anything new to report: no sign of Jenna Dobrosova or any suspicious activity, yet.

Patrick had relayed his conversation with Jamie Daniel to him, especially the message from China, *"A remarkable day the world will never forget"*. That had really scared him. He, Daddy's little boy Julian, the awkward nerd, was going to be right there when Doomsday, whatever that meant, unfolded. Or exploded?

For the first time in an hour, he was free to take a good look at the forty-odd chefs, sous-chefs, assistants and the other waiters, trying to spot anything unusual. For sure, some of them were showing tiny signs of nerves as they went about their professional duties but no more than he would have expected. Patrick had taught him, from the day he first arrived at the lab, that, if he wanted to reach the top, he should never rest on his laurels, never allow himself to settle for 'That's good enough'. As the great jazz musician Miles Davis once said, 'If you aren't nervous, then you aren't paying attention.'

He paid particular attention to the waiters who would join him on duty in the main reception. While it was Sir Norman who had arranged for Julian to be part of this team, one of the selection criteria for the others was evidently their looks.

The two men, who had both clearly spent ages getting their hair to look just right, had already indicated their interest in Julian, brushing past him a little too closely on occasion. From casual observation during the plate-wiping session, Julian concluded that they had both done all this on countless occasions. Which only left the lone woman, a quiet, well-spoken person in her mid-thirties, wearing a wedding ring, attractive but not in a sexy way. She had kept herself to herself all morning, getting on with her work without joining in the general chat.

He knew he was being stupid but, given his track record over recent years, he was surprised that she had not passed a single glance in his direction. Women always did – why not her?

He decided to wander over. 'Hello. My name's Sebastian. Have you done this sort of thing before?'

Of course she has, you idiot. Why else would she be here?

She turned and smiled, rather condescendingly. 'I'm Heather,' she said. 'I do *this sort of thing* for a living, actually.'

'Ah, of course,' said Julian, looking and feeling embarrassed. 'Sorry. Didn't mean to cause offence.'

'No offence taken.' She turned away, closing the conversation.

Five minutes later, the head waiter appeared.

'Right, reception team. To your places, please. They're on their way.'

Julian and the others strode single file into the main hall, where the seats were filled with reporters and invited guests. The head waiter directed them to take up station along the walls where trays of soft drinks, water, ice and glasses had already been laid. Julian looked towards the rear of the room and spotted Patrick standing in one corner, having a brief word with the passing head waiter as he scanned the rows of chairs. Patrick caught Julian's eye and gave a tiny shrug. No sign of Jenna Dobrosova.

At that moment a side door opened and a group of men and women, clearly from many different parts of the world, trooped in, each wearing a dark suit and an insignia on a ribbon round their neck. The ambassadors.

Hold on, isn't that Hong Jintao?

Julian recognised him immediately. What was he doing here? He glanced back at Patrick, who appeared unperturbed: indeed, unless Julian was mistaken, he seemed to be wearing a satisfied smile.

The game is on.

A guest approached him for a couple of glasses of water. Julian attended to the order, then another and another.

A journey that would have taken at least an hour and a half without a military escort had been accomplished in a little over half the time. As the convoy drew to a halt outside a discreet rear entrance to Lancaster House, Sir Norman packed away his phone and notebook. He had just managed to complete his list of calls and the man he was expecting was there waiting for him.

'Good morning Sir Norman,' he said, opening the car door. 'A bit of a rush, but everyone's in position. There's some coffee waiting for you inside so you can whet your whistle before the briefing.'

'Thank you, Wing Commander. I've tried to cover every eventuality but, frankly, as I told you, we have absolutely no idea where it's going to come from. So, for the time being, all we can do is watch and wait. I trust your employer is not too worried.'

'You know him, sir. Unflappable.'

He followed the other man into the building, along a service corridor and into a small meeting room, where a group of men and women - some in uniform, others in dark suits, was assembled around the table. Among them, he spied all three fellow members of the Last Resort Squad. How on earth they had each managed to get to Lancaster House so quickly was a puzzle he would have to leave to one side until this was all over.

The others were the tiny number of people who the Last Resort Squad referred to as their "Trusties" – all of them were senior enough to make things happen in their own arena and had proved themselves utterly trustworthy, so much so that they could be called upon when the national interest was at stake. In most cases, not even their immediate superior was aware of their involvement.

Sir Norman knew he had no need to remind them but, for the sake of good order, he began by emphasising that this entire operation, in particular this discussion, were subject to the highest level of secrecy: no notes would be taken, no record or report would be produced. Nothing was to be disclosed to any personnel other than the issuing of direct orders.

'I arranged for photographs of the key suspects to be transmitted to your phones. Can we take a look at them now, please?'

Everyone picked up their phone and located the file.

'The two men in the group coded "Us" are our own people, both working under assumed identities, which is why they look a trifle odd.'

A trickle of laughter.

'The other group, appropriately coded "Them", are the ones who concern us and who will either definitely or, in some cases, possibly be in Lancaster House this morning. Some may already be here. Please scroll through to the woman code-named Hydra.'

'Excuse me, sir.' The speaker was deputy commander of 22 SAS Squadron, based in Regent's Park. 'Before we do that, are you sure there hasn't been a mistake here? I know the face of the man you've code-named Locksmith. He works in Downing Street!'

Sir Norman looked briefly at the other Squad members who all nodded. 'This is true, Major. Let's leave it at that, shall we?' No further comment was required.

'Let me make it absolutely clear that, if you spot them, none of these people are to be detained until I authorise it by phone. Now . . . Hydra,' he continued. 'She is a dangerous professional killer. One thing I can guarantee is that she will look very different from the photos in front of you. As you can see, she changes her appearance for every operation, so the only thing you can go on is her height, five feet eleven inches, but even that can be disguised these days. Her weakness, in case you were wondering, is her vanity. She appears to take a pride in getting as close as possible to being discovered, then disappearing without trace before the security forces can nab her.'

'Is there any chance she is in the building now, sir?', asked the Senior Counsel at the Crown Prosecution Service, a woman QC who was renowned for scaring the living daylights out of the less up-to-date judges.

'Not as far as we know, Judith. But you'd expect me to say that, wouldn't you?' He smiled, which went some way to breaking the ice in the room.

'But we have reason to understand that she may use a weapon disguised as, of all things, an elbow crutch. We can't for the life of us believe that she would bring anything so obvious into the building, but you never know. Any more questions? No? I have activated the emergency phone network so we can all speak to each other in confidence. Now, if those of you with teams on duty would return to your post and the others take your seat in the main room, I have rather a lot to do.'

The room was empty in seconds.

Richard Merriott and the Prime Minister were met at the door of Lancaster House by the Under-Secretary of State for Commonwealth Affairs and, without ceremony, were led up the magnificent sweeping staircase to the room where the audience waited. The other senior hosts were already there: officials from the Commonwealth Secretariat, the Foreign Secretary, other ministers from the Foreign Office, and a representative of the Organisation for African Unity.

Richard Merriott led the PM to the head of the line, shaking hands as he passed with the Foreign Secretary, a popular man of huge experience, before turning away to take his seat.

Patrick was on full alert, watching Merriott's and Hong's every move. He moved to one side as someone brushed past him. Sir Norman thanked him and found a seat in the back row close by, crossed his legs and muttered a polite greeting to his neighbour.

Once the receiving line was in place, another door opened and

His Royal Highness the Prince of Wales entered, smiled at everyone as he passed, had a brief word here and there, a wave to someone in the audience, then took his place beside the Prime Minister. His immaculate pale grey double-breasted suit, white shirt and slightly flamboyant silk tie were, as ever, in "extreme, quiet good taste", as the editor of a leading outfitting journal had once noted.

The master of ceremonies checked her watch, no doubt noting, as they all had, that they were exactly ninety minutes behind schedule, and signalled to one of her staff.

The double doors at the far end opened and the African presidents filed in, followed by Vanmali Mehta.

To Patrick's surprise, they all looked quite expressionless, unnervingly so, with the notable exception of Vanmali Mehta. As he passed through the audience, his whole demeanour was that of a small boy at his first Premier League soccer match, wide-eyed, excited and fidgety, looking all round the room, his face a picture of wonderment.

One by one, the presidents worked their way along the reception line, shaking hands and moving on, stone-faced, without a word. Until the first of them arrived in front of the Prince, who held out his hand with a welcoming smile.

The tall African looked the heir to the British throne in the eyes and said, too quietly for the media microphones to pick up his words, 'Sir, I shake your hand but I spit in your face.'

Richard Merriott, seated in the front row, looked on as the brilliant plot he had been so privileged to co-author played out on stage, in the presence of such a distinguished audience and the world's media. So far, every actor, including himself, had performed perfectly – some under duress, some for a nice fee, others out of pure ideological loyalty.

His own small part in this final act had gone as planned. The next phase was now unstoppable. All he had to do was sit, watch and enjoy.

CHAPTER 35

Jenna Dobrosova was starting to feel uncomfortable and bored. The air in the vehicle was stifling and the conversation had hardly ever risen above the banal. The others had each been hand-picked for the job, so they had to be professionals, like her. But, their level of conversation was getting on her nerves.

Once they had extensively analysed last night's TV programmes and London traffic hold-ups, they then embarked on a string of rather tasteless stories, each ostensibly from their own professional experiences, that always seemed to begin with, 'I swear this really did happen . . .' and end with a graphic description of the extraordinary variety of items they had seen extracted from people's fundamental orifices or something equally unpleasant, followed by gales of laughter.

She had encountered gallows humour many times before, particularly in her days in the Russian military; for men and women who were paid to face life and death on a daily basis, it was a natural reaction, a way of binding the team together. But, after a while, it could become intensely boring.

She allowed her mind to wander across old ground. As her own career had developed, her one big regret was that, because she would never be apprehended, her name would never enter the lists of world-famous assassins alongside the likes of Brutus, John Wilkes Booth, Lee Harvey Oswald, Gabril Princip, who shot Archduke Ferdinand, and John Lennon's murderer, Mark David Chapman.

They were all a bunch of amateurs, for God's sake! It's the pro's like me who deserve recognition. We've put away far more celebrities than they did.

She was far more skilled than any of them, of that she was sure. Her special talents should be publicly acknowledged, as with anyone else at the top of their profession; one day she would be wealthy enough to retire and it was only right that her achievements should be honoured in some way.

She would give this some thought. Perhaps this assignment would provide her with the opportunity. She would come up with an answer; she always did.

Later, she had resolved to celebrate with a bottle of Krug and dinner at a discreet Michelin-starred restaurant, followed by sex, lots of sex with . . . She checked her phone to make sure she still had the number for Sebastian or Julian, that gorgeous young man who had taken her to pleasure pastures new only a few days before. He would be perfect.

Patrick was so busy keeping an eye on Merriott and Mehta that he was late spotting the look of consternation on the Prince of Wales' face as, one by one, the Africans arrived to shake his hand. The courteous smile was still there but the eyes told a very different story. Something had happened, someone had said something; or was he unwell?

He glanced across the room and caught a look from Julian who nodded towards the seat in a rear row where Sir Norman was looking hard at the far end of the receiving line.

Vanmali Mehta had finally arrived at the Prime Minister. He appeared even more twitchy now, but the PM, cool as a cucumber, greeted him with her normal media smile and said a few words before passing him on to the Prince on her right.

Even from where Patrick was stationed, the tiny dribbles of sweat on the Prince's brow were clearly visible. After speaking to the last president, he took a handkerchief from his jacket pocket and mopped his face before turning to Vanmali Mehta.

That was when Patrick noticed something else: while the Prince was making a fine job of pretending that nothing was wrong, the person standing next to him appeared totally oblivious – the Prime Minister.

Of all people, she must have noticed or heard whatever it was that upset him.

Only a limited number of camera crews had been allowed to cover the event and they were stationed at a discreet distance from the greeting line. But Patrick knew they all carried highly sensitive microphones. He made a mental note to get hold of their recordings after the event.

Sensing that somebody's eyes were on him, he found Sir Norman now looking straight at him. This was a risky breach of security, which could only be condoned in extreme circumstances.

As he returned the stare, Sir Norman slid his chair back quietly, stood up and brushed past Patrick on his way towards a door. In the second or so that it took the older man to pass him, Sir Norman caught Patrick's eye and looked down. Only once he was sure that Patrick had received the message, did he move silently on.

'Your Royal Highness, your Excellencies, my lords, ladies and gentlemen.' The voice over the speakers was that of the civil servant acting as master – or in this case – mistress of ceremonies for the day. She looked a little flustered.

The greeting line had now broken up and the dignitaries were standing around in small groups, the Africans and Mehta together close to the speaker's dais.

'There will now be a short, ten-minute break before the welcome speeches. This will be followed by a brief question time before the delegates, dignitaries and His Royal Highness take lunch in the banqueting room. During the break, the staff can offer you refreshments.' She waved in the direction of Julian and his colleagues.

Most of the audience stood to stretch their legs and Julian quickly found himself surrounded by thirsty customers. When he had time to look up, he was surprised to see that Patrick had disappeared. His phone was buzzing – a message.

The mechanical voice in his ear began to speak, just as he was pouring a drink,

'Stay where you are. Keep a close eye on Mehta and Merriott. Let me know if they do anything odd.'

Until that moment, Richard Merriott had been feeling life was pretty good. Now, he was close to panic. He had just spotted Sir Norman of the Last Resort Squad leaving the room.

What the hell is he doing here? He never appears in public these days. Surely the Squad can't be onto us. I've been so meticulous. But, if they are . . . Shit!

He searched the room, looking for Hong Jintao. He found him chatting to the British Foreign Secretary and a couple of ambassadors. He looked utterly calm, almost serene, Merriott thought. A man at peace with himself.

I love and admire the Chinese, Merriott thought. But I'm damned if I'll ever understand them.

Suddenly, his mind clicked into action. He knew what he had to do. He moved quickly into the corridor which was now full of people talking and laughing as they recognised old friends. No sign of Sir Norman. Round to the top of the staircase, pushing people out of his way – still no sign. Where the fuck had the man gone?

I have to find him. We cannot be stopped. My Master must have his revenge!

He thrust his hand into his jacket pocket, located and gripped his fingers around the tiny syringe he had been told to carry, and rushed down the stairs, two at a time.

Patrick found Sir Norman, waiting for him at the agreed place, checking his watch.

'Nice idea, sir,' he said. As he brushed past Patrick, Sir Norman had formed the letter "P" with his fingers, then pointed downwards towards the floor. The signal could not have been more clear. They were now standing by a wash basin in the ground floor men's toilet. As there were plenty of other facilities upstairs, this one was empty. There was also an 'Out of order' sign hanging on the door.

The older man smiled. 'Right, now listen. You are now going to take part in a conversation which you will never disclose,' he said. 'To anyone, ever, for reasons you will soon appreciate.'

At that moment, one of the cubicle doors opened and a man emerged.

His Royal Highness the Prince of Wales, Royal Knight Companion of the Most Noble Order of the Garter, Extra Knight of the Most Ancient and Most Noble Order of the Thistle, Grand Master and Principal Knight Grand Cross of the Most Honourable Order of the Bath, Member of the Order of Merit ... and lots of other things as well.

Patrick did his best not to look surprised as the Prince shook his hand.

'Doctor Cameron. A great pleasure to meet you. I'm most grateful to you for sparing the time as I gather you're about to become a father. Tell me, how is your wife? By the way, would you mind if

I call you Patrick? I'm afraid you'll have to call me Sir. Fusty old protocol, you know.'

Since embarking on this assignment, thanks to the untraceable phone Andy Fields had given him, Patrick had managed to get a call, however brief, through to Angela at least once every twenty-four hours. She was well; her mother had arrived from Scotland to be with her, and young Rory was not expected to arrive on the early bus, as she put it.

In all that time, the only people who'd enquired after her welfare had been his dear departed friend Andy Fields and now the heir to the Crown of the United Kingdom.

'She's fine, thank you, sir,' replied Patrick, adjusting to the fact that this man, with one of the most well-known faces in the world, was standing right there in front of him.

Sir Norman spoke. 'I should explain that His Royal Highness has a rather close connection with the Last Resort Squad, Patrick.'

'Yes, I'm their "pater familias"; from the Latin, it means father of the family. Silly title really, as they are all far older than I am.'

Suddenly, it made absolute sense. After all, to imagine that the Royal Family were purely a ceremonial tourist attraction, without any power in the land, was utterly naïve. Non-political, the quintessential embodiment of everything British, its heritage, character and spirit . . . The word "Establishment" sprang to Patrick's mind. But remote, dispassionate, uninvolved? No way.

After all, this is a bloody kingdom, not a republic. And certainly not a people's republic.

Which brought him back to the real world. In the next two minutes, the Prince explained what each of the African presidents had said to him in the receiving line.

'"I shake your hand but I spit in your face." I'm used to that sort of stuff from the Mugabes of this world. We can all laugh them off. But this, I felt, was quite genuine and totally unexpected. I'd met them all before and they were always perfectly pleasant. Any questions so far?' he asked Patrick.

'No, sir.' He looked at Sir Norman. 'I'm assuming that His Royal Highness . . .'

HRH interrupted: 'Oh, for heaven's sake, call me "the Prince". Far easier.'

Sir Norman had guessed what he was going to ask.

'Yes, the Prince knows everything and has approved our strategy at every stage.'

'So all I can ask you to do, sir . . .' Patrick looked at his watch.

'Don't worry,' said the Prince. 'They can't start without me. Call of nature, don't you know.'

Patrick continued. 'Sir, please just carry on as normal. I will be very visible, as will my colleague, so keep an eye out for signals from us.'

'How will I recognise your colleague?' asked the Prince.

'He's one of the waiters, sir. Six feet tall, slim, with a hairstyle that makes him look rather, shall I say, flamboyant?'

The Prince laughed aloud. 'I look forward to meeting him. Alright, thank you both. I must be on my way. Good luck to us all.'

He shook both men by the hand and left the room.

'Sir Norman,' said Patrick. 'Do you mind if I ask a question? I was wondering why the Prime Minister didn't join us for that discussion.'

The older man shrugged. 'That's the way we always work in the Squad. Better to keep it all non-political, old boy. Politicians have a nasty habit of buggering things up. Let's go back upstairs.'

As he turned, the door crashed open, revealing a wild-eyed Richard Merriott.

'There you are, you bastard,' he yelled, and launched himself at Sir Norman, brandishing a small syringe.

Patrick grabbed the man's other arm and pulled down, throwing him off-balance. Merriott swung the syringe round, missing Sir Norman, who had crossed his arms to protect himself, by a fraction. As he continued to pull, Patrick hooked his foot around the man's ankle. Merriott fell towards the floor, face down, his right arm underneath his body, and screamed. His head twisted round, a look of sheer terror on his features, as Patrick's knee pinned him to the floor. Sir Norman, panting, kneeled beside Merriott.

'You're under arrest, Richard Merriott. The charge – high treason,' he growled.

'Too late, too late,' Merriott murmured. 'My work is complete. You and your people . . .'

His eyes seemed to bulge then go blank as he exhaled.

Patrick released his hold and rolled Merriott over onto his back. There was the syringe protruding hideously from his stomach.

'Your Royal Highness, your Excellencies, my lords, ladies and gentlemen. We're running rather late, so I would now like to invite our visitors, His Royal Highness and the other senior guests to take their seats on the platform.'

Once the top table had assembled, the MC invited the Prince to formally welcome the delegation. His speech was brief and courteous, emphasising the strong, longstanding links between their countries and the importance of the Commonwealth. He appeared to be perfectly under control.

This was followed by a welcome from the Prime Minister. A natural speaker, charming and gently amusing, she spoke more about international aid, world trade and the value to Britain of food and mineral imports from Africa.

After a short address from the Commonwealth Secretary-General, it was the turn of Vanmali Mehta. He rose and walked quickly to the dais, carrying what looked like a barrister's briefcase, large enough to hold several bulging wads of court papers. There was a murmur of comment as he placed it on the table in front of him.

He looked down at the audience, cleared his throat, and then appeared to fix his eyes on a point on the far wall for several seconds, without speaking.

Patrick turned and looked at the wall above his head. It was so small that, even as close as this, he could have easily missed it. It looked like a tiny CCTV unit. What made it even more difficult to pick out was its colour, almost exactly the same as the wood panelled wall on which it had been mounted.

From where Patrick was standing, directly underneath, he could just make out a faint green flashing light.

Meanwhile, Vanmali Mehta had begun to speak, or rather read, continuing to stare at the same spot. After he had completed the formal opening words, he said,

'Thank you for welcoming us. I have brought something to show you.'

He then clicked open the large briefcase and removed a substantial sheaf of papers, held together by a thick elastic band. Holding them in his right hand, he removed the band and laid them on the table, where they could be clearly seen by everyone in the room. Those sitting in the front rows could observe that the papers were yellowing, their corners turning upwards. This was not a new file.

Mehta proceeded, 'This file does not make for comfortable reading. It lives in the National Archive, here in London, along with many, many others, in a section known as "Migrated". Only a tiny number of British officials are aware of its existence. Even fewer have access. You may wonder why. Well, I am going to tell you.'

Mehta was now speaking in a creepy, almost mechanical monotone, his eyes fixed in a glassy stare when, without warning, the British Foreign Secretary, one of the most respected figures in international affairs, stood bolt upright in the front row, pointed his finger at the top table, let out a piercing shriek, and collapsed on the floor.

In seconds, Mehta's voice was drowned out as the whole audience rose to their feet, pushing forward, trying to see what had happened. Camera crews were attempting to hold people back, officials trying to clear a space for the stricken man.

The woman MC rushed to the microphone, pushed Mehta aside and, trying to make her voice heard in the chaos, announced that the proceedings would resume as soon as the emergency services had attended to the Foreign Secretary.

The man was lying inert; a couple of aides were trying to gain his attention, while another placed a cushion under his head.

Patrick looked round. The Prince was standing, showing evident concern for the Foreign Secretary. The Prime Minister was closing her phone and returning it to her briefcase. The African presidents, who had formed a huddle around Vanmali Mehta, had all begun to shout at him, apparently very unhappy.

CHAPTER 36

'Cheetah. Go, go, go!' The voice on the speaker-phone was calm but insistent.

The driver already had the engine running, so it was simply a matter of buckle up, flick on the lights and siren and they were on their way.

The planning had been thorough: the crew, each one a former mercenary skilled in emergency response procedures, had been put through their paces. After hours of rehearsal, everyone knew their role. Jenna, the only novice at this kind of work, had slotted in easily, impressing the others with her ability to learn and perform everything she was asked to do, right first time. Nobody questioned her right to be there: it was not their place to ask.

On the day, Merriott had pulled Downing Street rank to ensure that his people were stationed inside Lancaster House. They would ensure the crew smooth access. What had happened to the in-house medical team was not made clear; all they needed to know was that they had been "relocated" and relieved of their phones.

The handshake that knocked out the Foreign Secretary had been Jenna's idea. The tiny injector Richard Merriott carried attached to his right thumb was in fact an adaptation of an old KGB weapon, this time containing just enough delayed action incapacitating agent to render the man delirious fifteen minutes later. It wasn't her fault that the drug had knocked him out earlier than planned: she'd warned Merriott this could happen but he'd ignored her. The Foreign Secretary would recover; he was not their target.

The moment he succumbed, the plan was that Merriott, under cover of the ensuing mayhem, would call them, using one of three agreed code words, each equivalent to red, amber or green. When the call came through, the voice was not Merriott's but who cared? The message was clear: "Cheetah" meant go.

In less than two minutes, they arrived at the rear entrance, where the door was held open by a uniformed security guard.

'First floor, right at the top of the stairs,' he said, adding the code word that identified him as one of them.

For a fleeting moment, as they rushed along the corridor, it crossed Jenna's mind how easy it was, almost too easy, for them to get into an important government building that was playing host, right now, to princes, presidents and prime ministers. She had been here before, on many occasions: there came a moment when you had to put all doubts to one side and trust the word of the puppet-masters that they had taken care of all the details.

The team leader had decided earlier they would take the lift rather than labouring up the fifty-tread staircase. It was a bit of a squeeze with all their equipment and Jenna had to hold the bag containing her elbow crutches close to her body. For the umpteenth time, she cursed them:

Damn these things. I could think of a hundred more discreet weapons than these.

She wasn't happy using such a cumbersome implement in a crowded space and she'd said so pointedly, even to the point of threatening to cancel the whole thing.

But, she reminded herself yet again, *if the big boss insists on using this technology for such a high profile assassination, so he can demonstrate to the rest of the world's armed forces how far ahead his people are, who am I to argue? Ego conquers all, it seems, no matter how great the risk.*

As the lift slowed to a halt, she pulled the peak of her baseball cap lower over her eyes and, with the rest of the crew, yanked the surgical mask up to cover her nose and mouth. Not routine paramedic procedure, they had agreed, but nobody would know the difference in all the fuss.

'New regulations, madam. Health and safety . . .' they would answer if asked.

By the time the paramedics arrived on the scene, the staff, including Patrick, had succeeded in clearing a space around the Foreign Secretary, who was already beginning to regain consciousness.

Patrick watched as the two men and two women, all wearing surgical masks, went to work quickly, setting up the equipment they needed and placing bags containing the rest in a tidy pile where they could see them.

Neat idea, the masks. Welcome to the party, Miss Dobrosova.

Patrick looked round the crowd again to check on his other leading actors.

The Prince had resumed his seat at the top table. He was deep in conversation with his private secretary but his eyes were sweeping the room. Occasionally, he would look down and make notes with a black fountain pen.

Hong Jintao was continuing to hover in the background, within a few feet of the action. He was watching, calm, poised . . . but poised to do what? Patrick prayed that he had guessed right.

Sir Norman was missing, which was as expected. He was no doubt waiting in the wings, making sure the others were ready for their cue.

The Prime Minister was standing closest to the fallen man, her body language a jumble of emotions. Patrick thought he could spot, in ascending order, concern for her sick colleague, frustration at the delay, and a fierce battle between the need to look calm in a crisis and something else, something approaching . . .

No, I must be mistaken. Are you sure?

He checked again. There it was, the same look.

Patrick turned away and typed a brief text message to Julian and Sir Norman. He was now certain he knew the identity of Sleeping Beauty and who Jenna Dobrosova had been hired to assassinate: the two candidates they had entirely dismissed from their planning. They could still stop it but it was going to be down to individual initiative now.

Julian was ready. He had manoeuvred himself along the wall to a spot where he could have a clear run to centre stage. He had been joined there by another waiter, a woman.

He watched as Julian's face turned deathly pale. Patrick's message had arrived.

The two male paramedics were kneeling, talking to their patient as they checked his pulse and blood pressure. The two women, both wearing caps and masks, had finished assembling their equipment. One was standing close, ready for instructions, while the other's hands hovered over the oxygen kit.

Patrick had a big decision to make. Which one was Jenna? Both were of a similar build; with the uniform, caps and masks, it was hard to tell them apart. If he picked the wrong one, it would be all over. He looked up at Julian.

Jenna was checking the scene thoroughly, memorising where each of the key players was located. Where was Merriott? He certainly wasn't in the room. No matter, he'd played his part; it was all down to her now.

There were no obvious armed security guards in the room or, if there were, they had relaxed and were chatting like everyone else. That would give her the time she needed to make the kill and get out.

The one advantage of this microwave weapon is that it's completely silent so any guards won't know where to look.

One last look around, check the doors, the . . .

What??? I know that guy, the one standing near the platform with the funny hair; he's looking at me now. I'd recognise those eyes anywhere. Bewitching. It's Sebastian or Julian or whatever his real name is.

A crack appeared in her world, which quickly widened into a gaping hole.

Julian had trained for this time and again; he'd been sure he could handle it. One of the paramedics' bags was the right shape, long and thin. It was less than ten feet away. But, when Jenna Dobrosova looked up and recognised him, he had to grip a nearby table to prevent himself from falling over. His throat tightened and a fierce urge to cough up his guts swept through him.

Those eyes. That's Jenna. She's spotted me among all these people. That was NOT supposed to happen.

Then, quite suddenly, a hand gripped his arm. It was Heather.

'It's OK, we'll do this together,' she whispered.

With that, she eased quietly to one side, her eyes also focused on Jenna, who had started to move.

Hong Jintao watched as his time approached. He had decided what he was going to do and was ready to accept the consequences.
Jenna Dobrosova, assassin extraordinaire, knew she was cornered. As she moved slowly away from the paramedics, options were racing

through her brain, arguments for and against each one, twisting and turning.

Give herself up, accept failure and spend the rest of her life in an unbearable women's high security jail?

A hasty exit? No chance.

Or go for it. Go out in a blaze of glory, her name forever quoted in the history books. Not just an assassin but the greatest assassin of all time.

Oh, what the fuck?

CHAPTER 37

China

Guo Dalong dropped the tablet on the table and called Harrison to his side.

'This is too small for my aging eyes,' he growled. 'Take me inside to the big screen. I have to be able to see what is happening.'

The direct feed, covertly hacked from one of the television cameras inside Lancaster House, was relaying every moment of the scenes the old man had waited so long to watch: the final act that meant he could die with peace in his heart. Each day, he was feeling weaker and weaker. Only that morning, the pains in his chest had woken him early and, for the first time, the morphine had failed to make him more comfortable. But his gods had spared him long enough to witness his family's revenge and for that he was thankful.

Harrison wheeled him through to sit in front of the large flat screen TV. He fitted the headphones and adjusted the volume until Guo signalled to him to stop.

The screen was showing the Prince deep in conversation with a man Guo did not recognise. The operator pulled back and turned to focus on the paramedics. A gaggle of people in the background were looking concerned.

Hong Jintao was standing slightly apart, watching impassively, his eyes flicking back and forth. There was something odd about his expression. Was he smiling? Not quite, but Guo had never seen him looking so . . . confident? Aroused? What was the word . . . fired up?

That worried him. Hong was a man who followed orders to the letter: what the Christians called "a good and faithful servant". He was never a man with whom he could ever entrust the whole truth but he could always be relied upon not to take the law into his own hands.

To Guo's frustration, the camera continued to switch shots between other members of the audience, dignitaries, officials, the doors and the paramedics, before he could get another good look at Hong.

Now he had moved away from the medical team to stand nearer the platform, that same look of anticipation on his face. Seemingly unnoticed by anyone, he was edging closer and closer to the platform steps. Then the camera suddenly moved back to show the casualty being helped to his feet and onto the mobile stretcher.

Guo shouted in anger at the screen. Something unexpected was about to happen, of that he was certain, and there was nothing he could do.

'Harrison!' he yelled. The butler was standing right behind him, watching the screen. His phone was in his hand.

Just before the camera moved on, both of them spotted one of the paramedics unzipping a long bag and removing an elbow crutch.

Harrison said nothing as he dialled a number.

Lancaster House, London

Jane Beaumont MP, Prime Minister of the United Kingdom of Great Britain and Northern Ireland, was trembling. This was to be her moment of triumph, the end of the long journey, when the country of her birth would begin its downward plunge, when her deep belief in the purity and practicality of Marxist-Leninist thought, of Mao Zedong thought, then later of the more flexible Deng Xiaoping theory, would come to fruition.

When her lover at Oxford University had recruited her, showing her a bright, more just path away from the degenerate, materialist ways of eighties Britain, she had grasped her mission willingly.

The speed with which she had mastered living a double life had brought her to the notice of senior officers while she was still in her mid-twenties. An intensive course in high level espionage followed, which she even managed to conceal from her fiancé, the son of a junior government minister, in the weeks before they were to be married.

Jane Beaumont became China's Sleeping Beauty, a name she rather liked. Her brief was to lie low, to remain sound asleep until she was called upon, however long that took.

Her progress through international management consultancy to running NGO's had been rewarding in many ways. She and her family spent their weeks in their Pinner four-bedroom home and, when time allowed, weekends at their cottage in Suffolk. She had no need to draw on her spying retainer fee so those funds had accumulated and were stashed away in an anonymous account in Macao, so she had been told.

For many years, indeed until the last few months, they had kept her updated but, other than that, her masters had left her undisturbed. Even now, as Prime Minister, her undercover work was restricted to monitoring the appointment of network members to key posts and ensuring, with help from Richard Merriott, that the information they passed to Beijing was untraceable.

As this day approached, she'd been so pleased at how calm she remained. After all, she was about to witness the humiliation and punishment of one of the great capitalist, imperialist powers of modern times. A resounding victory for socialist ideology over cruel, selfish pragmatism. And she would still be its Prime Minister, watching as it collapsed from the inside. As she looked across at the Prince, she could only feel contempt for everything he was and he represented. Deep, fierce contempt.

So why, so close to the culmination, had she begun to tremble so violently that she had to move over to a wall and grab a table to steady herself? Was she ill? Was she going to faint?

Patrick was the only other person in that room to notice Jane Beaumont's discomfort. At the last minute, it was he who had refilled the water glasses on the top table.

Julian reacted first. It was only a matter of six metres or so – two strides and a dive, he reckoned. The way that Jenna Dobrosova's eyes widened when she saw him showed that, for a brief few seconds, she was probably in a state of shock. Immediately, she had crouched down out of sight, re-emerging with an elbow crutch in her hand and begun to push onlookers to one side, shouting angrily. It was chaos.

Julian eased himself away from the wall, ready to attack, but found his way blocked by a woman who was clutching at him as she fell to her knees.

'Get out of the my . . .' he began, at which point he realised, to his horror, that it was the Prime Minister who was wrapping her arms round his thighs, gasping for help. He couldn't move. He looked around in desperation. Jenna, standing, had a clear line of fire now.

From nowhere, Patrick and Heather arrived and took the now semi-conscious woman from him. And, before the TV cameras could swing round, she was gone, through a side door.

Julian heard nothing of this. He had launched himself in the direction of Jenna, who had ripped off her mask and was aiming her weapon directly at the chest of the Prince of Wales.

Eye witnesses of cataclysmic events often insist that "everything seemed to happen in slow motion". What happened next in that room in Lancaster House can only have taken a second or two.

All Julian remembered, as he hurled himself horizontally at the Russian woman, was a sense of heart-breaking disappointment: he was too late. His special phone was in his hand, the one he had sweated hours over and of which he was so, so proud. And, after all that, he was going to be too late.

She had fired the weapon. At the heir to the throne. At point blank range. He was a dead man.

I've failed. I've failed.

Then, as he collided with the assassin, sending her crashing across the room, he realised that he had heard another loud crash while he was in mid-air.

Looking up, as he pinned the woman to the floor, he saw a body lying prone across the top table.

Oh, no. OH, NO!

Dobrosova was struggling. She was stronger than he expected, much stronger. And she was still grasping the elbow crutch between her body and his, grunting and pushing with all her strength. With one desperate heave, she managed to break Julian's grip and force the weapon under his chin.

An evil smile spread across her face.

'This one's for you, you sexy bastard,' she growled and fired.

Her expression changed to one of horror. Nothing had happened. Julian was now the one with a grin on his face as he shoved his phone in front of her eyes.

'Wonderful thing, technology,' was all he said.

Jenna Dobrosova released her weapon and sank back on the floor, a beaten woman. A uniformed soldier eased Julian aside, hauled her to her feet and took her away.

Patrick had reappeared and was offering him his hand. 'Up you come, mate. I'll get you something to drink,' he said gently.

It was all action at the top table. The body of the Prince was being carefully lifted onto a stretcher. Glass in hand, Julian looked on as his face came into view, his mind unable to handle the consequences of the death of the future King, a death he could have prevented.

Then - consternation. That was not the Prince of Wales. The dead man was Hong Jintao.

Julian looked at Patrick and pointed, speechless.

'I know. He must have seen what was about to happen and flung himself in front of the Prince, taking the full force of the microwave blast into his body,' said Patrick.

'You mean, the Chinese Foreign Minister, a man we always thought was a prime suspect, has given his life to save a British Royal? It doesn't make sense.'

'Perhaps he was on our side, after all,' said Patrick softly.

The doors were now locked and guarded by Sir Norman's unit of Special Services troops. The "paramedics" and a couple of stewards had also given themselves up and been taken into custody. The Foreign Secretary was in the care of genuine paramedics.

The Prince, the Prime Minister, the African Presidents and the rest of the dignitaries were nowhere to be seen but everyone else, including the media, was still in the room. Most were still in a state of utter shock, some standing, some seated, many weeping.

Nobody appeared to question why it was a little old man, dressed as a waiter, who took charge, standing alongside a uniformed senior police officer. Sir Norman had taken that decision: as he explained, the politicians and diplomats would make a hash of it and he had to remain anonymous. He knew he could trust Cameron to deliver.

'Ladies and gentlemen, your attention, please.' Patrick's voice was firm and authoritative, but reassuring.

'It goes without saying that, following the shocking events of the last hour, we have to call a halt to this occasion. I know that many of you have been profoundly disturbed by what you have witnessed and we are expecting more medically qualified staff here within a couple of minutes to help you. I am a doctor myself.

'Meanwhile, I must stress that, on occasions such as this, it is government policy, and a very sensible one I'm sure you'll agree, to place a complete blackout on everything that happened here today. For the security of the nation. The media are being given strict instructions to "bury" all coverage of the event – fortunately nothing was being broadcast live by any of the networks. And I have to warn you, every single one of you, that, from here on, you may never reveal anything of you have seen today to anyone. Ever. Not to your partner, not to your family, in particular not on Facebook, Twitter, Instagram, or any other social media. This is not a request, it is an order.

'I can assure you that the Prince of Wales is perfectly well . . .'

Sir Norman slipped into the room. He had just left the group of African presidents. At first, they refused to believe him when he explained how they had all, including Vanmali Mehta, been manipulated by China; how they had become innocent accessories to a devious, complex conspiracy; how nobody and nothing had been quite what they seemed.

Gradually, after a barrage of questions, these men, all highly intelligent figures of great stature in their own continent, came round to accepting the facts as they were presented and turned their attention to the welfare of their friend, Vanmali Mehta. Like him, Sir Norman was a man they instinctively felt they could trust.

He listened for a while and decided he could leave Patrick and the policeman to take questions. Outside, the other members of the Last Resort Squad were in conversation with the Prince, while soldiers and Special Branch officers scurried back and forth.

He spied Julian walking around a little unsteadily.

'Are you alright, young man?' Sir Norman shook Julian's hand and placed the other on his shoulder.

'You did an excellent job, you know. Congratulations.'

Julian grimaced. 'Right place, almost the right time, but not quite, I'm afraid, sir.'

Sir Norman looked him straight in the eye and said,

'Julian, your country owes you a great debt of gratitude for what you did today,' and shook his hand again.

At that moment, Heather emerged from the main reception room and approached them. Sir Norman turned away.

Heather was smiling as she took his arm and guided him away from the crowd. 'Julian,' she said. 'I was wondering whether . . .'

The room was starting to empty, people drifting towards the stairs, still looking bemused. Patrick stayed behind, checking his phone.

'Oh, my God!' he shouted staring at the screen, a look of horror on his face.

Sir Norman looked round, startled and rushed over.

Patrick showed him the screen.

I've gone into labour. John Radcliffe Hospital. Love you, A

China

Guo Dalong switched off the television and sighed. He turned to Harrison.

'You had better contact our friend in Beijing. We have no need to apologise for what happened today. Tell him I am not well and will not be taking calls for the foreseeable future. He will have to construct a fresh strategy himself, without my help. Tell him that I release him from any obligation to me. He will understand what you mean.'

The old man stood and walked slowly to his favourite chair. He closed his eyes. This day had now become the first day of the final brief chapter of his life and he was determined to enjoy it. Eventually, he heard Harrison return.

'Now, my friend,' he said without opening his eyes. 'Would you care to join me for a game of chess? Oh, and you might bring over that excellent bottle of Single Malt and two glasses.'

'This is the BBC News. We apologise for interrupting this programme but it has just been announced from Downing Street that the Prime Minister has tended her resignation on the grounds of ill health. After being taken ill at a reception in London today, she has revealed that she was recently diagnosed with a malignant tumour of the brain and that, while the prognosis is relatively encouraging, today's episode has persuaded her that it would be in the nation's best interest if she relinquished her responsibilities and retired immediately to her home and family. She asks that her privacy be respected at this difficult time.

'We will bring you further reaction and news in our regular bulletins.'

Angela managed to force a smile. The contractions were becoming more frequent and the midwife was busy.

'You got here quickly,' she said.

'Friends in high places. How are you, darling?'

'Pregnant, if you remember. But not for long. Thanks for staying in touch, sweetheart. Everything OK in the big world? Job done?'

'Job done,' he replied, smiling.

Rory Cameron announced his arrival on planet Earth with a triumphant bellow. The birth had been thankfully straightforward and Angela was already looking relaxed and happy.

As Patrick leaned forward to get a closer look at his new son, he could swear the baby opened one eye and looked at him. The expression said it all:

'Where the hell have you been?'

Bronzefield Prison, Kent, England

She had often wondered what life would be like for a Category A inmate in a women's jail.

Following her arrest, Jenna Dobrosova had been smuggled out of Lancaster House and taken to a locked but reasonably comfortable room in the Security Service's HQ.

After four long days of questioning, by a series of people she assumed to be police and espionage officers, she had managed to send them down enough blind alleys for them to abort the entire exercise.

She reasoned that, if she was clearly going to be detained "at His Majesty's pleasure" – such an elegant phrase - for an indeterminate length of time, she still had plenty to gain by keeping schtum. One day she would tell her tales, but not now.

One morning, a distinguished looking elderly man came to visit her. From his manner, she concluded that this was the top man, almost certainly the one who had outwitted her. None of your tedious British bluster or arrogance: this man was charming, sheer class. She was impressed.

He began by informing her that the UK security services had succeeded in exposing the entire Chinese spy network. And that it involved 'one or two rather senior people'.

'For that reason alone, Miss Dobrosova, it would be, shall I say, unwise for you to come to trial in the usual way. There will be a short, formal procedure in front of a High Court judge, at which I assume you'll plead guilty, and that will be that. The best I can offer you is a very long stay here, under a new name . . .'

'Under a new name? You mean nobody will know who I am? That I am the woman who almost assassinated the Prince of Wales?' Her face dropped.

'I'm afraid not. Not even the prison staff. It's much better that way, don't you think?'

Jenna Dobrosova was certainly thinking. Sir Norman could see that.

'You can choose your new name, if you like.'

And now, three months into her endless sentence, Joanna D'Arcy's partner in crime and in bed, an utterly sensual blonde con-artist, had managed to get her everything she needed. Her route to immortality was beginning to take shape:

"A Lust to Kill - the true life experiences of the world's most successful assassin, by Jenna Dobrosova". Or perhaps by yet another J D.

Self-published online, naturally. Her place in history would be assured. The royalties would keep her in comfort after her escape.

THE END